D0464848

the secret of snow

Also by Viola Shipman

THE CLOVER GIRLS
THE HEIRLOOM GARDEN
THE SUMMER COTTAGE

For a complete list of books by Viola Shipman,
please visit www.violashipman.com.

VIOLA SHIPMAN

the secret of snow

ISBN-13: 978-1-525-89981-2

The Secret of Snow

This edition published by arrangement with Harlequin Books S.A.

Graydon House
22 Adelaide St. West, 41st Floor
Toronto, Ontario M5H 4E3, Canada
www.GraydonHouseBooks.com
www.BookClubbish.com

Printed in U.S.A.

To my friends in Michigan who taught me to love and embrace winter all over again (and not to wear fancy shoes in the snow).

And to my brother, Todd, who loved winter and snow most of all.

the secret of snow

chapter 1

DECEMBER 2021

"And look at this! A storm system is making its way across the country, and it will bring heavy snow to the Upper Midwest and Great Lakes before wreaking havoc on the East Coast. This is an especially early and nasty start to winter for much of the country. In fact, early models indicate that parts of western and northern Michigan—the lake effect snowbelts, as we call them—will receive over 150 inches of snow this year. One hundred fifty inches!"

I turn away from the green screen in my red wrap dress and heels.

"But here in the desert…" I wait for the graphic to pop onscreen, which declares, *Sonny Says It's Sonny… Again!*

When the camera refocuses on me, I toss an adhesive sunshine with my face on it toward the green screen behind me. It sticks directly on Palm Springs, California.

"…it's wall-to-wall sunshine!"

I expand my arms like a raven in the mountains taking flight. The weekly forecast pops up. Every day features a smiling sunshine that resembles yours truly: golden, shining, beaming.

"And it will stay that way all week long, with temperatures in the midseventies and lows in the midfifties. Not bad for this time of year, huh? It's chamber of commerce weather here in the desert, perfect for all those design lovers in town for Mid-Century Modernism Week." I walk over to the news desk. The camera follows. I lean against the desk and turn to the news anchors, Eva Fernandez and Cliff Moore. "Or for someone who loves to play golf, right, Cliff?"

He laughs his faux laugh, the one that makes his mouth resemble those old windup chattering teeth from when I was a girl.

"You betcha, Sonny!"

"That's why we live here, isn't it?" I ask.

"I sure feel sorry for the rest of the country," says Eva, her blinding white smile as bright as the camera lights. I'm convinced every one of Eva's caps has a cap.

"Those poor Michigan folk won't be golfing in shorts like I will be tomorrow, will they?" Cliff says with a laugh and his pantomime golf swing. He twitches his bushy brows and gives me a giant wink. "Thank you, Sonny Dunes."

I nod, my hands on my hips as if I'm a *Price Is Right* model and not a meteorologist.

"Martinis on the mountain? Yes, please," Eva says with her signature head tilt. "Next on the news: a look at some of the big events at this year's Mid-Century Modernism Week. Back in a moment."

I end the newscast with the same forecast—a row of smiling sunshine emojis that look just like my face—and then banter with the anchors about the perfect pool temperature before another graphic—THE DESERT'S #1 NIGHTLY NEWS TEAM!—pops onto the screen, and we fade to commercial.

"Anyone want to go get a drink?" Cliff asks within seconds of the end of the newscast. "It's Friday night."

"It's always Friday night to you, Cliff," Eva says.

She stands and pulls off her mic. The top half of Eva Fernandez is J.Lo perfection: luminescent locks, long lashes, glam gloss, a skintight top in emerald that matches her eyes, gold jewelry that sets off her glowing skin. But Eva's bottom half is draped in sweats, her feet in house slippers. It's the secret viewers never see.

"I'm half dressed for bed already anyway," she says with a dramatic sigh. Eva is *very* dramatic. "And I'm hosting the Girls Clubs Christmas breakfast tomorrow and then Eisenhower Hospital's Hope for the Holidays fundraiser tomorrow night. And Sonny and I are doing every local Christmas parade the next few weekends. You should think about giving back to the community, Cliff."

"Oh, I do," he says. "I keep small business alive in Palm Springs. Wouldn't be a bar afloat without my support."

Cliff roars, setting off his chattering teeth.

I call Cliff "The Unicorn" because he was actually born and raised in Palm Springs. He didn't migrate here like the older snowbirds to escape the cold, he didn't snap up midcentury houses with cash like the Silicon Valley techies who realized this was a real estate gold mine, and he didn't suddenly "discover" how hip Palm Springs was like the millennials who flocked here for the Coachella Music Festival and to catch a glimpse of Drake, Beyoncé or the Kardashians.

No, Cliff is old school. He was Palm Springs when tumbleweed still blew right through downtown, when Bob Hope pumped gas next to you and when Frank Sinatra might take a seat beside you at the bar, order a martini and nobody acted like it was a big deal.

I admire Cliff because—

The set suddenly spins, and I have to grab the arm of a passing sound guy to steady myself. He looks at me, and I let go.

—he didn't run away from where he grew up.

"How about you, sunshine?" Cliff asks me. "Wanna grab a drink?"

"I'm gonna pass tonight, Cliff. I'm wiped from this week. Rain check?"

"Never rains in the desert, sunshine," Cliff jokes. "You oughta know that."

He stops and looks at me. "What would Frank Sinatra do?"

I laugh. I adore Cliff's corniness.

"You're not Frank Sinatra," Eva calls.

"My martini awaits with or without you." Cliff salutes, as if he's Bob Hope on a USO tour, and begins to walk out of the studio.

"Ratings come in this weekend!" a voice yells. "That's when we party."

We all turn. Our producer, Ronan, is standing in the middle of the studio. Ronan is all of thirty. He's dressed in flip-flops, board shorts and a T-shirt that says, SUNS OUT, GUNS OUT! like he just returned from Coachella. Oh, and he's wearing sunglasses. At night. In a studio that's gone dim. Ronan is the grandson of the man who owns our network, DSRT. Jack Clark of ClarkStar pretty much owns every network across the US these days. He put his grandson in charge because Ro-Ro's father bought an NFL franchise, and he's too obsessed with his new fancy toy to pay attention to his old fancy toy. Before DSRT, Ronan was a surfer living in Hawaii who found it hard to believe there wasn't an ocean in the middle of the California desert.

He showed up to our very first official news meeting wearing a tank top with an arrow pointing straight up that read, This Dude's the CEO!

"You can call me Ro-Ro," he'd announced upon introduction.

"No," Cliff said. "I can't."

Ronan had turned his bleary gaze upon me and said, "Yo. Weather's, like, not really my thing. You can just, like, look outside and see what's going on. And it's, like, on my phone. Just so we're clear…get it? Like the weather."

My heart nearly stopped. "People need to know how to plan their days, sir," I protested. "Weather is a vital part of all our lives. It's daily news. And, what I study and disseminate can save lives."

"Ratings party if we're still number one!" Ronan yells, knocking me from my thoughts.

I look at Eva, and she rolls her eyes. She sidles up next to me and whispers, "You know all the jokes about millennials? He's the punchline for all of them."

I stifle a laugh.

We walk each other to the parking lot.

"See you Monday," I say.

"Are we still wearing our matching Santa hats for the parade next Saturday?"

I laugh and nod. "We're his best elves," I say.

"You mean his sexiest news elves," she says. She winks and waves, and I watch her shiny SUV pull away. I look at my car and get inside with a smile. Palm Springs locals are fixated on their cars. Not the make or the color, but the cleanliness. Since there is so little rain in Palm Springs, locals keep their cars washed and polished constantly. It's like a competition.

I pull onto Dinah Shore Drive and head toward home.

Palm Springs is dark. There is a light ordinance in the city that limits the number of streetlights. In a city this beautiful, it would be a crime to have tall posts obstructing the view of the mountains or bright light overpowering the brightness of the stars.

I decide to cut through downtown Palm Springs to check out the Friday night action. I drive along Palm Canyon Drive, the main strip in town. The restaurants are packed. People sit outside in shorts—in December!—enjoying a glass of wine. Music blasts from bars. Palm Springs is alive, the town teeming with life even near midnight.

I stop at a red light, and a bachelorette party in sashes and tiaras pulls up next to me peddling a party bike. It's like a self-propelled trolley with seats and pedals, but you can drink—a lot—on it. I call these party trolleys "Woo-Hoo Bikes" because…

I honk and wave.

The bachelorette party shrieks, holds up their glasses and yells, "WOO-HOO!"

The light changes, and I take off, knowing these ladies will likely find themselves in a load of trouble in about an hour, probably at a tiki bar where the drinks are as deadly as the skulls on the glasses.

I continue north on Palm Canyon—heading past Copley's Restaurant, which once was Cary Grant's guesthouse in the 1940s, and a plethora of design and vintage home furnishings stores. I stop at another light and glance over as an absolutely filthy SUV, which looks like it just ended a mud run, pulls up next to me. The front window is caked in gray-white sludge and the doors are encrusted in crud. An older man is hunched over the steering wheel, wearing a winter coat, and I can see the woman seated next to him pointing at the navigation on the dashboard. I know immediately they are not only trying to find their Airbnb on one of the impossible-to-locate side streets in Palm Springs, but also that they are from somewhere wintry, somewhere cold, somewhere the sun doesn't shine again until May.

Which state? I wonder, as the light changes, and the car pulls ahead of me.

"Bingo!" I yell in my car. "Michigan license plates!"

We all run from Michigan in the winter.

I look back at the road in front of me, and it's suddenly blurry.

A car honks, scaring the wits out of me, and I shake my head clear, wave an apology and head home.

My house is located in the Movie Colony neighborhood of Palm Springs, a quiet enclave of historic homes tucked behind the northern part of the city. It has wide streets lined with large homes hidden behind huge hedges. Many movie stars lived here, or in the vicinity, during their heyday—Bob Hope, Liberace, Ann Miller, Steve McQueen, Howard Hughes, Elvis, Marilyn Monroe, Truman Capote—hence the neighborhood's name.

I live in a Hollywood B-list actress's home. She was famous for being the first woman killed in all of the old murder mysteries, the best friend who's mistaken for someone else, the only waitress at the late-night burger joint, the maid who wanders in on a crime, the nosy sister who knows the boyfriend is bad news. You would know her if you saw her in a movie; you just wouldn't know her name. But she made a ton of money being killed.

Ironically, America's fascination with celebrity never dies.

Especially in Palm Springs.

Endless streams of tourists amble through my neighborhood every single day, maps of stars' homes in their hands, stopping in the middle of the street to snap selfies in front of where their idols once dwelled. During Modernism Week, double-decker buses will drive by every hour on the hour, the voice of the tour guide booming at a decibel level only slightly lower than an airport runway, sightseers able to peer over hedges into our homes and yards. I have a front-load pool, and I have on occasion—after a glass or two of wine—gone topless to get a little more sun. I looked up once to see an entire family peering at me: the teenage son and husband snapping photos, the wife trying to cover their eyes with her hands. I still credit her as the primary reason those photos never went public.

Though I am not a famous celebrity, I am a local celebrity, meaning the buses stop at the top of the hour, and the guide bellows, "This 1920s Spanish bungalow was once owned by Lexi LaMar, famed for being the damsel in distress who was murdered first in every Hitchcock movie. In her later years, she was the voice of Velma in *Scooby-Doo.* The home is now owned by local celebrity and Palm Springs' number one meteorologist Sonny Dunes, who promised us chamber of commerce weather all week long. Everyone yell, 'Sonny says it's sunny…again!'"

I hit the remote to my gate, and it opens, my car sliding behind the ten-foot ficus hedge. We call it a Hollywood hedge out here, because it's so insanely green and lush, it seems fake. I pull past the glimmering pool and into the garage. I park and walk into the house, turning on lights as I go.

My house is nothing like what people picture a Palm Springs home to be—minimal, modern, clean, white, angular. It's actually original Palm Springs: a low-slung terra-cotta tiled home with thick white stucco walls, arched windows, dark-beamed ceilings, multiple Spanish revival fireplaces and bougainvillea-drenched courtyards. I head toward my bedroom and kick off my shoes. I toss my dress into the hamper and turn on the shower.

I step underneath the showerhead and let the hot water pour over me. At first, my hair doesn't move. It's frozen by so much hair spray that the water slides right off it, like it might an otter's back. Finally, my hair softens, and I lather it with shampoo. I turn and lift my face to the water and then look at the drain, watching the rainbow of makeup swirl away, as if I'd dropped a still-wet watercolor in the shower. On your TV set, I may look like perfection, but up close and in person, I look like, well, what you might kindly call a clown. Even Cliff wears more makeup than a Lancôme counter girl at the mall. It feels good to shower, to—quite literally—wash away Sonny's sunniness.

I am so not that person.

I slip into my favorite pair of sweats, pour a glass of a Sancerre and head into my garden. I sit, sip and inhale. The glorious scent of Natal Plum, which I call my Desert Star, fills the air. The deep green shrub, which I have planted as a low shrub on the far side of my pool, is as intensely fragrant as gardenia. The white star-shaped flowers dance against the dense green leaves, mimicking the stars in the sky. I love to cut the flowers and float them in a vintage turquoise Bauer tray so that my house—like the world right now—is filled with their heavenly perfume.

I sip my wine and take in the perfection of my world: a warm breeze, the silhouette of the mountains—lit by starlight and moonlight—seeming to hug the world, my glorious gardens filled with surreal color from blooming poppies, lavender and cacti.

I finish my wine and head to my kitchen for one more glass, this time opting to sit by the pool. I like to do this in the morning and evening, before and after work, switch locations to enjoy my different views, because the stunning vantage points are limitless: gardens to mountains, patio to pool. I take a seat in a turquoise lounger, resting my head against its orange bolster, and sip my Sancerre. I lift my head when I hear a voice. Then two.

"Where is that house?"

"Shh, you're drunk."

"No, I'm not." Silence. "Yes, I am." Laughter.

Then singing. "'When the moon hits your eye like a big pizza pie…'"

These lost tourists are as lit as the moon, I quickly realize, too buzzed to realize Dean Martin's former house is next to mine. So I let them dream. It's what this town is all about.

Much of the year, the desert is dreamy, and Palm Springs one of the best places to live. Summer is hot, hot, hot, but a few weeks of heat versus six months of winter is a wondrous trade-off.

"Can you believe this weather," the woman's voice says. "Remember what we left?"

"Buried in snow this morning," the man says in a Shakespearian whisper. "I had to call the plow guy just so we could get out of our driveway." Silence. "I'll have to call him again to get back in, too. But now? Perfection."

"I don't ever want to go home again," she says.

"Me, either," he says.

Me, either.

Their kisses are carried on the breeze.

One of the hallmarks of living in the desert is its silence. I can hear a raven flap its wide wings a mile high in the sky, or a coyote howl on a distant peak. Most things in the desert seem to go it alone, and at the age of fifty I have grown comfortable with my own solitude. It's now as much a part of me as the mountains that surround Palm Springs. But when I hear a couple talk about the winter, or plan a holiday, my heart cracks open like the dry, desert floor. I wonder what my life might have been like if…

"At least we'll have a white Christmas," she whispers. "And I'll be tucked inside with you."

I smile, before I hear them shuffle off to drunkenly search for another house in the dark.

I inhale the perfumed night air and stare at my pool. It is aglow, and the blue tiles shimmer in the light. I have orange accents scattered around the pool—Palm Springs orange, we call it, a specific shade that closely resembles Hermès orange—and between my gardens, the pool, my patio, the green grass, I am surrounded in a Technicolor dream.

Michigan would be white, I think. And soon it will turn gray. The whole world gray: the overcast sky, the sludgy snow, the dank mood. No difference between dawn and dusk, day or night, morning or evening. Gray all day. There really aren't four seasons in Michigan. There's one big one—winter!—with three tiny friends named Summer, Spring and Autumn. Winter in Michigan is interminable. Bitterly cold. Dark. So dark, as if Mother Nature turned off all the lights in her house, shut the curtains, closed the blinds and left the door wide open.

Even at midnight, I am warm here in the desert. Inside and out.

I am happy. I am not the person I used to be.

That person is gone, I think. *Faded to gray. Now, everything is sunny, isn't it, Sonny?*

I finish my wine, set my glass down on the colorful, round drum side table and shut my eyes.

"Wake up, Amberrose!"

I feel my bed shake, and I open my sleepy eyes to see my little sister, Joncee, jumping on the end of the mattress.

"Wake! Up!"

"What?"

"Look!"

She is pointing toward the window. The curtains are wide open, and the entire world is white.

"It's still snowing! We got a foot! Get up! We have to get outside! NOW!"

Joncee leaps off the bed in a giant bound, screaming, "I'm cool! No school!"

She races around the window doing a little jig in her footed pajamas and then out of the bedroom. I rub my eyes. Last night, Joncee did her snow dance, which she guaranteed would always bring enough snow to cancel school, which they never do in Michigan. The only times they cancel school for snow is when it obscures the Stop signs.

But this time, it worked. Her little dance worked.

I yawn, stand and look out the window.

It worked big time.

The snow is still falling heavily, almost in chunks, the flakes giant-sized. The snow on the yard lifts and dances across the ground in tiny tornadoes. I look up at the sky, squinting in the bright white, and then out toward the icy bay and back at the woods that ring our yard. My heart begins to race.

I love everything about snow. I love everything about weather.

"What's taking you so long?"

Joncee appears at my door again. She's already dressed, a ski mask over her entire face, only her electric blue eyes and mouth exposed. "Get moving, slowpoke!" She comes over and grabs me by the hand, yanking me to the closet. She begins tossing out turtlenecks and ski pants and thermal underwear. "What do you want to do first? Sled? Build a snowman? No, wait! Snow angels! No, a snowman and then a snow fort. Then we can snowshoe or ski. Hurry, Amberrose! Hurry! Time's wasting!"

Joncee races out the door so quickly, her thick, wooly socks slide across the wooden floor and she bounces off the wall in the hallway.

"I'm good!" she yells, before racing down the stairs. "Mom! I want hot chocolate and pancakes in the shape of a snowman!"

I laugh.

No, I think, the thing I love most about winter in Michigan is my sister.

"You'll never hear Sonny Dunes talk about snow in the winter in Palm Springs. Sonny says it's always sunny!"

I wake with a start.

"Everyone yell, 'Sonny says it's sunny…again!'"

I look up, and the upper deck of a tourist bus is taking my picture. I leap from my chaise, my neck aching, and race inside.

I look at the clock on my microwave: 8:05 a.m.

I must have been exhausted. I haven't slept outside since I was a girl in…

I think of my dream and shake my head. Hard.

Stop it right now.

I make some coffee, head to the bathroom, brush my teeth, then pour a cup of caffeine, grab my cell and slide into bed. Maybe a couple of hours of normal sleep, then a hike, then a nap, then I'll meet my girlfriends at The Parker for a drink…

It's nice to have a normal day and night. TV anchors never have a "normal" day.

It's nice to have friends who know me now, without a trace of my past. I sip my coffee and glance at my phone.

An endless scroll of texts appear. I click on the first. It's from Ronan.

Emergency meeting at noon! Be there!

I look at the other texts, from Cliff and Eva, asking what the meeting is about. No response from Ronan.

I call Cliff.

"I have no idea what's going on," he says. "Do you?"

I call Eva. Voice mail. She's at her breakfast event.

What in the world could this be about?

I get out of bed and down my coffee, trying to clear my bleary head. I grab a second cup, go for a swim in the pool and then head to the station.

I am stunned to see the entire staff—and I mean the entire staff—in the conference room on a Saturday at noon. Eva is dressed to the nines in holiday red. She shrugs when our eyes meet, and I grab an empty chair at the end of the table next to Cliff. Ronan enters in workout clothes and a baseball cap that reads, Chill, Bro!

"Thank you all for being here on such short notice, but it's important." He stops and takes a big drink from his DYLN alkaline water bottle. Ronan is all about pH. He's told us all that about a million times. "Ratings came in overnight." He looks around the room and then stops, looking directly at me. "Not good. Not good at all."

My heart stops.

"What's not good?" Eva asks. "Did we slip to second place? What's going on?"

"No, we're still number one overall," Ronan says.

I exhale, and the entire room explodes into applause.

"No, not good," Ronan repeats, exasperated, sipping from his water bottle as if it's life. "We've fallen to second place in the key demographic of 18-49."

"There are viewers in Palm Springs in that age range?" Cliff asks. The room bursts into laughter.

"Yes, Cliff!" Ronan suddenly yells. "And they're the influencers today. They're the ones who are out spending money and running the world, if you haven't noticed."

The room goes quiet.

"We can't continue to succeed with an advertising base that consists of denture creams, hearing aids, wheelchairs and walk-in bathtubs!"

"Don't forget senior medical alert buttons," Cliff says.

The room titters.

"You're fired, Cliff!" Ronan yells.

"What?" Cliff says. His smooth anchor voice is suddenly shaky.

"Done. Over. Today."

"You can't do that," I say.

"Oh, I can't?" Ronan says. "Well, I can, and I did. And you're fired, too, Sonny."

My eyes widen. The room spins. I want to stand, but my legs are jelly.

"Excuse me?" I manage to gasp.

"Meet your replacement."

Ronan turns off the lights and flicks on the giant TV on the wall.

An anime woman appears on screen. The name *AImee* appears beneath her. She is a stunningly realistic-looking Amazonian Barbie doll come to life: blond, blue-eyed, with what looks to be double D breasts. She is wearing a pink dress with a big bow around her four-inch waist.

"Hi, I'm AImee, the world's most accurate and reliable artificial intelligence meteorologist."

I look around the room for people's reactions. AImee continues. "I compile the latest computer models every sixty seconds to provide the most up-to-date weather forecast in your area and throughout the world," AImee says in a creepy voice that sounds like you misdialed and reached a sex hotline run by Alexa. "And I can be with you everywhere and at any time: on your phone, laptop, watch, or in your very own home."

Ronan hits pause on his remote. AImee stops midmotion, her big, doll eyes focused directly on me. Ronan smiles, and then hits play again.

"The weather today in Palm Springs is expected to be sunny and eighty-two degrees. And it will stay that way all week long in the desert."

"Wait for her catchphrase," Ronan says, his voice absolutely giddy.

"Wall-to-wall sunshine," AImee says, jumping up and down excitedly, her anime chest bouncing. "It's gonna be sunny, honey!"

Ronan hits stop.

"Is this some kind of joke?" I ask.

"No," Ronan says, turning, silhouetted in front of the TV with AImee behind him. "Isn't she the bomb? AImee's the wave of the future."

"You can't fire me," I say, finally getting my wits about me. "I have a contract."

"We're buying you out." Ronan stops and looks at me. "I really thought you'd like her."

His voice sounds wounded. Ronan ducks his head. He's acting like the one who's actually getting hurt here.

"Let's talk about this," I say, voice calm. "People don't want their weather from a robot."

"She's not a robot," Ronan says.

"No, but you are," Cliff says. "You have no idea what you're doing."

"Oh," Ronan says, as if an important thought just returned to his head. "I'm buying you out, too, Cliff. Eva, you're safe. For now. AImee gets introduced tonight."

"Do we even get to say goodbye to our viewers?" Cliff asks, incredulous. "I've been on air here for forty years. Sonny has been here since 1993."

"Monday will be your final telecast. Thank you all. Eva, if you can stay behind? We need to talk about a few things."

Eva looks at me all wild-eyed as she is ushered away. The news crew stands in a line, waiting to hug me and Cliff, as if we're at a funeral.

"Wanna get that drink now?" Cliff asks, when everyone is gone.

"Just one?" I ask. "I'll meet you after I call my agent."

The Purple Room is an old jazz bar and club where the Rat Pack used to drink and hold impromptu performances. It's a mostly windowless joint, now a wonderful restaurant and jazz club, with stiff drinks and an owner who does the world's best Judy Garland impersonation and show.

A cosmo is waiting for me when I arrive.

"You're a mind reader," I say.

"Cheers to our demise," Cliff says, raising his glass.

I take a healthy sip and look at Cliff. "What the hell just happened?"

"We got canned, sister," he says, sipping his Manhattan. "By a little man with a big ego and a tiny—"

"I got it, Cliff," I say.

He doesn't stop. "Who's trying to prove himself to even smaller men with even bigger egos," Cliff says. "Daddy's boys can never become their own men. Especially rich daddy's boys."

"What are we going to do?" I sigh.

"I had a long, wonderful career at my local station," Cliff says. "Able to live in the paradise where I was born and raised. I didn't have to move my family all over the country from Des Moines to Denver, starting over every few years in a new city. I'm proud of what I've accomplished. You should be as well." Cliff looks at me and raises one of those bushy brows. "You can't control crazy. And Ronan is squirrel-hiding-his-nuts-for-the-winter crazy. I actually feel sorrier for Eva than us right now. Imagine what she'll have to endure. And for who knows how long before he tires of her, too."

Cliff stops and takes a sip of his drink. "This allows us time to reassess and reinvent. I might do radio. I can do all that volunteering Eva wants me to do. I might write a book." He pauses for a moment. "Or, I might do nothing. I might actually take my wife to dinner on a weeknight, or watch the news in bed like the rest of the world. It's been decades since I've had a normal week." He takes another sip of his cocktail. "What this Ronan kid doesn't seem to care about is that I've covered wars, I've covered race riots, I've covered presidential elections. This dimwit doesn't realize that you were on air 24/7 after the '94 earthquake, sleeping in the studio so you could give viewers the latest news, provide emergency response and, most importantly, reassure them. That weather robot will never be able to do that. And Ronan will find that out when it's too late, when there is a crisis. You did more before you turned twenty-five than he will ever do his entire life." Cliff raises his glass. "It's been an honor to be a newsman. And it's been an honor to work alongside you for all these years."

I shake my head at Cliff and will myself not to cry. "I admire the hell out of you."

"But? There's a but in there. I can tell."

"But I'm *fifty*, Cliff. I need to work. I need to earn a living. I still love what I do."

"Then you're probably going to have to uproot your life from Palm Springs and head somewhere else."

"I don't want to," I say.

"You can fight for your job," Cliff suggests. "Maybe Ronan will reconsider."

I look at Cliff, and he laughs before I do.

"You can sue," Cliff says. "But his pockets are way deeper than yours." He hesitates for a second. "Don't ever forget the world is yours, Sonny. It's always sunny for you, isn't it?" He grabs my hand and gives it a squeeze. "What would Frank do?"

I nod, allowing myself to tear up just a bit, and another drink is ordered. That cosmo leads to another, which leads to a shot of tequila and then me standing on the bar singing songs by the Rat Pack, the world spinning before my eyes.

The next thing I know is that I feel hands around my waist lifting me from the bar and leading me to the lobby. I collapse into one of the circular 1960s sofas.

"I'm calling you a Lyft," Cliff says. "You can pick up your car tomorrow."

I watch two Cliffs try to dial one cell and start to laugh. Then I notice, directly behind him, the large mural that is painted on one of the lobby walls. I close one eye to stop the room and concentrate on reading it.

Alcohol may be a man's worst enemy, but the Bible says love your enemy.—Frank Sinatra.

"Ride's here," Cliff says, pulling me from the sofa and guiding me out the doors and into the car.

"Take her straight home," Cliff says to the driver.

Cliff leans into the car. "I'll call you in an hour to make sure you're home, okay? My wife will be here any minute for me." He stops. "Sonny? Sonny!"

I try to focus on Cliff. "Love you," he says. "You're gonna be okay."

He shuts the door and walks—or rather, stumbles—back into the lobby.

I nod off briefly, and wake up to notice we are heading back to my house.

A voice in my head asks, *What would Frank do?*

"Three twenty-one Dinah Shore," I say to the driver.

"That's not what I have here," he says, checking his phone.

"Change of plans," I say.

He repeats the address, I nod, and he adjusts his navigation. I smile. He keeps looking at me in the mirror. "Hey, aren't you—?" he starts.

"No," I say.

My lids grow heavy, and I blink, once, twice…

"Ma'am? Ma'am? We're here."

I wake up slumped across the back seat as if my spine is made of a Slinky.

I sit up and shake my head.

"You live at the TV station?" the driver asks.

"It's a temporary thing," I say, my words slurred.

I try to find my credit card but can't so I hand the driver my entire bag.

"Your friend already paid before I picked you up," he says, passing it back.

"Thank you," I say. "And tell him thanks when you see him."

"Are you okay?" he asks.

The driver is all of twenty, probably. He's all sparkly eyes and good skin and sunny skies ahead.

I stumble out of the car and then lean into his driver's window.

"Jury's still out," I reply, before drunk-walking into my TV station.

I look around. Saturdays are quiet. The big clock in the waiting area reads 6:10 p.m.

Perfect.

A sign over the door blinks, LIVE! ON AIR!

I think I'm being stealthy as I tiptoe inside the studio, but I collide into the back of a cameraman.

"Sonny?" he asks. "What are you doing here?"

"I wanted to see my replacement in action," I say, but the words come out in a slurred jumble.

"Are you drunk?" he asks.

"Are *you*?"

Eva is stationed behind the news desk with one of the weekend anchors, Brant, who looks as if he just graduated junior high.

Ronan must have asked Eva to make the big announcements.

"Welcome back," Eva says. "Well, DSRT is undergoing a number of wonderful changes meant to enrich the lives of our viewers and make our great station even better. One of those changes is a new meteorologist joining the team. I'd like to introduce our desert viewers to AImee, one of the world's first artificial intelligence meteorologists. AImee is fed the latest weather data every minute and, thus, can bring you the most accurate information not only in Palm Springs but also throughout the world. And, for those who wonder where Sonny is, well, she'll be back on Monday to say goodbye and tell us all about all the amazing things she has planned for the future. Hi, AImee! And welcome!"

Eva looks to the left, where I would usually be standing. One of the hardest tricks I had to learn as a meteorologist was to act natural in front of the green screen. I had to learn where to point on a blank screen that to viewers looks like a live feed of the weather map.

If you think that's a lot to grasp, try doing it.

AImee doesn't even have to point. She doesn't even have to study the weather. She doesn't have to put it into context for viewers. She doesn't have to do anything. Graphics just pop up behind her, like in a Pixar cartoon.

"Hello, Eva. Hello, Brant. What a pleasure to be here."

"That's so creepy," I say too loudly to the cameraman. I start to act and speak like a robot. “Hel-lo. I sound like R2D2 but have bigger boobs.”

Eva hears my voice and looks over at me.

No, Sonny, she mouths.

But it’s too late. I’m already beelining toward the set.

“Shut up, AImee,” I say, bursting before the cameras.

AImee keeps going because she’s not real. I can see the cameraman looking between me and AImee, unsure as to what he should do.

“Hi, DSRT viewers. Wanna know what’s really going on? I was fired. By a spoiled, rich brat. For being too old. For getting a few wrinkles and occasionally putting on a pound or two. For being too real. For having a contract. For this…*thing*.”

I pound the green screen with my hand. “There is nothing real about her. Not her face, her shape, her voice… Look.” I start kicking the green screen, over and over. I take off my shoe and begin beating it, tearing at it, until it collapses. AImee’s image vanishes, but her voice continues like a robotic ghost.

I turn to the camera. I start yelling.

“She’s not real! Nothing about her is real. Is this where we’re all headed in life? Replaced by robots? Until nothing is real anymore?”

Over me, AImee says, “It’s gonna be sunny, honey!”

“Oh, hell no!” I say. “Sonny’s the one who always says it’s gonna be sunny again! You can’t rip off MY trademark line. HONEY!”

I reach down under the news desk. *They’re still there.*

I grab two of the adhesive suns with my face on them and stick them on my chest, one on each breast. I walk toward the camera.

“You wanna know what’s real, AImee?” I shake my bosom. The cameraman spits out his gum. “*Me!* Everything about me is real!”

I look over and can see that the station has finally cut to a commercial. I have a moment of clarity: they kept me on for so long because they knew it would be good for their ratings. *Anything* for ratings.

Eva stands up, walks over to me and holds me.

I weep in her arms.

The last text I remember seeing when I get home and fall into bed is one from Cliff.

You didn't go home, did you?

I pass out, and I dream of snow.

chapter 2

I wake up with the most miserable migraine since my sorority's Pledge Night in college. I woke up that day at four in the afternoon in a dress I had not been wearing the night before with pizza adhered to my thigh.

I remembered none of it.

I remember very little of last night, except…

I have flashes of doing shots, dancing, doing bad things with adhesive sunshines.

I groan.

"Please, God," I pray out loud, shutting my eyes. "Make it all a bad dream. If you do, I promise I'll never do anything bad again in my life."

I chuckle at my prayer, my head hurting even more.

Why do we only barter and make promises with God when we want something from Him or know we've messed up?

I brace myself, take a deep breath and sit up, the room all Tilt-

A-Whirl. I search for my cell. It is encased in my thigh, just like the pizza from so long ago.

A scrolling line of texts, longer than a royal decree, awaits.

It seems my daughter has gone—what do you kids call it—viral? Even made the news here in Michigan. Call me. When you sober up.

My mom. The former nurse and current hospice nurse who thinks she's Ellen.

I click the link my mother has shared from her news station in Traverse City, Michigan.

A Palm Springs meteorologist flashed, well, her high-pressure system to viewers in a tirade now heard 'round the world...

I throw my cell across the room.

The video continues to play.

...if she looks familiar to you, she is. That's Amberrose Murphy, who was born and raised in Traverse City and now goes by the name Sonny Dunes...

Sonny. Sunny.

I squint, the sun glinting into my bedroom.

How ironic, Amberrose, I think.

I groan getting out of bed, my stomach lurching. I kick my cell toward the bathroom and finally bend down, pick it up and turn it off, the simplest of actions making me dizzy when I stand up again. My mouth is drier than the desert, and my tongue feels as if it's been stung by bees. I splash my face with water and then just stick my mouth under the faucet, lapping water like a thirsty dog. I look at my face in the mirror. It is blotchy and swollen. My eyes have more bags than Macy's.

The bags have bags.

I take a shower, and when I'm finished, I feel maybe an ounce better. *Better* being relative in perspective. *Better* meaning that I no longer feel like I perhaps might die, although I am still walking dead, like a zombie. I head to the kitchen, make coffee, take three aspirin, drink an entire bottle of pH water that I had stolen earlier this week from Ro-Ro and a glass of orange juice and then put my head on my countertop and watch the coffee drip.

When we'd play games in my family growing up, my sister was always the timekeeper, my dad always the scorekeeper, my mother and I the entertainment. Joncee would hold the little plastic hourglass and—when no one was looking—tap it, hard. She'd look at me and wink, put a finger over her lips and mouth, *Shh.*

In the winter, after we'd played in the snow all day and the world grew dark in the late afternoon, my dad would make a fire, and my sister would pull out all the games from the cabinet beside it: Operation, Yahtzee, Monopoly, Trouble, Battleship, Uno, Sorry!, Candyland.

More than anything, Joncee loved jigsaw puzzles, the ones with a thousand pieces that took forever to complete. Her favorites, of course, were winter scenes, cardinals in snowy branches, a cabin in the woods with smoke billowing from the stone chimney, a girl sledding down a hill. Often, I would catch her with a puzzle piece in her hand seated in front of the fire, just watching us. She loved games and puzzles, I finally realized, not to win or for the fun of it all but because the entire family was together on a cold, winter's night. We were one.

I watch the coffee drip, thinking of not just how fleeting time is but how the truly magical moments in our lives are the simplest, and how we let them pass without a thought. We foolishly believe that somehow they will all last forever, that destiny will not show up at our door unannounced and knock when we least expect it.

I believed that.

I forgot that time is cruel. I pretended things would be different.

First, my sister.

Then, my dad.

Now, my career.

I am alone at fifty. Hungover, my head on the counter, waiting for coffee to revive me from a funk that has no end.

I grab a mug and then the pot of coffee. I fill it and add a touch of cream and head to the patio with my cell.

After I knock down half a mug and can feel the caffeine pulse though my system, revive my brain and lift my lids, I finally look at my texts.

Three hundred eighty-one.

I take a deep breath, another slug of coffee and start to read.

Most have the same theme: Are you okay? Did you need to talk? Are you going into rehab?

Many are from those entertainment shows—*Access Hollywood*, *Entertainment Tonight*, even The Weather Channel—wanting an interview.

My phone begins to ring.

My mother.

I do not answer.

That's when I see my hedge moving. I sit up. There is a camera lens poking through the green.

What the…

I stand and race at full sprint toward the ficus before the photographer can react. I grab the camera and yank it free.

"What the…?" a man's voice says. He's peering at me through the hedge from the street.

"No, that's my question," I say. "What do you think you're doing?"

"I'm with *Hollywood Gossip*," he says. "The celebrity news site."

News site?

"We'd love an interview about your breakdown."

Breakdown. So that's what they're calling it.

"I didn't have a breakdown," I say indignantly. "I was angry that I lost my job. I perhaps had too much to drink."

I peer through the hedge. He is recording me on his cell.

"I'm not trespassing," he says. "I'm on public property."

"I'm *not* doing an interview," I say. "I'm not allowing you to use anything I say. And if you want your camera back, you will go away quietly. Otherwise it's going in the pool. Deal?"

"Deal," he says.

"I want to see you erase that."

He lifts his cell and I see him hit a button. He turns the screen toward me. "See? It's all gone."

I poke his camera back through the thick hedge, and he grabs it.

"Go away," I say. "Please. If you need a quote, talk to my agent."

He is quiet for a moment. "She said to talk to you."

Oh, JoAnne, I think. Anything for publicity. That's why I call her, "Oh, no, Jo!"

"Go away," I tell him again. "I'm a bit under the weather."

I watch him move away, and then I hear a car start and drive away.

There's only one place I can go to be alone right now, I think, turning to look at the mountains behind me. On a hike.

Despite my hangover, I nab my backpack, fill its inner reservoir with water, and place an apple, some nuts and a protein bar inside. I grab another cup of coffee and drink it as I slather on sunscreen. I change into my hiking clothes and, on my way out, pull a ball cap from a hook in the garage. The hat reads: DSRT: The Desert's #1 Newscast.

I put it back and grab a yellow one: Sonny Says It's Sunny Again!

I take both caps and throw them in the trash, before pulling free another one. It's a purple cap with a big block *N* from my alma mater, Northwestern.

More like N for Nincompoop, I think.

My cell lights up as I drive, but I ignore it. When I reach the Frank Bogert Trailhead, I head into the lot, my car spewing gravel, dust flying. I shove my cell into my backpack, step out of the car, pull on my pack and look into the sky. Murray Peak hovers in the distance.

It is the highest spot in Palm Springs, and it rises from the desert floor, ominously but magically. For some reason, Murray Peak always reminds me of Witch Mountain from the old Disney movie.

I start the hike and—within moments—am gasping for breath. Even with sunglasses on, the sun is bright, and I squint. My head pounds with each step I take, but the higher I go and the more my body labors, the better I actually feel. Exercise, no matter the season, has always made my body—and mind—better. The hike is a series of quick ascents—one small peak leading to a higher one. About an hour in, the path flattens and meanders through the high desert. All of a sudden, the world stills. I can no longer hear any traffic. There is no one around. The tourists generally don't hike this far. I stop, take a long draw of water and look out over the desert floor. Some years, when we've had an abundance of moisture, Palm Springs will have what's known as a superbloom, when the desert literally explodes in color. We have not had enough rain or cool temperatures to have a superbloom for a while, but it's super close to one this year due to a couple of late summer monsoons and some fall showers.

The usuals—the yellow desert sunflowers, which sort of resemble small daisies, the cactus and the purple lupine—are in bloom. But their friends—sand verbena, brown-eyed evening primrose, desert moon flower—are, as well.

I pull my backpack off, set it on a nearby rock and reach for my cell to take photos of this display.

Perhaps some video would make a nice lead-in story to the forecast Monday night, I think.

Without warning, I nearly burst into tears.

I lift my face to the sun to steady my nerves.

The sun has been a constant companion to me the past few decades. Many think being a meteorologist in the desert is easy—and I *am* a meteorologist, not a "weatherman." I earned my degree in climate-space sciences and engineering and worked in research for the university after graduating—but it's not. The sun can be as unforgiving as a Michigan winter, and the constant tracking of earthquakes is more frequent and much scarier than any thunderstorm or blizzard.

I have grown used to the sun. I ran from the clouds and the snow because they were like memories: they hovered and refused to dissipate. They darkened my days and my mood.

So, Amberrose became Sonny.

Literally.

And now who am I?

I glance at the desert in bloom, and it can't help but make me smile. I suddenly think of Michigan in bloom—after winter—and what a *Wizard of Oz* Technicolor dream that was: the sunny daffodils followed by the lollipop tulips, and that canopy of green that just pops out of nowhere one warm day when you look out and every bush and tree has come to life again.

Northern Michigan. Southern California.

Before. After.

I reach down and pick a stem of lupine.

What a spectacular show of life emerging from the harshest of conditions.

Reenergized, I move with a purpose toward Murray Peak. The last fifteen minutes of the hike are straight up. There are no switchbacks. It's simply a serpentine staircase to heaven. Without warning, I start running, my hiking shoes spitting rocks, and I don't stop until I reach the peak.

I lift my arms into the sky, take a seat at one of the two picnic tables, which I still wonder how they managed to get up here.

I eat my lunch and realize my hangover is fading. I am as high as the ravens. They circle just below where I am sitting, wings out, casting dramatic shadows on the mountain ridges. I sit in silence, shut my eyes and let the breeze calm me. When I open my eyes, a constant stream of baby monarch butterflies float by. They are born, in droves, when it warms in the winter, and they quite literally float along the same path like a yellow river. The butterflies are so tiny, so delicate, so beautiful that it makes my heart ache, and I do not want it to end because I need any sign of hope that I can get.

"Be safe," I yell at them. "Be happy."

I hear the shuffling of rocks, and a hiker has emerged at the peak and is staring at me.

"Butterflies," I say, pointing. "See?"

"Oh, my gosh, are you...?"

"No," I say, grabbing my backpack and rushing down the steep path, rocks flying.

I stop when I'm out of sight. Usually, I run a good part of the path back to the lot. I feel it's good for my balance, eyesight, ankles and agility. Today, I meander.

There's nothing waiting for me. Nothing to return to.

When I reach my car, my cell begins to ding repeatedly. I reluctantly free it from my pack, take a seat in my car, opening all the windows to cool the interior.

"Amberrose? It's Mom. Call me. I'm worried." Pause. "But do not send a video. I repeat. Do not send a video."

You're a hoot, Mom.

"Sonny, it's Cliff. Call me."

"Hi, it's Eva. Are you okay, honey? Call me."

I scan my texts.

Oh, no.

I open a link one of my friends has sent. It's a clip from *Hollywood Gossip*, with that annoying, overly dramatic, staccato music and a headline that screams, Are Sonny Days Behind Her?

It's the video of me from this morning, running toward the paparazzi in the bushes, no makeup, hungover, an enraged look on my face. I grab the camera, and the video shakes. Then my voice yelling, "I have a breakdown. Angry. I drink too much. Go away!"

That little sleazebag, I think. He not only didn't erase anything, he edited it to make me sound even worse.

The cell rings. My mom.

"This day can't get any worse," I say.

"Well, good day to you, too, sweetheart." She laughs at her joke. She always does. She pauses. "I've been worried about you. Why didn't you call me? How are you?"

I take a deep breath and will myself not to cry.

"Not good," I say. "I went for a hike to forget about everything and returned to see that I'm trending as a psychotic drunk."

"You never could handle your alcohol, dear."

We both make jokes to deflect our pain. Always have, always will.

"Mother. You're not helping."

"Why don't you come home for a little while. Rest. Recoup. I'll cook for you. You can hide out while you figure out next steps."

"Isn't there a blizzard right now?"

"It's a little snow. And it's so beautiful, honey. The whole world is white. Coated in magic dust. You used to love the snow."

I don't answer.

"It's almost Christmas. I always come to you. Why not come back here for a change?"

Don't say it, Mom. Don't say it.

"And there's no reason for you to be there right now. We can have a white Christmas in Michigan."

She said it.

"No holiday parades for you to host. No work. No Christmas specials."

And she keeps going.

"I'll think about it," I say to stop her.

"Do," she says. "Nothing more magical than the holidays in Michigan." I can hear my mom take a deep breath. "I miss you, honey. Desperately. And I'm sick with worry. Come home. *Please*."

This is real. Too real.

"I have to go, Mom."

"You can't run from this forever."

"I love you, Mom."

"I love you, too."

I hang up and put my head on the steering wheel. I bang it once just for good measure. My cell rings again, and I bang my head once more.

Pause. "Is this Amberrose? Amberrose Murphy?"

I look at the number.

"Yes? Who is this?"

"Lisa Kirk. From college. Remember?"

Kirk the Lurk? The girl who always sat in the common room alone watching movies. The one who ordered Domino's nonstop as a way to bribe girls to join the university news station? Or march for the environment? The girl who made T-shirts for everyone on the fourth floor of Allison Hall that read, Alli's Pallys?

"Lisa? It's been a long time. What can I do for you?"

"I'm the news director at TRVC now, in Traverse City. I saw what happened yesterday."

Everyone wants a story. This time with the local girl gone crazy.

"Listen, Lisa," I say. "It's been a rough couple of days. I'm not interested in doing any interviews about what happened."

"I'm actually calling about a job," she says. "We're looking for a new meteorologist to anchor our nightly newscast. I'm trying to build something special here. The area is booming. I want a station that mirrors that growth and spirit."

"Are you joking?" I ask. "Did you see the video? I humiliated myself. No one will want to hire me."

"I do."

"Why?"

"I just have a gut feeling about you," she says. "I think you've changed." Lisa hesitates. "The hometown girl returns. Sonny turns snowy."

"I'm really not interested, Lisa. Thank you, though."

"May I ask why?"

"I just—" my head spins "—can't."

"Well, you have my number," she says. "I'll be filling the position within the next week, so if you change your mind—"

"I won't," I cut her off.

"Okay, well, it was nice to talk with you, Amberrose," she says. "I mean, Sonny."

"Take care, Lisa."

"Oh, and I've forgiven you," she adds.

My heart lurches.

"For what?" I ask, playing dumb.

"You don't remember college?" she asks. "*Kirk the Lurk?* All the pranks? Ignoring me? I sure do."

"That wasn't me," I say.

There is a ringing in my ears.

I can picture the first snowfall on campus. I am trudging through the newly fallen snow, which slides into my too-low boots. Even though it is bitterly cold, the wind is whipping, my backpack weighs a ton and the snow is still falling, I head to Lake Michigan and stare into it for what feels like eternity. I am at college. Away from home. Nearly an adult. But still tethered to my past by this water and this winter.

"Are you okay?"

I turn, and Lisa is standing there, a mug of hot chocolate extended in her hand. "For you," she says.

I stare at her without saying a word.

"You looked like you were going to cry in class," she says. "Just staring out the window, like you wanted to run away. I thought you could use a little pick-me-up."

Just like Joncee. Always reading my emotions. Always there to make me feel better. Always there in the snow with a hot chocolate and melting marshmallows.

"I don't want your hot chocolate," I can hear myself saying. "I don't need your pity or your friendship."

A raven's wings flap overhead. I am back in the desert, back in the present.

I am not lying to Lisa. It wasn't me.

"Oh," Lisa says. Her voice has changed. "You're right. I'm forgetting. That was Amberrose. Not Sonny. Take care. Bye."

I hang up, my mind racing, and immediately call my agent.

"Well, well, well, if it isn't Mata Hari."

"I'm not *that* infamous," I say.

"Really," Jo says. "You were breaking news on CNN. Scrolling red ticker tape and everything. I mean, Sonny. C'mon."

"Isn't bad publicity good publicity?"

"Not in this case," she says. Jo takes a deep breath and then a sip of something I'm pretty sure is whiskey instead of water. That's how Jo rolls. "Let me break it down for you. Weathermen…"

"Meteorologists," I correct.

"Whatever," Jo says. "You're the person people trust. Think of Willard Scott. Ginger Zee. You're the best friend. The one people call when they need advice. You're spun sugar. The pretty girl next door who always waves at the neighbors when she leaves the house. You can't go on TV blind drunk, pretend to flash your goodies and tear down half the studio. It's not a good look."

"What are my options?"

"You have no options," she says. "Well, you have one. Did that news director from somewhere in one of those flyover states call you?"

"You knew about that?"

"I gave her your number."

"Why?"

"Because you need a job."

"I can't take that job."

"Take the job, Sonny. Now. Keep your head down and your mouth shut. Do a good job."

"I can't go back there."

I do not state this. I am pleading my case.

A gust of wind picks up as it so often does in the desert. A current will sweep along the slopes of the mountain and gather steam until it becomes a heaving sigh of dry air and dust. The dust swirls in mini-tornadoes just like the snow does when it sweeps across the lake. I look again, and I can see my little sister in her stocking cap and little mittens turning when she hears me trudging through the snow. She takes off running as soon as she sees me, arms extended, calling, "Amberrose is home! Amberrose is home! What should we do first in the snow?"

"I can't go home," I tell Jo again.

I already know I am pleading my case with the wrong person.

"Then start looking at a different career path. Like Starbucks." She doesn't laugh. "Take the job, Sonny," Jo says very slowly, drawing out each word. "At least for a little while. Then you can head west again…or maybe even to a bigger market once you prove yourself again. America *loves* a comeback story. Girl gone bad goes home and does good. I can sell that. But you have to start over again somewhere."

The world around me spins, like the tornadoes of dust.

"Want me to call and negotiate?" I don't answer. "I'll get you the best salary I can, I promise. And bonuses if their ratings soar. But it won't be what you were making here." She stops. "Then after a while, I can start selling your comeback story to different stations."

"You expect me to move back and live with my mother?" I ask, my voice raspy and weak.

"You're a grown-ass woman," Jo says in her Jo-way. "You can afford your own place. You don't have to live with your mother."

But I do have to live with my mother. I can't return to Michigan and leave my mother alone.

Again.

My sister and father are gone. I am gone. I can't do that to her. And what if I were to move into a condo somewhere and be surrounded by people I knew from childhood that I couldn't avoid every day? My past in my face, every single day.

But then I picture my childhood bedroom…and Joncee's down the hall.

But can I do that to myself?

"I can't do it. I'm sorry."

"You can," Jo says, her voice like steel. "And you will." Silence. "Honestly, the whole scene sounds very sweet. Just don't expect me to visit. Especially in the winter."

She hangs up, and I place my head on the steering wheel.

This time I bang it really hard.

When I look up, as if on cue, the sun slides behind a cloud.

chapter 3

I open my eyes and Rick Springfield is staring directly at me.

This can't be happening.

I do not move my head. I shift my eyes right.

Hi, Madonna. Hi, Duran Duran.

I shift my eyes left.

My high school and college mortarboards, along with my high school cheerleading pom-poms and college sorority formal photos, hang over a mammoth cork bulletin board crammed with hundreds of pins from bands and bars that I used to wear on my jean jackets. Stacked beside that are wall shelves stuffed with framed photos from my school days along with awards and trophies as well as a pink boom box.

I scan my eyes back across the room.

There are faded squares on my too-pink walls, missing moments from my life, edited scenes that can be deleted from my bedroom but not my memory.

My neck aches. I am still too exhausted to move after a three-day drive filled with all the angst of Thelma and Louise's getaway. I pull the covers over my head and try to shut out the world.

"Good morning!"

My mom flings open my bedroom door. She is carrying a cup of coffee, which she sets down on my little nightstand. She walks over and pulls open the curtains.

"It snowed last night!" she says. "Michigan is welcoming you home in grand style."

The room explodes in blinding white. So blinding, in fact, I have to squint. It's like the winter equivalent of the desert sun. My eyes try to adjust. When they do, my mother is seated next to me.

"How did you sleep?" she asks.

"I'm a fifty-year-old woman who just drove across the country after having a meltdown on TV. I'm back in my parents' house, in my childhood bedroom, sleeping on a twin mattress that obviously has a box spring made of nails. You do the math, Mother."

She scrunches her face as if she is counting. "So, we're calling ourselves fifty now, are we?"

She bursts out laughing and shakes my leg under the blanket. "I'm just teasing. Here." She reaches for my coffee and hands it to me. "Black with a touch of cream. Just the way you like it."

"Thanks."

I take a sip of my coffee—my mom can still make better coffee than I can—and look at my mother, really for the first time since I arrived home once again.

I was so exhausted, depressed and stressed from my cross-country drive from Palm Springs—it literally started snowing the minute I crossed the Michigan state line—that I dragged my overnight bag into my mom's house, hugged her and fell into bed.

My mother is already in full makeup.

Let me set the record straight: my mother is quite a pretty woman. Her features are not delicate like a desert rose teacup, rather she is more Katharine Hepburn, regal and strong. She could get by with a little mascara and blush, but she still paints her face as if it is a blank canvas and she wants to reimagine the entire thing. And yet it works. My mother was ahead of the curve: she let her hair go gray long before millennials were coloring it to look cool. She wears it short, in a longer-style bob, a beautiful bang swept across her forehead.

My mom has been in full makeup her entire life. My college friends were once taking about what our earliest childhood memory was, and I told them mine was seeing my mother in her makeup. When I was just out of the womb.

In fact, her face was resplendent in the first photos she took while holding me in the maternity ward as a newborn.

Ironically, my mother is the least vain person I've ever known. As a nurse, and now as a part-time hospice nurse, nothing bothers her, not blood or any bodily fluid. As a nurse, she worked the floor, ER and ICU, before becoming an administrator at Cherry Capital Hospital. When my father was diagnosed with cancer, my mother gave up everything to help care for him. She stopped wearing makeup, she stopped telling jokes, she just stopped. Over the course of a few months, however, she became amazed by the care, compassion, professionalism and empathy the hospice workers provided my father every single day. Within a month of his death, she was back at work, this time for hospice.

I once asked her how she could go back to work. "How could I not?" she asked.

I look at my mom, who is staring at me adoringly.

I also once asked my mom when I was little why she always wore so much makeup.

"Maybe it's my own superhero mask." She winked with a big, mascaraed lash.

Maybe, I think, *it's why Sonny Dunes does, too.*

My mother is already dressed in scrubs, her name tag pinned to her chest: PATTY ROSE.

We are a family that was shattered by horror and death, masking taped again by hope and faith, our broken pieces Krazy Glued together with copious amounts of love, hope and dreams before being reassembled into something that once again resembled a family. We were reassembled by the strength of my mother, though perhaps not reassembled in exactly the right emotional pattern.

We are also a mishmash of a family made up of big personalities and odd quirks.

I mean, even our names. My mother is Patty Rose, named after her mother and grandmother. My father was John. My sister, Joncee, was a mix of my dad's name and his mother's name, Cecilia. And me? After my mom and my aunt, Amber.

If we were a song, we'd be a mash-up on *Glee.* If we were dinner, we'd be goulash.

Now, only two ingredients remain.

"It's good to have you home," my mom says. "I missed you on Christmas Day."

My heart pings.

"I'm sorry. I had so many loose ends to tie up. Packing, getting my house ready to rent, saying goodbye to friends, last holiday parties..."

My mom nods. She's not a good liar, but she knows a really bad liar when she hears one, and she knows I'm lying. I haven't done Christmas here in years. When my dad was alive, I used to grit my teeth and come back every few years, but most of the time, I made them fly to visit me to celebrate Christmas in the desert, something my parents always considered downright apocalyptic.

"Sunny and seventy-five on Christmas?" my dad used to say. "Decorated cactus? It's not right."

I would nod and make all their favorites, and then take them for drinks at all the places Sinatra used to go. Retro bands would play Rat Pack Christmas music, and my dad would slowly chill. But my mom? She always wanted to be in Michigan.

I just couldn't do it, I don't say to my mom.

"Well, I have a couple of gifts still waiting under the tree," she says. "We can open them when I get home. I have to go to work."

"Really, Mom? It's New Year's Eve. I just got home. And you're seventy-five and still working?"

My mom shakes my leg. My mother has always shaken my leg, as if to wake me from a trance. "I know it's not how you imagined your life might go, but, as we well know, lives—especially ours—rarely go in the way we imagined."

"But, Mom," I start.

"Young lady," she says, "and I use that moniker very ironically—" she stops to laugh at herself "—I didn't know you were coming home until a few days ago, my job still makes me feel vital and worthwhile, and I do think a dying man takes precedence over your current woes, don't you?"

She shakes my leg again for emphasis.

That's my mom. Cuts right to the heart of the matter and then asks you to respond directly to your own selfishness.

"Attagirl," she says. "I'll be home at noon." She stands. "Be dressed. And semicoherent. I love you."

"Love you, too, Mom."

I hear her pad down the stairs, the garage door opening and her monster SUV starting. When it is quiet, I stand, go to the window and watch her drive away.

Her headlights briefly illuminate the dark, icy bay, a tunnel of haunting light on the spot where our dock lies in the summer.

I hold my breath until I see the lights of my mom's car fade away, and then I shut my eyes and count to fifty. I gasp for air. I rub the lock on the windowsill ten times, walk to the light switch and turn it on and off twenty-five times and then touch every object on my dresser.

Only then do I feel safe.

Without warning, I begin to cry.

The repetitive routine I had established and worked hard to overcome with years of counseling in the desert—the one I used after Joncee died whenever my parents left the house in the winter, the one I believed would somehow keep them safe from harm—has returned like a ghost you believed was no longer around to haunt your life. I don't know how it started or why, but it did one night when my parents went out to dinner and left me alone, and I counted, over and over again, until they returned.

I continued this obsessive pattern in college until I finally moved far enough away that I believed the ghost couldn't find me. My therapist said the fear would never go away, but I had to learn to control it, or it would rule my life.

Keep me alone.

But this winter ghost has always been around, haven't you? Haunting me. Driving away men I've dated and loved. Putting distance between me and my family. Coldly turning away from potential friends who wanted to get a bit more than surface level with me. Forcing me to sever relationships.

All because it's easier to be alone than it is to lose someone you love. Again.

I walk to my closet and yank out a sorority hoodie from my college days. I dry my eyes with the soft sleeves and then pull it on, along with some sweats and thick socks, wash my face and begin to head downstairs with my coffee.

Before I do, I turn back and make my bed. My dad was in the army, and the first thing he did every day was make the bed. He taught us to do the same.

"If you start your day by completing one task, it sets an intention," he always preached. "You will go on to accomplish many every day."

I still have my father's accomplishment-driven nature, which is why I feel like such a colossal failure right now.

I behaved like an idiot. I lost my job. I moved back home.

Yes, Dad. I've accomplished a lot recently.

I start to head down the stairs but stop yet again.

I turn. I can hear my pulse beat in my temples. I put my hand on the doorknob and open it.

Joncee's room.

I rarely went into her room after… I had tried to forget everything. I click on the lights and exhale.

I had forgotten that my parents turned her bedroom into a study when I was in high school.

"We have to move on in some way," my mom had said.

"What are you going to study in here?" I had yelled at my parents. "Episodes of *Matlock*?"

But I had been secretly relieved to know that her ghost did not live just down the hall from me anymore. I couldn't bear to see photos of us on her bulletin board, or see her little soccer outfit hanging off the closet door, or the little Charlie Brown Christmas tree she left decorated on her desk all year long.

I close the door, my heart still racing, and head down the big staircase. I pause on the landing. The entire two-story wall is filled with family photos. Unlike me, my mother has not removed a single picture. There are photos of the four of us, at Christmas, Easter, the Fourth of July, birthdays. Me and Joncee building a snowman and sledding.

How can she look at these every day?

I grab the banister to steady myself and when I reach the first floor, I turn again and look up the staircase.

How many times did we race up and down these stairs?

How many memories were stolen, how many photos not taken? No descents down the stairs in prom gowns, no surprise parties, no more wedding anniversaries, no more knocking over Dad's golf bags stacked against the bottom steps.

The downstairs is one massive room: living, dining, kitchen all rolled into one. My mother was open-concept before open-concept was a thing. For years, this space was a playground. I could ride my wheelie bike round and round in circles without ever having to go outside. I head into the kitchen.

A huge floor-to-ceiling fireplace made of Michigan lake stones of various shapes, colors and sizes fills the living room. I run my hand over the stones, cool and smooth.

And that's when I smell it before I even see it: a huge Christmas tree stands in the corner, soaring toward heaven. It's a Fraser fir, of course, my father's all-time favorite. We could never have any other kind for a Christmas tree.

"The perfect Christmas tree," my dad used to always say as we decorated. He loved its dark green needles and upturned branches, which showcased our colorful, vintage ornaments. He loved that it didn't drop its needles and that, when lit, the tree had an almost frosty underlying glow.

But we all loved the way it smelled, a fragrance that filled that house with a perfumed outdoorsy scent that could only be described as "Christmas."

The glass ornaments—so fragile, so pretty—are tucked into every crevice of the tree.

How long did it take her to decorate this? I think. *It must've taken days. Who does she do this for anymore?*

I crane my neck and look up.

The star!

One year, Joncee and I were playing, and we rode our little bikes directly into the tree. It fell with a mighty crash, and my mother was nearly inconsolable as my father swept up broken ornaments that had been passed down by her mother and grandmother. Joncee and I retrieved the big pieces from the trash and made a giant patchwork star. It was like a Frankenstein ornament, but my mother thought it was beautiful.

She wept when we showed it to her, and placed it atop the tree every year since.

"It's like our hearts," she said. "Sometimes they get shattered, and we have to piece them back together and still shine for the world to see."

You never realized how prophetic your words would be, did you, Mom?

I stare at the star.

Did she get it up there by herself? Did she cut the tree and drag it back here, or have a neighbor kid help? How little do I know about my mom's life? How little does she know about mine?

In the kitchen, a halved grapefruit, lightly sugared, is waiting with a note. I smile.

Didn't want you to miss California too much. Love, Mom.

I refill my coffee mug, grab the grapefruit and sit at the long counter where we used to do our homework and watch Mom make dinner.

I pluck a segment of grapefruit free with the serrated spoon and sigh when I taste it.

Tastes like sunshine.

The snow is still falling. The large deck that sits just off the kitchen facing the woods is thick with snow. The snow continues to pile up, and the railing looks as if it's been covered in a foot of whipped cream. I know the outdoor table and chairs are out there only because I can still, barely, make out their shapes. My mother has bird feeders hanging from shepherd's hooks, looped around barren tree branches, off of railings—essentially anyplace she can hang one—and she has recently scattered seed on the deck. Fat birds eat, occasionally fluffing their feathers in the snow. I stand and crack the patio door, not wanting to startle them.

Cardinals sit in the branches of the pines, shocking red among the dense green. Snow buntings, which my mom calls *snowflakes*, with their white plumage and rusty collars, forage for all the sunflower seeds, some fluttering into the snow for a winter bath while others tunnel into its cold depths for roosting warmth.

The scene is so unfamiliar to me, so strangely beautiful, that I can't help but pull on my mother's coat and boots that she has stationed by the door and walk onto the deck as if in a trance.

The world is hushed. Not just quiet, but silent. As silent as being atop Murray Peak. The only noise is the hiss of the snow and the occasional rustling of the birds. Flakes gather on my lashes. I close my eyes.

Stick out your tongue, I can hear my sister say. *Eat some snow, it'll make you grow.*

It'll make you look like a snowman, I'd tease.

Perfect!

I open my eyes and stick my tongue out. Flakes float onto it and quickly melt.

There is a rustling and then a *plop*. A squirrel is sitting in a branch of a Fraser fir watching me, snow falling from the tree's limbs.

I race back inside, out of the snow, away from my memories.

I am sitting at the counter sipping a peppery Syrah, watching my mom make enough appetizers to feed the University of Michigan football team. She is making a charcuterie platter, and the massive slab of wood is overflowing with cheeses, meats, olives, grapes and dates.

This is just the start of my mother's appetizer blitz.

She is also making spinach artichoke dip, baked Brie with fig jam, wontons, rollups, crostinis, stuffed mushrooms, spring rolls, caprese kabobs, mini pizzas, potato skins, deviled eggs, phyllo tarts, not to mention dessert.

Ever since I was young, my mother has loved making apps,

more so than normal meals. It started in the late '70s when a surprise blizzard canceled my parents' annual New Year's Eve party. Appetizers for seventy-five guests, and no one to eat them.

Except for us.

And we did. For weeks.

My mother figured out that none of us got sick of eating them. It wasn't like we were eating pot roast or lasagna for a week straight. It was like eating a new dinner every night. We could pick and choose, mix and match. We could go from New Year's Eve, to the football bowl games on New Year's Day, through our winter break and right into school again on that smorgasbord.

"Your appetizer fetish is a sickness, you know," I say.

"So's watching me do all the work," she says, pushing dough into a muffin tin. "Grab a knife."

I'm not what you would call a chef. Or even a capable cook. I'm what you'd call a good reservation-maker. My job has made my eating schedule a bit off-kilter, to say the least. Since I anchor—*used* to anchor—the evening newscasts at 6:00 p.m., 10:00 p.m. and 11:00 p.m., I would usually eat a healthy breakfast and a bigger lunch, as I didn't like to feel bloated or puffy on air. I would often workout midday and then head out for a lunch at a local restaurant when it was quiet. Then I'd head home to get ready, arriving at the station early to prep my segment and meet with my weather team.

"Here," my mom says. She takes the knife from my hand and slides it across some green onions. "Do it on a bias. Makes it look prettier."

"Is that what you used to tell the doctors in surgery?" I tease.

"No. I used to say, 'Let me do it, if you want it done right.'"

She laughs and takes a sip of her wine.

My mother should have been a doctor, but that wasn't a real option for her—like so many women of her era—growing up. So she became a nurse, and she was a damn good one. I've never been able to go anywhere in town without a stranger stopping to tell us how my mom saved a relative's life, or stayed in touch after someone passed. My mom has always been an open book. I've always seemed like an open book. On TV, you think you know everything about me.

But you don't.

I look at my mom, her cheeks flushed from the heat of the kitchen. She has always been beyond proud of me, especially for building a successful career in what was once a male-dominated profession. She has not been so proud of me for running away.

"Like your sweatshirt?"

I look down at one of the Christmas gifts my mom got for me, which reads in big letters across the front: EAT, SLEEP, PLOW, REPEAT.

"I love it," I say.

"You don't sound convinced," she says.

"Just tired," I lie.

"I bet," my mom says. She walks over and hugs me. It takes every fiber of my body not to collapse into tears.

"Thank you," I say instead. "For everything. Opening your home back up to me for who knows how long. For listening. For not judging. For every gift..." I stop and stretch out my sweatshirt. "All of which seem to have a common theme, by the way. Winter coat, scarf, mittens, boots, hand balm..."

"Sweetheart, you're a hothouse flower. You haven't lived anyplace where the temperature drops below fifty degrees for decades."

"I will be now," I say. "I took the job."

My mother stops cold. "You buried the lede, sweetheart! When?"

"Before I left California. My agent said it was the right thing to do."

"Again, you don't sound convinced." She puts her hand under my chin and looks me in the eye. "Well, I'm thrilled to pieces, but are you ready for this?"

"That's a loaded question," I say.

"I know this is hard." My mom continues to look me in the eye. "I'm here for you."

She turns back to cooking. "And, do you even remember what snow is? How to predict it? How to survive it?" She stops and grabs my face yet again, just like she does my leg. "How to *enjoy* it?"

I start chopping again.

"That would be a no then?" My mom laughs at herself. "Well, then, I have an idea after we eat." She walks over and grabs the bottle of Syrah. "And after you have another glass of wine."

"You told me the other day I couldn't handle my liquor," I say with a laugh.

"You can't," she says, before looking around the kitchen very dramatically. "But I don't see any TV cameras around, so I think we're safe."

"Ha-ha, Mother."

We listen to old holiday songs and eat our fill of appetizers while gazing at the tree in front of the blazing fire. The wine, food and warmth make me sleepy, and my eyes begin to droop.

"No, way, Amberrose!" my mother shouts, her legs curled beneath her in an oversize chair, a blanket over her lap. "If I can stay up, you can stay up! We have to make it to midnight."

"Why?"

"It's a big year," my mom says. "And it requires big dreams and wishes."

My mom clicks on the TV, and we watch for a while, waiting for the ball to drop. When it does, she leaps up and pulls me to my feet. We count down, "Ten! Nine!" And then she hugs me with all her might when we get to one. "To 2022!"

"Happy New Year, Mom!"

I give her a kiss.

"Do you know the importance of the number two?" she asks.

I look at her. "Am I supposed to make a potty joke right now?"

She laughs. "No. The number two is associated with harmony, balance, consideration and love. When the number comes to you, it means that you should have more faith in your angels."

My mom has always been the queen of obscure facts. I think it's because she had to learn to make conversation with patients who don't often talk back to her. But my mother's trivia always seems to make perfect sense at the moment.

"It's 2022!" she says. "Lots of twos. Lots of harmony. Lots of balance."

My mom twirls me. I spin out of her grip and begin to head toward the stairs.

"Hey!" she yells. "I had an idea, remember?"

"Does it involve my pillow and sleep?"

"Humor me," she says.

"I've been doing that my whole life, Mother."

She walks over and grabs my opened gifts, which are still sitting under the tree. "Here, put all this on," she says, handing me my coat, scarf, mittens and boots.

"Why?"

"Put it on and follow me."

I sigh dramatically, but do as I'm told.

My mom pulls on her winter garb, opens the kitchen slider and steps out onto the patio. I follow her and shut the door. The cold air sobers me instantly. The wind chills my cheeks, and my eyes water. It has stopped snowing, and the sky is crystal clear.

The moon is bright, and I watch two moms—real and shadow—walk into the backyard. I follow, and when I step into the yard, the snow is up past my knees. It's thick and heavy, and I have to trudge through it. My mom walks into the middle of our yard, into a giant clearing, and by the time I reach her, I am out of breath.

"What are we doing out here?"

"We're going to make snow angels. Have you forgotten?"

I don't answer. I can't answer.

"Oh, honey." She squeezes my hand. "You need to remember. You *have* to remember."

She doesn't add *your sister, your father, the holidays, winter, the snow,* to the end of her sentence because she knows I already understand.

"It's not as if not remembering has allowed you to forget, has it?" She shakes my hand. Hard.

I can hear my heart pound in my head.

"We're going to fall straight back in the snow, just like you used to do as a kid. The snow is fresh and powdery, so it'll be like a pillow. But you already know that, right? You're a weather professional."

I nod.

"Try to land in a T, with your arms out. Makes for a better angel, remember? I'm going to let go of your hand now, okay? We're going to jump now, okay?"

My mom grabs my hand and gives it a squeeze.

"Together."

"What on earth, Mother?"

"Just trust me. One, two, three… Go!"

My mother, at seventy-five, is a force of nature, and she literally pulls me through the air. She lets go of my hand in midair.

We fall backward together, and I can't help but scream from the excitement. We land with a big *Poof!* and snow billows up and around our bodies. My heart is racing, and I giggle.

"You remember the rest now, right?" my mom asks. "Just move your arms and legs like you're doing jumping jacks, then gently press your head into the snow to make an indentation."

We push our arms and legs through the powder, and I can feel chunks of icy snow sneak down the back of my coat and underneath my shirt. The cold takes my breath away but makes me feel incredibly alive.

I look over at my mom. In the moonlight, her face ruddy from the cold, her now wet bangs hanging from her stocking cap, she looks like a girl.

She looks just like Joncee.

I inhale the cold air sharply. In fact, she looks so much like her that I feel as if I'm trapped in a dream from forty years ago.

"What are you thinking about?"

"Nothing," I lie.

She reaches over and hits my shoulder, without messing up the snow between our two angels. "Ope, I'm sorry," she says with a laugh. "You're a terrible liar."

My mom even sounds like my sister. She has the Michigan accent. "Ope," for "Oops."

"About" sounds like "a boat." The vowels are often pronounced differently in certain words.

I lost my Michigan accent long ago. In J-school, my broadcast journalism instructors worked with students to lose their accents, so we could be hired at any station around the country. It was something to hear my Southern classmates end up sounding just like me. I'm sure it was instrumental in me getting hired—I mean, does a Californian want their news from a Michigander or someone with a Jersey accent?—but it's also sad that our uniqueness was washed away, our personalities watered down, our voices—quite literally—silenced.

"Pick a star and recite the poem."

"Mom," I start.

"Pick a star and recite the poem."

It's not really a poem, I want to say. *It's a song. Joncee's favorite from* Pinocchio.

"'When you wish upon a star, makes no difference who you are...'" I say in unison with my mom.

We did this ritual every New Year when Joncee was alive. She believed there was nothing more pure than newly fallen snow, and that if you made an angel on New Year's Eve then

God would most certainly see it and all your wishes for the new year would come true and—like the song's lyrics promised—anything your heart desired would come to you.

"Now, we have to stand up as carefully as we can, so our angels—and our wishes—remain intact," my mom says.

I sit up and try to position my legs underneath me, so I can stand without messing up my creation. But I am not used to the snow, and I slip and fall back on my rear.

"Here," my mom says. "Take my hand."

She reaches out, her arm sliding across the snow. I take it, and we stand. Together.

We leap from our snowy silhouettes and turn around. There is a muddled line attaching the two angels, thanks to my mother's assistance in helping me stand.

"We ruined them," I say.

"No, sweetheart," my mom says. "We made them better. They're connected."

I look at my mom. My heart feels like it's made of ice, and her warmth is making it crack.

"It's good to have you home," she says. She hesitates. "What did you wish for?"

"Mom! You know I can't say. Then it won't come true."

"Mine already has," she says, looking at me, her voice as hopeful as church bells in the cold air.

I look at my angel. I wished for so many things right now, I don't know if God can even make heads or tails of them. I wished for everything—and everyone—I used to have, all of which is gone now. I wished for a new start. I wished that life wasn't so painful and God wasn't so cruel.

I just want to spread my wings and fly, I can hear my sister say. *Just like an angel.*

I stare at my angel, and then I look up into the sky. I don't just see one star tonight, I see the entire Winter Hexagon. While not one of the officially designated eighty-eight constellations, it is easily recognizable because of its six-sided pattern of bright stars in the Michigan winter night sky. The Winter Hexagon is really an asterism, which are imaginative ways to connect the stars.

Looks like a baseball diamond, Joncee used to say.

This has six sides, not four, I'd correct her.

I don't care. I just want to hop from star to star.

How could she always see the light in the dark?

Just make a wish and shut up. Don't be so sciencey, she'd say to me.

I think of what my mom just said about the number two: 2022. A year of harmony. I look back one last time at our two snow angels.

A year to have more faith in my angels.

I shake my head.

I just wish that wishes actually came true.

chapter 4

JANUARY 2022

"You do realize it's about a hundred degrees in here?"

I look up at my mom. I am curled up on the couch drinking coffee in flannel pajamas, thick, wool socks, a plushy, hooded robe. The fire is blazing, the heat is running, and I'm still cold.

"And?" I ask.

"And," she says, walking over to turn down the thermostat, "I feel like I'm living in a petri dish. And I don't want a three-hundred-dollar electric bill, since I'm the one who'll be paying it. Besides, it's not that cold out."

"It's twenty degrees outside, Mom." I hold up the weather app on my cell.

"That's not bad for January. And it's sunny!" She walks over and shakes my leg. I move it so she can sit next to me. "You better start remembering what Michiganians love about winter."

My mom. The backward hypnotist. Asking me to remember things I want to forget again.

"What's that again, Mom?"

"We love a sunny day after a newly fallen snow," she says. "We love being warm enough to be outside without the temperature being warm enough to melt all the snow away. We love a forecast with lots of snow in it so we can do all the things we love to do here in the winter: sled, ski, snowshoe, build snowmen, enjoy our winter festivals…"

My mom grabs the remote and turns on the TV. She scrolls through and stops on TRVC.

"It's like the first day of school," she says. "What time is your interview?"

"It's a meeting, Mom. I've already been hired." I sip my coffee. "I'm meeting Lisa and my weather team today."

"That nice Lisa Kirk from college? The one who used to make the cookies for Parents Day?"

"Uh-huh," I say. "She's the news director. She hired me."

"That's right," my mom says, looking into space. "I've seen her around town a few times. Such a sweet girl." My mom shakes me. "Well, you be nice to her then. You weren't very cordial to her in college, if I remember correctly."

"I *was* nice to her," I say defensively. "She was just…odd. She didn't join a sorority. She didn't party or socialize much. She didn't have a lot of friends."

"Because you wouldn't let her be one," my mother says, the tone of her voice as direct as it is to meddling families who seem more interested in a dying person's will than their well-being. "I think she reminded you too much of Joncee. She was so energetic. So smart. So willing to wear her heart on her sleeve. She *wanted* friends."

I begin to protest, but I don't, finally remembering Lisa in the dorm on our very first Parents Day. She *had* made cookies for all the visiting parents. I just don't remember hers being there.

"Well, she's your boss now," my mom reminds me.

I think of Ronan, and my stomach lurches. I think of Lisa from college, and my stomach somersaults again.

"Is it your stomach?" my mom asks. "Your face always gets that strange look on it when you're nervous. Do you want me to make you some cinnamon toast?"

Suddenly, I feel like little girl again. Nothing made me feel better and safer than my mom's cinnamon toast.

"Don't you have to go to work?" I ask.

"I took the day off so I could drive you to the station," she says.

"I'm not five, Mother. This isn't the first day of kindergarten."

She cocks her head just-so and laughs. "Pretty darn close, though, right?"

I nod.

"So, you want the cinnamon toast then?"

I nod again, she stands, tossing me the remote, laughing all the way to the kitchen.

I turn up the volume and try not to cringe as the newscast returns from commercial.

The set is—let's just say—not as swanky as what I'm used to. The anchor desk is very small, almost like a child's desk, and the graphics behind the anchors are also childish, the typography…

"Is that Courier?" I say out loud.

I hate Courier font. It looks like an old typewriter. Courier doesn't make the news newsier. Just like Comic Sans doesn't make something funnier.

The reporters look, well, childlike, too. They are very young. Straight out of college young, and most look like Lily Tomlin's character, Edith Ann: kids wearing grown-up suits. The lead anchor, however, resembles a caveman who was recently thawed back to life. He has unkempt gray hair and a too-long white beard, and, if I'm not mistaken, what looks like a doughnut sitting beside him on the anchor desk.

"How's the weather looking, Polly Sue?"

"Sunny and beautiful!" she says. "We might hit thirty today. A heat wave is upon us! Back in a sec!"

A heat wave? Sunny and beautiful? Back in a sec? Is she out of her mind?

My mother brings me my cinnamon toast, straight from under the broiler, and it's even better than I remember: crunchy, golden and sweet on top, the white bread soft, warm and buttery underneath. I feel momentarily better, until the newscast returns.

Polly Sue is using a pointing stick, which I haven't seen anyone use since the 1970s. I think Johnny Carson used one in a skit. She's jabbing it around in the air like she's taming a lion. She points to the seven-day forecast, which now looks as bleak as my life, before sending it back to the anchor.

"Later this week, we say goodbye to Mighty Merle the Meteorologist, who's retiring after decades of snowy service. He's off to hunt and snowmobile, and we'll welcome our new lead meteorologist, a former Traverse City girl who up and left us but has returned. What do you think of all that, Pol?"

"Not much," she says.

"What the actual hell!" I yell, crumbs flying from my mouth. "Are you seeing this?"

"I think they're just having a little fun?" my mother says.

"A little fun? Fun to them must be waking up sleeping puppies and babies."

The newscast ends with a screaming graphic in giant Courier type that reads: *The fastest growing news station in Traverse City!*

That is *not* good. In news terms, "fastest growing" usually means a station has horrendous ratings, and in the latest sampling viewership went up by a millimeter, meaning they will tout any increase in any age demographic and try to make it into something when, in reality, the station is celebrating simply because its ratings didn't go any lower.

Either you're #1 or you're nothing.

"You better go get ready." My mother shakes my leg. "I think it's going to take you a while."

"Ha-ha, Mom," I say. I wipe my face. Cinnamon toast crumbs fall onto my robe.

My mom looks at her watch. "Should I set a timer?"

Two hours later, I emerge from my childhood bathroom feeling not much different than I did decades ago when I was getting ready for my first day of high school.

My stomach is a flurry of butterflies, I'm wearing too much makeup and my hair is way too big. The one thing that is different is that my back hurts from slouching over the too-low bathroom cabinet, which my parents never updated.

I nearly fall down the stairs in my heels when I notice my mom at the bottom snapping photos.

"What are you doing?" I ask.

"We always need to capture big moments," my mom says. "And this house has been without one for much too long." When I reach the bottom of the stairs, she asks, "What are you wearing?"

"What I normally wear to work," I say.

My mother eyes me from top to bottom, her eyes lingering on my dress and shoes. Like actresses on a red carpet, female meteorologists must abide by certain fashion rules: the dresses we wear must be what I term "alluringly modest." They must be formfitting and show off our figures, but they cannot be so overtly sexy as to offend viewers. Our dresses must be free of distracting prints and lace, and they are generally brightly colored, but never green, or else our bodies disappear in front of the green screen and become weather maps. The dress I'm wearing is red with a black piping that runs down the front of the dress, around the waist and then along the edge of the hips. It's known as "the dress," and I'm not joking. It's the dress that nearly every female meteorologist wears as it's flattering for nearly every body type, and it comes in about a hundred different colors. There are Reddit threads devoted to the dress.

Warm, however, it is not.

Nor are my shoes.

"You realize this is Michigan, not California," my mother says. "You realize this is Traverse City, not Palm Springs."

"Thank you, Miss Lentz," I say, referencing my middle school geography teacher.

"Miss Lentz knew the difference between the west and the north."

My mother heads to the coat closet. "You need this and this and this and this," she says, tossing a coat, a scarf, some gloves and boots my way.

"I'm not Ralphie in *A Christmas Story*, Mother."

"No," she says. "You're more like the kid who got his tongue stuck to the frozen flagpole." My mom stops and looks at me, shaking her head. "You have so much to relearn about Michigan."

I layer my winter garb, and my mom walks with me to the garage. "Ready?" she asks.

"What are you doing?"

"I told you, I'm driving you."

"Again, mother, I'm fifty. Not five."

"Okay, fine. Do you know where you're going?"

"My car has navigation."

"But no snow tires. And do you even remember how to drive in the snow?"

I shake my head and give my mom a look as bad as any I'd given Ronan.

She opens the garage door and heads through it and into the immense driveway.

"Phil already plowed," she says.

I look, and the driveway is clear of snow, knee-high walls of white framing it.

Michigan snowplow drivers are like mythical creatures. They appear in the middle of the night, risking life and limb, so Michiganders can pull out of their homes and make it to work in the morning. Many can make a small fortune in a bad winter—doing homes and businesses—and then spend summers doing nothing more than fishing, boating and drinking beer.

"Phil is still plowing?" I ask. "He must be a hundred."

My mom shrugs.

I'm not sure my mother has ever seen Phil's face or would even recognize him in public. For decades, I've only seen features of Phil, a green eye and a chapped lip. Phil always shows up in a stocking cap atop a full face mask ensconced in a thermal winter suit, a cigarette butt dangling from his mouth. My mom leaves checks for him that are wedged into the seasonal wreaths on the front door: Halloween witches turn into a Thanksgiving cornucopia that transforms into bright Christmas balls, Valentine's hearts, St. Patrick's green and happy spring daffodils.

Yes, it still snows in the spring up here.

My mom lifts her cell phone.

"What are you doing?" I ask.

"I'm going to film this," she says matter-of-factly.

I roll my eyes, get in my SUV, buckle myself in and begin to back out of the garage. As I pull out, I glance up at the house, and a memory pulses through my mind. There is a window above the front door, at the top of the staircase, a little nook where Joncee and I used to read. On snowy predawn mornings, Joncee would sneak to this window and try to catch Phil's attention with a flashlight and a sign: *STOP PLOWING! I DON'T WANT TO GO TO SCHOOL!*

When I would join her, I could see the light from Phil's cigarette dance in the dark, and I knew he was laughing at my little sister. One day, after a bad snow, Phil didn't plow.

You got your wish, sis, I remember.

Without thinking, I hit the gas and then slam on the brake.

There is a layer of ice, where the snow has been plowed and then melted and run off in the sun before refreezing on the concrete. My SUV fishtails. I panic and turn the wheel as if I'm driving at a go-kart track, do a full 360 and slam into a pile of snow.

There is a knock on my window.

"Want me to drive now?"

I unbuckle my belt and get out, dejected, like I just failed my driver's exam.

"We're taking my car," my mother says. She moves my car, and we slide into hers. She repeats what she said earlier. "You have a lot to relearn about Michigan."

I slump into the seat like a kid and stare out the window.

My parents' home is situated on a deep, heavily wooded lot a few miles outside of Traverse City as you head toward Suttons Bay. It is perched on a hillside overlooking the West Bay and Old Mission Peninsula, M-22 running between the lot and the water. As girls, we'd stop at the road—looking both ways—and then grab hands and cross it, running as fast as we could, sprinting down the long dock before flying into the water.

The dock is up for the winter, packed away, like my memories.

My childhood home, like so many along this stretch, is what I call "quintessentially Michigan." Rustic lodge homes made of natural materials consistent with the northern environment: wood, stone, and timber crossbeams.

Growing up, I hated where we lived. It was too far out of town, too far away from my friends, and our house seemed like a strange cabin compared to all the ranch homes and trilevels. But now, after living in Palm Springs, I get it. The house fits the rustic environment, much like the minimalist architecture fits the desert landscape.

My mother turns on my radio and immediately finds a station that plays holiday music 24/7. That's a thing in Michigan: the day after Halloween, many radio stations immediately begin playing Christmas songs. And it doesn't ever seem to stop, even after the holidays have long passed.

Anything to get you through winter, I guess.

My mom lets me stew in my embarrassment as she drives. It's one of her specialties. As we proceed through Traverse, there is no denying—even in the middle of winter—that the town has changed greatly over the last few decades and is booming. Young people bustle about, restaurants, bars, bookstores, coffeehouses and cute touristy shops line the streets. The downtown is decorated for winter, and people seem nonplussed by the snow and cold.

Finally, my mom pulls into a giant development in Traverse City.

"Where are we?" I finally ask.

"The Commons," my mom says.

"For some reason, I thought the station was still on the other side of town."

"Just moved here," she says, "with about everything else."

"Didn't this used to be...?" I start.

"An asylum?" my mom finishes. "It did."

"Fitting," I say.

"I brought you here a few times to shop after it opened," she says. "Remember?"

I nod.

When I was young, this huge new development now known as the Village at Grand Traverse Commons, and called "The Commons" by the locals, was the Northern Michigan Asylum, a hospital dedicated to the idea that fresh air and beautiful surroundings could ease the suffering of the mentally ill. After Joncee died, I would come down here and sit, wondering how any of us could even get on with our lives after such tragedy. I felt as if I needed to leave the world and not be bothered. I would watch everyone continue with their lives as if nothing had changed, when all I wanted to do was stop the world and go back in time.

I watched kids bike. I watched teenagers laugh. I watched parents walk with families.

I wondered about the patients, actually inquired about what was required to be committed.

"Honey," a woman at the front desk said, "I don't know what's troubling you, but you have your whole life ahead of you. Go enjoy the fresh air and all the beauty of our area. Celebrate every season of your life. Just know you can't control everything, or it will control you."

"*You* should be committed!" I yelled at her.

I walked out, and that's when everything clicked, just not in the way that stranger had suggested: maybe I *could* control everything—my life, my heart, even the weather.

And maybe, I knew in my soul, such control could even help save a life.

In the near distance, I hear a branch crack in the cold wind coming off the water, and the sound echoes how I feel inside. I take a deep breath and realize my mother has been talking the whole time.

"This project is the country's largest historic preservation and adaptive reuse development. The hospital closed in 1989, but its forested grounds and buildings have been preserved. Everyone now comes here to walk, run, ski and bird-watch. There are tons of restaurants, retail shops, wineries, even a brick-oven bakery."

"Thank you for the tour, Mom," I say. "How much do I owe you?"

My mother shoots me a glance even icier than the buildings' gutters. "More than you'll ever know," she says. I look at my mom, and my soul makes that sad cracking sound again. Standing here, in the cold, she looks so pretty. So much still like a girl. So much like Joncee. "This place embraced its history. Why can't you?"

She gets out of the car and heads toward one of the old buildings.

"Where are you going?"

"I'm going to get a cup of coffee," she says. "You've made it clear you don't want your mother embarrassing you any longer. Station is on the top floor in that building over there. Good luck."

My mother tosses me the keys. I just stand there, like I did the first day of kindergarten, scared to walk into class. I take off my boots, put on some strappy heels, place my boots back inside and lock the car.

I turn. The Commons resembles a European castle, or even an old prep school, towering on a hillside, a forest behind, the world its view. I slip-slide across the lot in my strappy heels, a feat that is like walking across a frozen high wire. I've forgotten what it's like to walk on ice. It is *not* fun.

There is a well-marked sign inside the building's doors, and I locate the elevator to head to TRVC. I hit the top floor and exit into an outer lobby, where I have to buzz to talk to a receptionist.

"I'm Sonny Dunes," I say. "I'm here to see Lisa Kirk. I'm the new meteorologist."

The receptionist looks at me as if I'm a Jehovah's Witness who showed up unannounced to hand her a pamphlet rather than the new hire who's going to save her station's tail.

I smile.

"You can have a seat," she says.

I hang up my scarf and my coat, stuffing my gloves into the pockets.

A few seconds later, Lisa comes rushing through the doors. She has two phones in her hands, Bluetooth in her ear, a badge around her neck and is carrying an iPad.

"Lisa," I say, the inflection in my voice dropping.

I practiced saying her name in the shower so I would sound enthusiastic when I met her, but my voice cannot hide my real emotions. I'm ashamed of how I treated Lisa in college and embarrassed my career has landed me here.

"Sonny!" she yelps.

Lisa throws her arms around me as if I'm a long-lost sister.

I can hear my mom's voice from the other night. *I think she reminded you too much of Joncee. She was so energetic. So smart. So willing to wear her heart on her sleeve.*

Is that why I've always been so distanced from her? As icy as the wind off the lake? I'm not a bully at heart.

She wanted friends.

Now I hear my therapist's voice. "All coping mechanisms," she is saying. "Just the wrong ones."

Lisa holds me at arm's length. "You look even more amazing in person!" she gushes.

"Thank you," I say. "Thank goodness you're not wearing your readers."

She laughs.

"You look the same, too," I say.

"Thank you!" she says.

Lisa truly looks like she did in college, save for her unruly, curly hair. It's gone gray at the roots, and her ringlets are tinged in silver. She has kept on the "freshmen fifteen" she gained her first year in college—from the late-night pizzas and the cereal bar and free ice cream at the cafeteria—and even retained a similar, albeit hipper, style of her signature cat eye frames. Lisa is wearing a pantsuit over which she's draped a long sweater, which has given her the look of someone who's just parachuted into the newsroom.

And forgotten to remove the parachute.

Stop it! I think to myself. *Stop being so catty. Your life and your past have nothing to do with her. She's the one being so kind. She's the one saving your career.*

"It's good to see you again, Amberrose..." She stops. "I mean, Sonny. Sorry...habit. How has your transition been going?"

"It's been going," I say. "Nothing like moving home to live with Mom," I joke.

"I adore your mother," she says.

"You remember her?"

"Of course! I've seen her a few times. And everyone in town adores her, too. She's a true Steel Magnolia. Although I prefer to call her our Cherry Queen."

In the summer, Traverse City is famous for its cherries, and its National Cherry Festival draws tourists from all around the world.

"I prefer to call her something else," I say completely out of nervousness. "I don't know why I said that. I love my mom, too."

"Well, you'll need to hit your edit button more often in these parts. A wicked sense of humor doesn't play well up here." She starts to walk. "Follow me."

The news station is an open work space enclosed by brick walls and tall, paned windows. Light flows in, and my heart floats. Sunshine always makes me feel better. Reporters talk on the phone and scribble notes, while others tap on laptops.

"I like this space," I say. "I thought the station was still on the other side of town."

"Just moved here. Big changes, like I told you. I thought we needed to be centered in town, be part of the community and part of the action."

Lisa pushes through double doors and leads me directly into a small studio, where the noon news is about to finish. The set doesn't look any more impressive in person than it did from the couch this morning. The midday anchors, who look as if they need to be put down for a nap, are showing footage of a black bear that wandered through downtown Traverse this morning, stopping to look in storefront windows as if it were out for a day of leisurely shopping.

"I think I know what he's looking for," one of the anchors says. "Gummy bears."

I groan out loud.

"And it looks like it will be a bear of a week coming up,

too," Polly Sue adds, using that pointing stick again as if she's an Olympic fencer. "A massive cold front will move in from Canada, bringing loads of snow and a big drop in temperatures. Enjoy the thirties while you can."

I feel dizzy and have to grab Lisa's arm for support.

"Are you okay?" she whispers.

"Blood sugar," I say.

Lisa pulls a sleeve of Oreos from her sweater pocket. "That's why I carry these," she says. "Want one?"

I shake my head.

"Of course not," she says, shoving one into her mouth. "Let's introduce you to Polly Sue."

"And we're clear," a director calls.

Lisa pulls me toward a young woman with electric red hair wearing a bright blue dress. My instinct is to salute her.

"Polly Sue Van Kampen, this is Sonny Dunes. Sonny, Polly."

I extend my hand, and Polly grabs it and then drops it quickly, as if I'm holding a grenade.

"It's nice to meet you," I say. "I have so many ideas to share with the team about making us the best station in Michigan."

"Team?" Polly Sue looks at me and gestures around with the pointer in her other hand. "It's just us, *Sonny*."

She makes my name sound like a dirty word.

"Just us?" I ask.

"Merle is retiring," Lisa explains. "Polly is our morning, noon and weekend meteorologist. Icicle handles all the behind-the-scenes stuff. He's our part-time cameraman, part-time graphics editor, part-time news writer, part-time researcher, guy Friday."

"Icicle?" I ask.

"Ron Lanier. Icicle is his nickname," Lisa says matter-of-factly.

I look at her. "And?" I ask. "With a nickname like that, there has to be more to the story."

"Oh," she continues. "He was shooting a bad traffic accident one morning and was standing under a building's overhang when a hospital helicopter buzzed overhead. It was coming to the scene to transfer the injured driver."

"No," I say.

"Yes," Lisa says. "About a hundred icicles came flying off the building. Nearly every one missed his body. It was a miracle."

"*Nearly* every one?" I ask.

"He survived." Lisa shrugs. "And we got it all on tape. Made for a great story. Our ratings shot up overnight."

I try not to shake my head, but I can't help it.

"It's winter in Michigan," Lisa says. "Get used to it. Oh, there's Icicle now! Let me grab him to introduce you."

As soon as Lisa is out of earshot, Polly Sue turns to me. "Let me be clear, *Amberrose*. I've worked here five years. This was supposed to be *my* gig. Lisa either felt sorry for you, or knew your pathetic story would be good for a quick ratings boost. But we don't like outsiders around here. Viewers know a fraud and a turncoat when they see one. They know when someone is just using this as a launching pad for another job. We're the station for the old-timers around here. They won't take to you at all."

I feel my face morph into a look of shock and then barely hidden rage.

"I'm not an outsider. I was born and raised here. And let *me* be clear: you work for me." I take a breath. "Listen, I know we're both under a lot of pressure here, but I want this to work, okay?"

"You were replaced by a virtual meteorologist," Polly Sue says. "What's that say about how your so-called career is going?"

I look at her and think about grabbing the pointer she's still holding in her hands. I picture myself saying, "PS. It's not 1972. Nobody uses these pointers anymore," and then snapping it in half and handing it back to her, but I don't. I've had great mentors in the past, and they've all treated me like gold. I will try to do the same with this wannabe villain.

"Glad you two had a chance to talk," Lisa says.

"Me, too!" I say, my voice a virtual bird's chirp.

"Good, good," Lisa says. "Sonny, this is Icicle. Icicle, Sonny."

Icicle looks a lot like one of the adorably cute but dorky actors in a teenage comedy film, the smart, science nerd who falls head over heels with the beautiful cheerleader and ends up making her fall in love with him by giving her a magic potion he invented. He's impossibly tall and lanky—like a human pogo stick—with a mop of hair that he's parted and slicked down, like he started playing with his grandfather's Brylcreem and used the entire jar. And yet there is something goofily appealing about him, like your best friend's kid brother who really wants to hang around with the older crowd.

"Hi, Sonny! It's so nice to meet you."

"You, too, Icicle." I stammer over his nickname, and he laughs. "Nice to break the ice."

"Speaking of which, everyone always wants to know how bad the accident was after hearing about my nickname." Icicle pulls up the sleeves of his shirt and shows off two horrible scars where the sharp ice pierced his skin even through a sweater and jacket. It looks like he was attacked by that black bear on TV. "Just got nicked here and here. Who knew icicles were so sharp?"

"Nicked?" I ask. "You poor thing. I'm so sorry. I can't imagine what that must have been like."

"Thank you," he says. "That's very nice of you to say. It certainly was not my best day, but you know what that's like."

His face immediately reddens. "Oh, my gosh. I'm sorry. That didn't come out right."

"That's okay," I say. "I do."

"I'm a survivor," he says, his gold eyes darting to the floor. "You know what that's like, too."

This time, my face reddens. And then it hits me.

"Oh, my gosh. Ron Lanier. You're Julie Smith's son, aren't you? I mean Julie Lanier."

He nods. I went to high school with Julie. She married her

high school sweetheart, who played college hockey at Michigan. I haven't spoken to Julie in forever. Because I never returned her calls. Like all of the ones I got from Cliff and Eva. Why do I never look back? Why do I never ask for help?

"Wow, I feel old," I continue.

I can see Polly Sue nod imperceptibly.

"Well, as I said, Icicle does it all around here," Lisa says.

"I'd really like to be a weatherman one day," he says.

"That'll be the day," Polly Sue blurts.

Icicle ducks his head.

"So, Sonny, I have your first assignment," Lisa says. She lifts her head from her notes. She has missed the whole incident.

"Today? I thought this was a day of introductions."

"It was," Lisa says. "That's over. Let's go to my office, and I'll tell you about it."

"It was so nice to meet you, Polly Sue," I say. "I look forward to working with you."

Polly beams as if all is A-OK. "Me, too!"

"Ice, meet us in five, okay?" Lisa says.

Lisa walks me into her tiny office and shuts the door. The chaos of the newsroom goes away, and it's suddenly just the two of us. Her office is filled with photos of politicians, celebrities and VIPs who have come through town—for the Michael Moore Film Festival, the Cherry Festival, or even just vacation—and stopped for an interview. Her office is filled with Northwestern memorabilia too, a swath of purple running along the brick walls. A bookshelf is lined with biographies of Edward R. Murrow, Walter Cronkite and Barbara Walters. And then I see a photo propped in a corner of one shelf, leaning against a stuffed wildcat: it's a group of freshman girls. The photo was taken in the hallway the day we moved into the dorms, and boxes are stacked around us. My arm is around Lisa, and her head is on my shoulder. She's flashing a #1 sign.

I don't even remember that photo being taken.

"Let me be as straightforward as I can," Lisa says. "You're the highest paid employee at TRVC, and you're a meteorologist. I've ruffled a lot of feathers to bring you here. The anchors are furious. Polly Sue already hates you..."

My eyes widen.

"Yes, I know. I know everything, so don't act surprised," she continues. "I saw you two arguing. The whole newsroom did. And that's probably a good move on your part to put her in her place. It puts everyone on their toes. Now, I realize folks aren't happy you're here. I realize you're not happy you're here. I still don't know if *I'm* happy you're here. But..." Lisa takes a deep breath and adjusts her glasses. "It's TV. I don't give a rat's patootie. My job is on the line. And I am going to turn this station's ratings around, and you're going to help me do it."

I remember her in college, running not only NNN—Northwestern News Network, the student-run news channel on campus—but also nearly every other student organization.

Did she annoy me so much because she was always so serious, or because I was only serious about having fun in order to run from my past?

My eyes skew to the window. Snow gently falls. I am back at Northwestern, pinned against the soda machine by Lisa.

"Amberrose, two students have been injured this year walking on the ice on Lake Michigan. Two! And we can do something to prevent that. I want to do a story on the need to mark those areas as unsafe. You want to be a meteorologist, you could do a wonderful angle on the exact science of why the lake is so unsafe even though students may think otherwise. They see ice, they think it's okay."

I remembered Joncee, the bay, the ice, and I clung to the soda machine to hold me upright.

"That sounds completely lame," I remember saying. "No one cares about that, Lisa."

"I care!" she had yelled. "You should, too! You just can't be a part of NNN to bolster your résumé and not do a damn thing."

"I'm planning Winter Formal for the sorority," I had said. "That takes priority."

Lisa began to walk away, but turned at the last minute. "I'm trying to help you," she said in a voice so sad it still breaks my heart. "I'm trying to be your friend."

"So, here's my game plan," Lisa says, knocking me back into the present. "I want people to see Sonny in the winter. In fact, that's the name of your new winter segment: Sonny in the Winter. I want the hometown girl back home doing the winter things she loves: sledding, snowshoeing, making snowmen, ice fishing, skiing, participating in all the winter festivals, including the Winter Ice Sculpture Contest."

"I'm more of an in-studio personality," I say. "I love brainstorming..."

"So do I!" Lisa's tone makes me sit up straighter. "I know you're used to perfect weather all the time. I remember you complaining about all the cold, snow and wind in Evanston and Chicago. Well, too bad. Act like you love it. I'm taking you live, all the time. Viewers want to see how the desert rat does in the winter snow. Viewers want to see the hometown girl come home." Lisa stops, and a small smile comes over her face. She tightens her long sweater around her as if she has to contain her enthusiasm. "Most of all, people want to see if you have another breakdown."

"Lisa," I say, my voice shaking. "That's not nice to say."

"That's TV, Sonny. You know that." She walks around her desk to stand beside my chair. "You're under contract for a year. If you fail, your career's over. If you fail, my career's over. We both have a lot riding on this little winter adventure."

Lisa continues, "Today, you're going to meet Mason Carrier. He's head of the chamber of commerce for Grand Traverse and Leelanau County. Mason organizes nearly every event in northern Michigan, winter, spring, summer and fall. TRVC is sponsoring most of the winter events this year. My idea, because of you! And you're going to be participating in every one."

"What?"

"Starting today." Lisa grabs my arm and pulls me from my chair. "Off we go."

"Wait, what am I supposed to be doing?"

"Icicle will show you. You can follow him to Suttons Bay," she says. "Mason is the perfect person to toss you into the snowbank, as it were."

I turn to look at her, as she nearly pushes me out the door into the lobby.

"Polly Sue says it's going to be a looong winter," Lisa continues. "I can't wait!"

And, just like that, she is gone.

"Ready?"

I jump. Icicle is tapping on his cell.

"Sorry," he says. "I do that all the time. Sometimes I make the best company anyway." He looks at me and smiles before standing and lugging the camera and equipment onto his shoulder. "Want to follow me over to Suttons Bay?"

"My mother drove me," I say. "Oh, my God, I sound like I'm twelve years old."

"I still live with my parents," he says with a nod. "It's cool."

"Can you drop me off at my house later?" I ask.

"No problem."

I text my mom to tell her that I'm leaving the car keys for her at the reception desk, and that I already have my first assignment. I also tell her that I'm sorry for being such a jerk earlier. Then I pull on my coat and gloves, wrap the scarf around my neck and follow Icicle to the news van.

I make it halfway through the parking lot, before my heels slide across the pavement and my feet fly out from underneath me. I land with a resounding thud.

"Are you okay?" Icicle asks. He sets his equipment down and helps me off the ground. "My grandma broke a hip doing that."

My day could not get any worse.

I brush the ice and snow off my butt. I glance around to see if anyone saw, in that embarrassed way we all do when we fall. In the window, I see a woman lift her latte in a silent salute saying *Cheers!*

It's my mother.

I give her the finger.

"My mom," I say to Icicle, as if that's the only explanation needed.

"My mom would so ground me if I did that to her," he says.

"Aren't you like twenty-five?" I ask, doing the math in my head, remembering when I heard Julie was pregnant so long ago.

"That's a really good point," he says.

I hurry back to my mother's car to retrieve my boots, having already learned my lesson.

My tailbone aches, and I already know I'm going to have a massive bruise by tonight.

But that's nothing in comparison to the one on my ego right now.

chapter 5

Icicle is driving the winding road—the famed M-22 highway that dips and bends along the lake and bay, the road that literally transports summer tourists into another world of picturesque wineries and orchards, unique resort towns, beautiful beaches and stunning water—as if he's a kid playing with Hot Wheels, and the highway is a plastic track.

"Are you okay?" he asks.

I am clutching the side of the van, holding on to the door handle as if I might—at any second—need to keep it from flying open or jump for my safety. My legs are straight out in front of me, and I keep pantomime pressing the brake to slow the van down.

"Can you slow down just a bit?"

The kid looks at me and tilts his head.

"I grew up driving these roads," he says.

"That doesn't matter," I say.

My voice is trembling, and I will tears from springing to my eyes. Icicle slows the van immediately.

"Sorry," he says.

"I'm not used to this," I say, lying to cover the truth.

"Sonny likes the sun, right," he says with a laugh.

"Right," I say.

"Boy, is this going to make good TV. Lisa was right about that."

At fifty, my career is a joke. My life is as dicey as the roads. My future is as dire as the long-term forecast. My mind is littered with more dangerous memories than this road is with winter-created potholes.

I look out over the bay. A front is approaching. The wind is picking up, the tree branches bend, and in the distance, I can see a curtain of snow falling over the water. Half of the world is still draped in sunlight, half of the world is now cloaked in darkness.

The irony.

The bay is iced over a long way out. I can feel the tires of the van slide just a little on a patch of frozen road.

I shut my eyes to gather myself. I touch the buckle on the seat belt…eight, nine, ten… It doesn't shut out the past.

Can you come pick me up? I can hear Joncee say.

I'm busy, I say, impatiently twirling the phone cord. I was always busy. With a boy. Or my friends. Cheerleading or a club.

Puh-leeze, she said in that way only a kid can say, drawing out a single syllable into a heart-wrenching plea.

I'm busy.

"It's busy."

I open my eyes.

Icicle is staring at me.

"It's really busy," he says again.

Traffic is at a standstill in downtown Suttons Bay. I mean, if you call a dozen cars a standstill. A police officer is standing in the middle of the road, as people run around willy-nilly through the street.

Icicle rolls down the van's window—*that's* how old my new news station's van is—and calls out, "Hey, Trent."

"Hey, Ice." The police officer lifts his head up and yells, "News is here! Make me look good!"

Icicle laughs. "Where should I park?"

"Where they won't eat ya! Ha!"

"What is going on?" I ask. "What am I doing here?"

"Oh, we got a newbie," Trent says. "Doesn't look like she's got much meat on her, though."

"Excuse me?" I say.

They both laugh, and Icicle follows the sweep of the officer's hands into a marina parking lot.

I pull on my boots before stepping out of the van.

"You're a quick study," Icicle says, laughing.

I laugh. "Quick like a turtle," I say. "Can I ask you a question?"

"Shoot."

"Do you like everyone calling you Icicle?"

"That's my name," he says, pulling his equipment from the van.

"No, your name is Ron. Like your dad."

He looks at me, then puts his hands on his hips. On the barren landscape, his long, lithe body resembles one of the frozen trees. "I never thought of it like that," he says.

"It's a matter of respect," I say.

"But your name is Amberrose, not Sonny," he says.

"That's TV," I say. "TV folk are like Hollywood actors. We change our names all the time to reinvent ourselves, to make us seem like something else in viewers' eyes."

Icicle stares at me like I'm a hole in a wall, and he can see right through me. "What's your mom think of that? I mean, isn't that a matter of respect to her?"

My heart suddenly twinges like a bad guitar string.

What does she think of that? What do I think of that, all these years later?

"I don't know," I say. "I never asked."

"Why?"

"I don't know."

"I bet you do."

I look at Icicle. "Wow, you are a good journalist. Vic Victor, my mentor at WGN, urged me to change my name."

"Vic Victor?"

I laugh. "See what I mean? Vic was a great guy, but he was old-school, and he believed simple, memorable names—like those old-time movie stars—resonated with viewers. 'Listen up,' he told me the first week, 'Amberrose Murphy sounds like the girl you barely trust with your coffee much less your weather.' Vic credited his name change as a big reason for his long-term popularity." I look around, scanning the barren landscape. "I went on vacation to Palm Springs to escape the winter and fell in love with the desert. I knew that's where I wanted to work. There's an area in Palm Springs called Sunny Dunes. It's spelled differently, but it stuck in my head. That's when I knew. But I really did it for myself. It was a way for me to have a clean break from my past, a new start. I thought I could be a different person, reborn, but it didn't really turn out that way. I actually ended up living dual lives: half as Amberrose Murphy and half as Sonny Dunes."

"I get it," he says. "Maybe you—maybe we—just need to merge the two again."

Who is this kid? I think.

"Maybe. Sooo," I say, changing direction. "Are you going to tell me what I'm doing here? I'm supposed to meet Mason Carrier. Why do you need a camera for that?"

"Oh, we're filming a local winter festival," Icicle says. "Just a little filler between news segments. Follow me."

I happily turn away from the wind coming off the bay. My eyes water, and I wipe them with my gloves, and follow Icicle into Suttons Bay.

I forgot just how quaint this adorable little resort town is, even in winter. The town of Suttons Bay, quite literally, sits on Suttons Bay, sort of an ice-cream scooped bay that flows into Grand

Traverse Bay, which flows into Lake Michigan. The town is all brightly painted little wooden storefronts and historic cottages that have been turned into retail stores, restaurants, wine bars, art galleries, gardening stores and ice cream shops. It still has its old movie theater, with the original marquee, that shows one movie at a time. Small Town Theater! World Class Cinema! a sign on the building says.

I used to come here to see movies when I was girl, especially in the winter. I loved going to the movies here: the old-time seats and the popcorn drenched in butter. Mostly, I loved dreaming of running away from here, to the magical places shown on screen, where the sun always shined, the sky was blue, the grass was forever green and love was just a mistaken-run-in-with-a-stranger-on-the-beach away.

It is spitting snow, and the only color pops from the painted shops. The storefronts remind me of tulips that implore Michiganders to remain hopeful even when it's still snowing in May.

I turn. I've lost Icicle in the snow.

He should be easy to spot, since he's like a walking lamppost.

"Icicle!" I yell, immediately feeling like an imbecile for saying that out loud.

I spin left and right, and then step into the street to get a clearer view. I turn toward the bay, thinking he perhaps forgot something in the lot. I squint my eyes.

What in the world?

I see something large, white and amorphous, moving toward town. At first, I think it's a cloud of snow that's been lifted off the ground, but it keeps getting bigger and bigger. As it grows closer, I can hear it.

It's grunting!

And that's when I can finally discern the white figure in all the white snow: a giant animal—a groaning beast—is charging me.

I scream, so loudly the entire town seems to stop and turn.

No one moves.

All anyone does is grab their cells to record my death.

I stare at it, paralyzed. Its eyes are yellow, its hands like tiger paws, its fur matted, its teeth like razors.

I think of running, but the beast is in full sprint, its dirty breath puffing out of its mouth like smoke from a train.

As it nears, I finally realize it's not a ten-foot-tall behemoth running on all fours with drool flying, but a person in a costume.

Suddenly, that seems even more terrifying than a wild beast. Why would someone be charging me in a rented Halloween costume? And why is no one trying to stop it?

That's when I remember taking a self-defense class as part of a news story. I square my body, and when the beast is nearly upon me, I knee it squarely in its nether regions.

"Ow!" it cries.

The creature is bent over, groaning, walking in circles.

It reaches up with its awful paws and pulls off its head.

"What's going on?" I yell. "What kind of bad joke is this?"

"Got it all!"

I turn, and Icicle is standing beside me, the camera directed on me.

"What the..." I start.

The person turns. The beast now looks a lot like Tom Brady, albeit at fifty-five: piercing cornflower blue eyes, a dimple in his chin deep enough to plant a good-sized tomato plant, dusty blond hair gone silver at the temples that still looks remarkably good after being flattened in a snowman costume. His cheeks are ruddy, and his nose looks as if it may have been broken and then healed at an adorable angle, and he has a scar on his forehead that tells a secret. In short, he's one of those men who looks amazing without even trying, so unlike the California guys—and especially the TV anchors—whose faces have been lifted and tucked, skin has endured Botox, filler and dermabrasions, whose bodies are so perfect they resemble rectangles, men who are pretty but not handsome.

"Are you okay?" he asks once he's recovered from my knee. "Are you in shock?"

I realize I've been staring, blinking, for way too long.

"You're not abominable at all," I finally say.

A booming laugh spills forth, one that sounds like the elusive thunder snow in Michigan.

"Thank you," he says. "Neither are you, Sonny."

"How did you know my name?"

"I'm Mason Carrier. Lisa wanted us to meet." He extends his hand.

"Wait a minute," I say, the lights finally coming on in my head. "You mean this was a setup."

He nods.

I turn toward Icicle. He lifts one hand as a sign of a truce. "Hey, this was all Lisa's idea," he says. "And, from this footage to introduce you to viewers, she's going to love it."

"Welcome to YetiFest," Mason says.

"YetiFest?"

"Can I buy you a cup of coffee?" Mason asks. "I think you need a little time to process everything."

"I need wine, Mason," I grumble. "We're not at a PTA meeting."

"That's where you need wine the most, right?" He winks, and I smile.

"I don't have kids," I say. "But I do have a mother."

He laughs. "I have kids," he says. "And how long do you have to talk about my mom?"

I laugh and turn to Icicle. "I'm going to edit this footage and send it Lisa," he says. "Go on. I'll catch up with you in a half hour, if that works."

"I'm not on air tonight, am I?" I ask Icicle.

"No," he says. "Tomorrow night."

"I don't want a repeat of my last newscast."

"You sure?" Mason asks. "Last time I looked, that clip was up to about five million views."

"You're buying, Mason," I say.

I follow the yeti to a nearby wine shop. It's downright adorable, with big oak barrels serving as tables and a sign made from corks that reads, Don't Wine About Winter!

We take a seat, and a waitress brings us a menu.

"Our yeti must be thirsty!"

She takes a free hand and musses the fur on his costume, until it mats.

"So," I start, "you're..."

"Freddy the Yeti," he says. "Each year, a local celebrity—" he stops and uses dramatic air quotes around *local celebrity* "—is chosen to be Freddy."

"And what does Freddy do?"

"Well," Mason starts, "Freddy is like the abominable emcee for all the events. The library holds a yeti story time and answers kids' questions like what do yetis smell like, or do yetis have friends. There's a big scavenger hunt around town, where people try to find me hidden in the snowy landscape, the movie theater is showing *Abominable*, and there's a chili cook-off."

"Do yetis have friends?" I ask.

"Depends if they're hungry," he says.

I laugh, too hard, and look at the menu.

"This place is a winter pop-up for a local winery that holds wine tastings on their spectacular orchards overlooking the water," Mason says. "The whites and reds are very good."

I guffaw, too hard.

"That laugh sounded sarcastic."

"Sorry," I say. "I've spent my whole adult life in California. They sort of know their wine there."

Mason waits until he can catch my eyes. "We sort of know our wine here, too. Things have changed. Michigan is famous for its wine now. Can I order for you?"

I nod, and he calls over the waitress.

"Two glasses of the Blustone 2018 Cab Franc Rosé," he says. "Typically, I'd go with a red, but considering it's early..." He looks at his watch and smiles. "Really early, and a drunk yeti can be a bad thing."

The waitress returns with our wine. Mason starts to pick up his glass, but realizes he's still wearing his yeti paws. He removes the oversize mitts, then swirls and sniffs, and lifts the glass of peachy-pink wine to his lips. I do the same, but steel myself as if I might be drinking bad milk. Instead, my taste buds explode.

"The aromas of gooseberry, apricot and strawberry are charmingly blended with more subtle hints of beach grass and white pepper. The palate is juicy and loaded with lemony acidity, ripe strawberry and cherry, ending on tangy cranberry and apple."

I look at him, impressed.

"Yetis like their wine." He shrugs. "I'm the chamber guy. I have to know everything about everything here. Cheers!"

He lifts his glass. I follow suit. We clink.

"So," Mason says. "What's it like to be home?"

I take another sip of my wine and tell him even more about my career debacle, moving back to live with my mom, my fight with Polly, my fall in the parking lot and my ride with Icicle.

"Great first day at work," he says. "Cheers again."

Mason looks at me, unzips the top of his yeti costume, and I can't help but stare.

"Did you grow up around here?" I ask.

"Northport," he says. "Born and raised. Married my high school sweetheart, and we had two kids. A boy and a girl. Both grown. Both flew the local coop. One works in Detroit, and one lives in Chicago. Both married with kids."

"So you're a grampa," I say. "Congratulations. Your wife must love being a grandmother."

Mason ducks his head and looks at me. "She passed away nearly ten years ago."

"Oh, my gosh," I say. "I'm so, so sorry."

"Andi committed suicide," Mason says. "She suffered from depression her whole life."

Mason takes a sip of wine. "Sorry, I didn't know we'd be getting into all this today," he says. "Especially just meeting and wearing this." Mason smiles, and the dimple on his chin expands. "I'm an open book, though. I don't like to keep secrets." He looks at me again as if I'm the only person in the world. "I believe in life. I believe the good outweighs the bad. I believe we're on a journey here that is filled with beauty and pain, happiness and horror, highs and lows, but it's a journey we must take because we never know the impact our lives and love will have on others."

I'm at a loss for words after that. I am anything but an open book. I am a diary with a lock and a hidden key. I shiver.

"Are you okay?" he asks. "I'd give you my costume to stay warm, but it's all I have."

I smile. "Readjusting to Michigan…to winter…pretty much everything." I turn and gesture toward the door. "I forgot that Michigan stores always keep a door cracked open, even in the winter."

"We get used to the cold, so we get hot easy," Mason says. "Remember what that was like?"

"I'm used to being hot all the time, and liking it," I say.

"You know," Mason says, "they just might ask you to be Freddy the Yeti next year."

"Oh, God, I hope I'm not here a year from now."

Mason gives me an odd look and sits back in his chair.

"I'm sorry," I say. "I didn't…"

"But you did, Sonny," he says, leaning forward again. "You did mean it." Mason swivels his chair toward me. "We're not yokels. You're actually one of us. Remember, Amberrose?"

I look at him.

"Stop stereotyping us. Maybe we'll stop stereotyping you. Have you ever considered that maybe we're just good people up here who love all four seasons just like Californians love the sun? To each his own?"

"Winter is the *longest* season by far here."

"I think it's the prettiest."

I turn from him and stare out the window. It is snowing like the dickens now. I can't even see across the street. I couldn't find the yeti in this lake-effect blizzard with a team of baying bloodhounds.

Am I angry I'm back in Michigan? Angry my career took a U-turn? Angry my past still holds me prisoner? Or embarrassed because this stranger just read me like a book? Is it possible to merge Amberrose and Sonny?

"I'm sorry," I say. "I'm a bit off-kilter. I wasn't expecting all of this today."

There is silence for a moment before Mason asks, "What is snow?"

"I'm sorry?" I ask. "I'm not following."

"What is snow?"

"Well, snow is precipitation in the form of ice crystals, mainly of intricately branched, hexagonal form and often agglomerated into snowflakes, formed directly from the freezing of the water vapor in the air at a temperature of less than thirty-two degrees Fahrenheit."

Mason laughs. "Spoken like a true meteorologist." Then he looks at me again, and the entire world drops away. It's just me and him. "But what is snow? What does it mean to you, as a person?"

I can feel my heart begin to flutter. I shake my head to try to knock the memories away. I look away from him. A young girl in a bright pink coat stops at the front window and puts her mouth to it. She blows on it, and the glass fogs. She traces a heart with her finger. Then she sticks out her tongue and catches snowflakes, before turning to run, her mother racing after her.

Joncee, I think. *Joncee is snow.*

"I have to go," I say, standing. I reach for my coat but realize I've never taken it off.

"Sonny, are you okay?"

I don't respond to his question. "Thank you for meeting me. I know Lisa wants you to show me around and get me involved in a lot of these winter festivals for live broadcasts. I'm sure we'll be in touch."

"I'll be seeing you tomorrow actually," he says.

I stop.

"We're going sledding," Mason explains. "Actually, cardboard sledding."

Can this day get any worse?

"Lisa already arranged it." He grins and holds up his hands. "Don't shoot the messenger."

"Can't wait," I say, heading toward the door.

"Sonny?"

I turn.

"Word of advice?"

What is he going to say now?

"Make sure your rear is padded."

I smile.

"One more thing?" Mason continues.

"Yes?"

"You can't stop the weather from happening," he says. "It's going to snow in Michigan. A lot. You already know that as a meteorologist. You just need to understand that as a person."

I start to head out the door when Mason yells, "You know, when it snows, you have two choices: you can shovel or you can make snow angels."

chapter 6

Same drive, different driver.

Same ole Sonny.

I am gripping the passenger door, touching the seat-belt buckle and air-braking as my mom drives me back to Suttons Bay.

I can barely see the road. The world is white. It is snowing as if snow has just been invented, and Mother Nature wants to test it out on the world for the very first time.

Meteorologist Sonny knows that lake-effect snow is produced during cooler atmospheric conditions when a cold air mass moves across long expanses of warmer lake water. I talk to myself in terms of science to calm myself.

Western Michigan and Northwestern Lower Michigan are known as "snowbelts." As winds cross over Lake Michigan, they generate snow, and areas north to south from Traverse City to South Haven can experience massive amounts of lake-effect snow, often up to two inches an hour in certain spots. These snowfall events are highly localized and under the right conditions of northerly winds, a single band of lake-effect snow may form down the length of Lake Michigan, producing intense snowfall, while a few miles inland it may be sunny and clear.

My mother's SUV is buffeted by the wind, and the car shudders.

I do the same.

Human Sonny believes that God is standing over the northern coast of Michigan dumping buckets on top of us, laughing—*at me!*—the entire time.

This is my punishment.

"Stop it right now, young lady," my mother says, as if reading my mind. "You're okay. You're safe."

I look over at my mom, and my body relaxes just a bit.

She reaches over to shake my leg, to shake me out of my funk.

"Keep your hands on the wheel!"

"My goodness, Amberrose. You're just like Marge."

Her out-of-the-blue reference actually makes me laugh.

"She was a smart dog," I say.

All of our dogs growing up were girls—my mother didn't like the thought of a boy dog taking aim on her beloved flowers—and they were all named after elderly matriarchs in our family. And our dogs were all as wise as those women, too. Marge, in particular.

Marge both loved and hated the snow. When she was in the snow, the eighty-five-pound auburn-furred mutt acted like the part husky she was. She dashed through the snow, she rolled in the snow, she caught snowballs we tossed in the air for her. Marge even let Joncee ride on her back when Joncee was small, like a tiny equestrian atop a pretty pony. The two were inseparable.

But when Marge got in the car and it was snowing, she was the equivalent of riding with a driving instructor. Her golden eyes were riveted on the road ahead as well as your navigation.

If your hands strayed from ten and two on the steering wheel, or if you reached to change the radio station, take a drink of water or eat a snack, she would whine and bark until both hands were firmly planted and full attention was given.

It's as if she could see the future, I think. *She knew she had to protect Joncee.*

"Aren't you excited?" my mom asks. "I am."

I look at my mom. She is dressed as if she's a girl going to a holiday party: beautiful blue coat, black gloves, pretty pink scarf, an adorable knit cap and, fittingly, dangly snowflake earrings bouncing happily around her face.

"I can't say that I'm excited," I say. "I feel like I'm being set up."

"Oh, honey, stop that negative thinking," she says. "You used to be such a little ray of sunshine all the time."

"There's no sunshine in my life anymore," I say. "Literally."

My mother slows the car, and I can't tell whether it's because the snow is coming down even harder or she wants to make a point to me.

"You made a mistake," she says.

Again, I don't know if this statement is referring to my career or my childhood.

"Is it so bad being back home? Is it so bad enjoying a real Michigan winter? Is it so bad being with me?"

Her voice cracks, and I look over at her. My heart pings.

"Of course not," I say. "It's just not how I expected my life to go."

"Me, either, sweetheart. I lost half my family. You moved three thousand miles away. I don't have a husband, I don't have grandchildren..."

"Mom, that's not fair."

"No, honey. That's just it. Life ain't fair." Her voice echoes in the car, over the incessant holiday music and the heat blaring from the defroster. "Do you know how long it's been since I've had a little fun?"

My heart pings again. I look at my mom and can finally see her clearly: living all alone in a big house once filled with family, trying to navigate a world without those she loves most in it. I want to say all of this, but I cannot find the words. I turn to humor yet again.

"I thought you were your own party," I say.

"Ha," my mom says. "I spend my days trying to make the world feel okay. I spend my days helping the dying and healing their broken families. I try to make the world feel better because I know what it's like to lose those you love. But that's life. How we choose to deal with all of that is living. So, if you want to have a pity party, then bring it on, because I get to wear the crown, pick out the china and fill the teacups with my own tears."

I feel my heart rise in my throat. As if on cue, "Sleigh Ride" begins to play on the radio. I turn it up so I don't have to say a word—so my emotions won't be known—and my mom begins to sing.

"'Come on, it's lovely weather for a sleigh ride together with you.'"

"Although," my mom says, as we pull into the park where the Cardboard Sled Race is being held, "I think you're going on this sleigh ride all by yourself." She stops and begins to laugh before she's even finished. "In a cardboard sled."

The parking lot is packed. Even in this snowstorm. Nothing, I remember, stops Michiganders from a day of fun, not even a lake-effect blizzard.

My initial thought was that this would be an event mostly for children, but this is more akin to an adult Pinewood Derby, except, it seems, with cardboard and loads of duct tape.

I turn to my mom once we're out of the car. "How do I look?"

She squints in the snow. "Very pretty, honey. Albeit not very practical for this type of thing."

"It's my first show," I say.

"But you still have to sled, right?"

Her words hit me hard.

I actually thought I might just be seated in one of the sleds for a shot, or talking to the participants in front of their sleds, but now it's dawning on me that Lisa—of course—would want me to get maimed for ratings. I dressed more ski bunny than Michigan sledder, opting not for puffy coat and thermal suit but rather a skintight black skiing ensemble with belt and embroidered vintage-inspired sunbursts in orange and yellow on the shoulders. When my friends and I would escape the desert to ski at Big Bear—a stunning snow-covered mountain and ski resort close to Palm Springs—we would dress to the nines. Instead, I should have dressed for the viewers—and survival.

"Hi, Mrs. Murphy! Don't you look pretty!" Lisa approaches. "Hi, Sonny!"

When Lisa sees me, she nearly stumbles in the snow. "Ope! Aren't you just a ray of sunshine in all of that."

I know that's her Michigan way of saying, "I hate what you're wearing," much like Southern women will say, "I just love your hat!" when they absolutely despise it.

Lisa is wearing essentially what she was wearing yesterday.

"Hi, Lisa. Aren't you freezing?"

"This is downright balmy for Michigan. Snow seems to make it warmer, doesn't it?"

No, I want to say. *It makes it colder.*

"We've got you set up at the starting line for the first broadcast," Lisa says. "I want you fully integrated into the entire newscast, start to finish. The anchors are going to welcome you and throw it to you here. You will interview participants about their homemade sleds, talk to Mason about where the money from the race goes, then we'll tease you racing downhill in your sled the entire show."

I knew it!

"I knew it!"

I say that out loud, and my mother laughs.

"What did you expect, Sonny? You're our star."

Every word of that sentence drips with sarcasm, and I inhale to steel myself, but begin coughing when the cold air plummets down my throat.

"Get her some water, Icicle."

He races off.

Lisa walks over and slips her arm around me. Management always attempts to keep the talent calm before a big show. She walks me toward the starting line, where hundreds are gathered.

"Now, as I said, you're going to race downhill. Icicle will be in with you, filming the whole thing. That will be the end of the show. So, you'll open, throw it back to the news desk, then you'll do a live forecast here, which will be beautiful—it's snowing for your first segment!—and your ride will end the show. I was thinking you would say something like, 'I look forward to the ride ahead with all of you and TRVC,' or something like that." Lisa stops. "Although I really like what I just said. Got it?"

I nod. I'm already frozen. There is an inch of snow on my perfectly coiffed hair. In a half hour, I'll look like a poodle that just got a bath.

"Oh, Mason! Hi! Over here!"

Lisa's enthusiasm is like water torture. I now remember why I avoided her in college. I can turn it on for a broadcast, but I can't muster faux happiness.

"It's snowing! You must be so excited!" Mason says to me with mock enthusiasm. He spans his arms wide and laughs. "Just teasing you!"

"You're a real hoot," I say, shaking my head at him. "Why didn't you change out of your yeti costume?"

"*You're* a real hoot," Mason laughs. "Let me show you around."

The hill at the park is storybook Michigan. It is lined with pine trees, thick with snow, a beautiful border to the hill, whose snow has been smoothed and polished, like a rock you'd find on the lakeshore. Above the park lies another hillside, rising toward the howling heavens, lined with eerily majestic winter vineyards.

"There's a warming hut up there if you get cold," Mason says, pointing at a little log cabin off to the side.

"I forgot about warming huts," I say.

"You can never forget about warming huts, but I guess there's not a need for many in California, right?" he asks.

"About or a-boat it?" I tease. "You sound like my mom."

"That's probably a good thing," he says with a wink.

Beyond the bottom of the hill sits the bay. I immediately imagine seeing myself taking flight on one of the knolls and flying into the bay.

"It's just a small hill," Mason says, as if reading my mind.

"Easy for you to say."

"From here, it does look like a miniature ski run you would see in the Olympics, but it's a bit of an optical illusion," he says. "It's not that big of a descent. And there are hay bales to stop the sleds along with a team of volunteers and EMTs."

"Hay bales? Gee, thanks. That doesn't make me feel any better."

Mason walks over, puts his arm around me and gives me a squeeze. "I promise you'll be okay."

He removes his arm, but the heat from his body remains, like his arm was a hot poker and my skin was bare.

I look up, and my mother's eyebrow is soaring above her face, like a sarcastic eagle. I narrow my eyes, and she gives me a cheesy thumbs-up.

"Are you sure?" I ask, trying to ignore both my mother and my emotions.

"You can trust me. I started the annual Cardboard Sled Race," he says.

"What? You?"

"I'm the Cardboard King," Mason says.

"Why?"

Mason's light blue eyes span the hillside, and for a moment, they perfectly match the color of the cold bay in the distance. "For my wife," he says. "For my kids." He turns. "For me." He tugs his stocking cap farther over his ears just like a boy. "Andi loved winter. She loved skiing with the kids. It turned her into a little girl again, if only for a moment." He stops. "I started this event to shine a light on depression and suicide, and to bring awareness through something she loved." He kicks the snow. "Suicide is the tenth leading cause of death in the US, and the fourth leading cause between the ages of thirty-five and fifty-four. There were nearly 1.5 million suicide attempts last year. Depression plays a role in more than half of all suicide attempts. People's minds are changed and their hearts are moved when you're engaging them in a cause rather than preaching at them. Every dollar we raise goes to our local hospital to talk to kids and adults about depression and suicide, and how to seek help."

How can he talk so openly about tragedy? How can he be so transparent with his emotions? He is a window. I am a wall.

"Ready?"

Lisa appears out of nowhere.

"We're just a few minutes from broadcast. We need to mic you up and test sound and the feed." She motions me toward the starting line. Lisa cannot hide how absolutely giddy she is with this entire debacle.

The majority of the participants are adults.

Who just want to act like kids.

The homemade sleds run the gamut: some are just large cardboard boxes that have been reinforced with additional cardboard, edges covered in duct tape. But most are insanely creative, not only works of art but also feats of engineering. There's one shaped like a pizza slice—complete with realistic-looking pepperoni and mushrooms covering it—a shark that looks like Jaws, Michigan cherries on a giant stem, boats, mail trucks with wheels, Michigan Wolverines helmets—in maize and blue—adults holding on to the face mask as if they were on a roller coaster. My favorite is the sled that looks exactly like the Mystery Machine from *Scooby-Doo*.

"Let me introduce you to your sled," Mason says.

"*My* sled?"

Icicle appears from the side of the hill pushing what I can only describe as the antithesis of Michigan right now: a bright, yellow sun.

"A sun for Sonny!" Icicle yells. He stops, his breath coming out in big puffs of smoke. "Get it?"

"Oh, I get it," I say. I walk over and look at the sled. A giant cutout of a cartoon sun—yellow as a daffodil, rays splaying into the snowy sky—sits atop a cardboard sled with the station's name, TRVC-8, painted on one side, and Northern Michigan Welcomes Sonny Dunes! on the other.

"You're going to stick your head through the cutout as you go downhill," Lisa says, "so your actual face will be the face of the sun. The face of weather in northern Michigan."

"Who did all of this?" I ask.

"It was Lisa's idea," Icicle says. "Mason and I made the sled for you."

I can't help but smile.

"I don't know what to say."

"How about 'Testing 1-2-3'?" Lisa asks, as Icicle mics me up.

Lisa gives me the once-over, and we test the feed. "Ready?" she asks.

I nod.

"Good, because our careers are riding on this." She looks at the sled, as if her joke was intentional and laughs. "Riding? Ha! I'm funny."

"How do I look?" I ask Lisa.

Mason smiles. "Perfect."

My heart begins to pump, and I'm unsure if it's because this is my first broadcast or because of Mason's unexpected compliment, but my first segment is a blur of excitement. I interview participants about their sleds, and when I talk to Mason about why he started the sled race, my voice breaks, and my eyes mist.

"Holy moly!" Lisa says as soon as we're clear. "You can really turn it on for TV. The emotion… I mean, I nearly teared up."

I smile and nod, and then I do my first forecast.

"Okay," Lisa says as we near the end of the broadcast. "Here we go." She stops. "I mean, here you go."

"Here's a helmet," Mason says, handing me a yellow one.

"My hair," I say.

"Your head," he says, putting it on me and giving it a thwack with his hand. "I think that's a bit more important."

"You don't know TV," I say.

My ski suit is so tight I can barely maneuver through the opening and into the sled. Icicle basically shoves me inside and then follows suit, Lisa handing him the camera.

"Pray for me," I say to Mason, who laughs.

"Sometimes, losing control is a good thing," he says. "I mean you lost it before, and didn't it feel good for just a split second?" Mason looks at me. "This always made Andi feel so free and happy. Just be a kid for a moment. Remember what that was like? Happy, joyful, in the moment, life's troubles don't matter as you're flying down a hill."

I nod.

"You're going to be racing against four other sleds," Lisa says. "Best time wins."

I look to my right and left. I'm racing against a giant beer can, Jaws, the pizza slice and the Batmobile.

"Oh, and your sled has to stay intact," Mason adds. "Don't worry. It will."

"What about me?"

Mason doesn't answer. Instead, he moves behind me.

I teeter at the tippy top of the snow-drenched dune, gripping my sled like a modern Mr. Grinch.

When an air horn shatters the silence, Mason pushes our sled with all his might.

"You'll pay for this!" I yell.

My final words.

I scream, and the sled begins shaking the faster we go. I feel like an astronaut in a space shuttle.

Made of cardboard. And held together by masking tape.

We pick up speed, and it feels like we are flying at the speed of light now. One of my false eyelashes loosens in the icy wind and flies away. I look at Icicle, who has the camera positioned inches from my face. I scream and pull the other lash free, tossing it out the sun.

As my death-defying descent continues, I have two revelations: one, I might not survive. And two, how did I—quite literally—get here?

I shut my eyes, and I can feel Joncee with me in this sled. She would love this. Just the two of us on a wild ride together, sisters screaming and laughing and holding on to one another on a perfect winter day.

After she died, I blamed myself. What more could I have done? What more should I have done?

Mason's voice shatters my thoughts.

I open my eyes. I can feel my sister right beside me.

Just hold on, Amberrose! Just hold on! she would always say when we were sledding.

Her words are prophetic in so many ways.

I grip the front of the sun, stick my head out and yell, "Wheeeeee!"

The crowd screams and applauds.

At least, I think they are people. We are going so fast that they could be blenders or dancing raccoons.

I look out, the bay blurred from the snow but the little town twinkling and glowing brightly, drenched in lights. The bay is frozen, geese flocking to a hole in the ice, and boats sit in an open shelter like ghost ships.

I look to the hillside. A cardinal, the brightest red I have ever seen, sits silhouetted on a branch. It flies as I whiz by, snow from the pine falling with a big thud.

In the distance, beyond the shroud of clouds and lake-effect snow, the horizon has broken, the snow band temporarily halted, and I can see the moon illuminating the unfrozen waters of the churning bay, the winter cold and shards of light turning it alternating colors of brilliant blue, deep green and steel gray.

It's mysteriously majestic, and I realize my mouth is open, but I am no longer screaming: instead, I am staring in awe at a coast I have never embraced, one draped in a peaceful, otherworldly, icy costume.

Isn't is beautiful? I can hear Joncee say.

I hear a loud shudder. In front of me, the shark is falling apart, in sections, from the middle out. A fin flies in front of my face, and then we sideswipe a man who looks like Grizzly Adams, and I laugh harder than I have in ages. The pizza slice flips and out fly human pepperonis.

Suddenly, Icicle screams, "Aim for the hay bales!", so I lean my body as far left as I can and the sled moves just enough for us to ram a stack of hay bales.

"I'm alive!" I yell.

My mother appears, a huge smile on her face.

"You won, Amberrose! You won!"

I stick my arms out the front and yell, "Sonny's here to win!"

"How do you feel?" my mom asks as I clamber out of the sled.

I look at her. "Like a kid, Mom," I say, my voice suddenly shaky. "Like a kid."

She holds open her arms and gives me a big hug.

I see Mason racing down the hill. "You won!" he says, bending over to catch his breath.

"I think you deserve a glass of wine," my mom says to me.

"I think I do, too," I say. "But first—" I look at Mason "—I think I want a repeat."

He shakes his head and beams. "I'll go with you this time," he says.

And then we grab the sled and begin the long climb back up the hill to do it all over again.

chapter 7

"Good news or bad news first?"

"I feel like I should be sitting in a doctor's office," I say.

Lisa looks at me and stands from her office chair. She moves in front of me and leans against her desk very dramatically.

"I always wanted to be a doctor on *Grey's Anatomy*," she says. "Yes, McDreamy, you may kiss me…*after* I save this woman's life."

I try not to roll my eyes.

"Okay then, good news first," Lisa says. She takes a big slug of her latte, sets the cup down and picks up a raft of papers. "Our ratings are up."

My mind spins. *Up? Going from nothing to something is still nothing.*

"Way up," she adds, as if reading it. "Forty percent after your first broadcast!"

Lisa stands and does a little dance that looks as if Elaine from *Seinfeld* just stuck a fork into an electric socket.

I smile at her in that way patrons do at parents in a restaurant when their child dumps a bowl of spaghetti onto its lap and begins screaming and throwing noodles.

"You want me to stop dancing, don't you?" Lisa asks.

"Only when you're done," I say.

Lisa cinches her long sweater around her waist, grabs her laptop off her desk and takes a seat in the chair beside me.

"The bad news is our competitors are already taking shots at you on social media."

"Already? What did I do?"

Lisa opens her laptop, clicks on a link to a competitor's Facebook page, pulls up a video and hits play.

"Sonny's here to win!"

It's me at the end of the sled race. My arms are raised in exultation and then I wave an "I'm #1" finger at the crowd.

Winner? Or Loser? blares the banner over the video. *Does this look like a good sport to you?*

"This has received few thousand views already and over a hundred comments, most of which are not so nice," Lisa says. "And there's more."

Another station has a video of me seeming to laugh at my competitors' travails. "Everyone was laughing when the pizza slice and shark fell apart!" I say.

"I know, I know," Lisa says. She types a Google search into her laptop. "And then the TV critic at the local paper wrote this about you just this morning, and I quote, 'Did anyone else happen to see—and I use that word very sarcastically here—the debut of Sonny Dunes on TRVC-8 last night? I did, and I have a lot of questions, including, who wears false eyelashes to a cardboard sled race? And a ski suit that looks like one of the Real Housewives of Orange County? Northern Michiganders don't just want our weather from a real person, we want it from a real Michigander who loves and understands our state.'"

I rise out of my chair and pound Lisa's desk with my hand, her latte cup spinning wildly on her desk.

"It was my FIRST day!" I yell. "That is just downright vicious!"

Lisa looks at me. "I know. It is. Take a deep breath."

I do.

"Now sit."

I sit.

"You're the new kid on the block. The other stations feel threatened." Lisa pats me on the leg. I think of my mom. "And that's a good thing, as you know from your years on TV." She sets her laptop back on her desk. "But I need to be smart about how I position you moving forward."

I sigh. *At least there's a silver lining.*

"I can stay in-studio," I say. "Everything can be controlled. That way no one can use any impromptu moments against us."

I expect Lisa to nod and pull a cookie from the pocket of her sweater. Instead, she shakes her head. "No, people want to see you out and about in Michigan. That's a big reason I think our ratings are up."

No, you want to see me out and about in Michigan, I think.

"I want Sonny to do something that connects her to the beauty of the area. I want Sonny to show viewers what they could be doing in the snow. I want Sonny to be the face of Michigan, just like Sonny was the face of Palm Springs."

"You're talking about me in third person. That scares me."

Lisa laughs. "I want you to head out this afternoon with Icicle to go snowshoeing. These outdoorsy, adventure segments seem to be resonating with viewers."

"We've done *one*," I say.

"This time, we'll tape and edit them, so you won't be live, but it will seem that way," Lisa says, lost in thought. "And we'll eliminate the Sonny in competition with others element. You can snowshoe, right? Any dummy can." Lisa stops. "I didn't mean that."

There is a small smile on her face.

Yes, you did.

Lisa stands. "So—" she waves her hands as if I'm a bee she's trying to shoo out the window "—off we go."

I stand. "To?"

"Empire," she says. "The Empire Bluff Trail."

When I reach the door, I turn to ask Lisa if she wants my forecasts in different locations, but she is already shutting the door on me.

"Ready?"

I jump.

Icicle is standing in front of me. "You're like Jacob Marley."

"Who?" he asks.

"One of the ghosts that visits Ebenezer Scrooge."

"Who?" he asks again. "Oh, are they like an old-timey band my mom listened to in the '80s? She still goes to all those tribute concerts."

"Never mind," I say. "Houston, we have a problem, though."

"My name's not Houston."

"Never mind again. I don't have anything to wear to snowshoe."

"Oh, you do," he says. "It's already in the van. You can change when we get there."

I cock my head at him, confused.

"Lisa bought you an outfit that is—and I quote—'more appropriate for northern Michigan.'"

I actually shudder. "Lisa bought clothes for me?"

I picture myself in sweatpants and a sweater with a glitter pine tree on the front.

"And she gave you her snowshoes, too."

"I'm all set then," I say.

"You're being sarcastic, aren't you? My mom says you were really funny as a kid."

I think of the two of us planning our cheerleading routines, and me pushing to use a chant I created.

We're number one
Can't be number two
And we're going to beat
The whoopsie out of you!

I shake my head. "That sounds like there's a 'but' in there," I continue.

"No, you are funny," Icicle says. "But it's not my kind of funny. I like *The Walking Dead* and stuff like that."

"That's not funny, though."

He looks at me like I'm crazy, and says, "We all walk around like we're zombies most of the time. Half dead. Half alive. I think it's amusing, or I'd be sad all the time."

The honesty of his words stuns me.

I can't help but think of myself, stuck right now in this in-between world. I think of my mom, her family half dead, half alive. I think of Lisa, trying to resurrect a dead station. And I think of this young man standing before me who has been marked—literally and figuratively—by a life-defining and life-changing near-miss moment and not his accomplishments and all the life he has ahead of him.

I zombie-walk to the van, and we head toward Empire. It is snowing lightly, and as we drive the flakes seem to dance in the headlights, weightless, carefree, happy. The roads are fairly decent, so I need not clamp the door handle, touch the buckle or air-brake the floorboard the entire drive, which makes Icicle relax a bit.

We head directly west from Traverse City and straight across the middle of the pinky finger of the Mitten. As we drive along

72 and cross M-22, the snow picks up a bit. Empire sits on the coast of Michigan south of Leland and Glen Arbor. If you were able to drive across Lake Michigan, you would end up in Egg Harbor, Wisconsin.

"Was TV always what you dreamed of doing?" I ask Icicle to distract myself from the roads.

He nods. "I always loved video games and sort of being lost in another world. I filmed a lot of shorts in high school and college. I did a short documentary on my dad's hockey career, which ESPN ran online."

"That's amazing," I say.

"Everybody else's world just seemed a little more interesting than mine."

I look at him and smile. "Why?"

"I mean, you know. My dad was pretty famous around here. My mom was so pretty and popular. I mean, you two were so close before..." He stops abruptly. His face twists in embarrassment and pain.

"It's okay," I say.

"She told me about your sister," he says. "I'm so sorry."

I nod. "Thank you," I squeak. I don't want to cry. "It's okay," I repeat. "Go on."

The red streaks across his face from his admission, and he takes a breath to calm himself. "And here I come, this too-tall, goofy-looking kid who's too lanky to play hockey and who is terrible at basketball. Not as social or as popular as my mom. I mean, I was not the kid my parents should have had."

You poor thing.

"And then the icicle incident made me into part folk legend and part bad luck symbol. Girls didn't want anything to do with me because they assumed I was bad luck and were scared some sort of natural disaster might befall them, too. So I just do my job and disappear into everyone's else's world. Like yours now."

"You do realize that not everyone else's life is perfect, much less any better than yours."

Icicle looks at me and then stares out at the road. "It's fun to pretend, though, isn't it?"

We sit in comfortable silence until we reach the Empire Bluff Trail. The parking lot is dotted with a few cars and trucks but not many. Most people are at work or at home, warm and safe, not having to snowshoe for their career.

In goodness knows what clothes, I think.

I jump out of the van and head to the back. Lisa's snowshoes are waiting along with a recyclable grocery bag filled with…

I pull the bag toward me and wince.

"Are these men's clothes?"

There is a handwritten note atop a pair of polyester pants and bright red turtleneck and fleece zip-up.

"Cotton is rotten!" the note from Lisa says. "Soaks up the moisture and makes you feel colder. And we all know Sonny hates being cold. Ha! Ha!"

"Don't worry, I won't look," Icicle says.

"I'm more worried about you seeing me dressed in this," I say.

He turns, and I hop into the back of the van and pretend I'm a Cirque du Soleil performer, bending and twisting to pull on the too-big black snow pants and fleece. I pull on a pair of thick socks Lisa has left, the boots I wore today and then hop out.

"How do I look?" I ask Icicle.

"Like Lisa?"

"You're funny," I say.

I jump back into the passenger seat and pull down the mirror. I apply some makeup—not too much—and smooth my hair. I grab my beloved Tom Ford sunglasses from my bag and put them on.

"Do you need the sunglasses?" Icicle asks.

"The snow is blinding," I say. "And they look good on camera."

"They seem a bit much." He stops and gives me look. "Lisa wouldn't like them."

I take them off and return them to my bag.

"If you hand me a pair of Oakleys to wear," I say, "I swear I will stick you with a snowshoe pole."

Lisa, of course, has old-school snowshoes that are wood framed with rawhide lacing. The ones I had growing up were aluminum and plastic. These are heavier than the ones I remember but seem sturdier. I can't recall the number of times I had to trudge home through the snow with a broken binding or torn plastic decking.

"Did you know snowshoeing was developed thousands of years ago specifically for winter travel by foot?" Icicle asks. "Native Americans innovated snowshoe design. Depending on snow conditions, they created different styles. The whole idea is to stay atop the deepest of the snow." He looks down. "See? In these, we only go down a few inches versus having to trudge through knee-deep snow in boots."

"You're a surprise every day," I say.

Icicle ducks his head and takes off.

I follow, clomping loudly out of the lot and toward the trailhead.

"Ready?" Icicle asks.

I nod.

It is snowing now with some intensity, and the temperature seems to be dropping.

"Lake effect is in full effect," Icicle comments.

"You know weather?" I ask.

"Isn't everyone in Michigan an expert?"

I laugh.

"They seem to be, anyway" he says.

"What causes lake-effect snow?" I ask.

Icicle explains as adeptly as I ever could.

"And why is this area so prone to it?"

He explains astutely.

"Good job," I say.

"Thanks," he says. "You know I'm a meteorologist, right?"

"What?"

"Double major," he says. "Along with broadcast journalism."

"Why aren't you on air?" I ask.

"Me?" He chuckles and shakes his head as if I'm joking. His laughter is sad and hollow, and he takes off ahead of me without saying another word.

By the time we reach the trailhead, I'm out of breath.

"This is a pretty easy trail," Icicle says as if to mock my exertion. "Especially for inexperienced snowshoers. It's only a mile-and-a-half loop, but it's got a great payoff at the end. That's why Lisa chose it."

"I used to come here with my family when I was little. I did grow up here, remember?"

Icicle smiles and trudges forth on snowshoes carrying heavy equipment.

Ah, to be twenty-five again. I stop. *Ah, to be forty again.*

The trail meanders through a beech-maple hardwood forest that is breathtaking in its solitary beauty.

"These trees always seem to know a secret," I say in the quiet of the woods.

Icicle turns, a long, lone silhouette in the snow.

"Oh, I think they do," he says. "Just think what they've witnessed over the centuries. Life springing forth here after the Ice Age, emerging after massive glaciers carved out the deep basins of the Great Lakes and created the perched dunes—formed by glacial sands deposited on plateaus high above the shore—like we're standing on now. We're talking ice so heavy that it actually pressed the Earth's crust down. Imagine the power of the forces and the length of time it took to form these hills and valleys, shorelines, lakes and streams of today. These trees emerged. Native Americans traversed through these very trails and spoke to them. Their love of this earth was carried on the wind, driven into the ground and took root where it grew in these trees. So, yes, I do think these trees know a lot more about life than we do."

I am staring at Icicle unable to speak. "You sure are a wise, old owl for someone so young." I finally manage to say.

"You grow up an outsider, you spend a lot of time alone in the woods reading," he says.

"What else do you know?" I ask.

"That we better keep moving or Lisa will have our heads."

We continue along the trail in silence, passing some old farm equipment buried in the snow.

"And there's the money shot!"

I look up, and Lake Michigan is laid out before me. The shoreline arcs in breathtaking fashion, and Lake Michigan seems to go on for infinity. The water churns in the wind, and the dunes seem even more dramatic in winter, sand coated in ice and snow.

"Pretty amazing, huh?" Icicle asks. "We're four hundred feet above the water." He points. "In the distance you can see Sleeping Bear Point and South Manitou Island."

I smile, remembering the legend my dad used to tell me about the Manitou Islands.

Long ago, the bear Mishe Mokwa and her twin cubs sought to cross Lake Michigan from the Wisconsin shore to escape a great forest fire, I can hear my father say decades ago as we stood at this very spot. *Mishe Mokwa made it safely across, but her cubs floundered and drowned in the lake. The mother bear crept to a resting place where she lay down facing the restless waters that covered her lost ones. As she watched, two beautiful islands slowly rose from the water to mark the graves of her twins. The Great Spirit Manitou had created two islands to mark the spot where the cubs disappeared and then formed a solitary dune to represent the faithful mother bear.*

A thick band of lake-effect clouds drifts inward, and the sun breaks out. It is simultaneously sunny and snowing. Lake Michigan suddenly turns from concrete gray to Caribbean blue. Without warning, I tear up, thinking of my mom as the mother bear and how she continued on without one of her cubs.

"Ready?" Icicle asks, grabbing the camera. "I think this is the perfect spot and moment."

"I agree."

"What a stunning winter's day, northern Michigan! I'm Sonny Dunes, and I'm coming to you today from the Empire Bluff Trail, where I've been enjoying a day of snowshoeing." I lift my snowshoe and shake my leg. "I've been humbled by the landscape and the lake today, and its beauty in winter. The sun has broken out, and right now, in the distance, you can see the Manitou Islands." Icicle turns and pans the lakeshore. "The legend reminded me of my own mom. She was one tough mama bear who loved her cubs more than anything, too." My voice breaks, and Icicle turns the camera on me. "It's good to be home."

I stop. "Sonny Dunes' Dunes Forecast is a winter wonderland!" I give the seven-day, knowing a graphic will appear later. "From the Empire Bluff Trail, I'm Sonny in the Winter. Have a Sonny day!"

"That was great!" Icicle says. "Did you just come up with that sign-off?"

"Like it?"

"I do!"

A family snowshoes past, a young mother and father and two little girls. The parents stop to admire the view and ask what we are doing. The girls are literally running through the snow, puffy coats that make them look like little snowmen come to life. One of the girls screams, and I look up. Her body disappears over a dune. One ski pole flies into the air. I take off running, instinctively, before the parents even move. My heart is in my throat. I reach the first little girl who is peering over the dune.

"Gotcha!"

Her sister appears, laughing. The hill was an optical illusion, the drop-off only a foot or so.

"Don't ever do that again!" I gasp. "Promise me! Ever! Don't do that to your sister!"

The little girl who played the trick begins to cry.

"What are you doing?" the mom asks when they approach a few seconds later. She pulls the little girl into her arms, and the dad holds the other sister protectively. "They play this game every time we come here."

"I'm so sorry," I say. "I didn't know. I'm so sorry. I was just worried. I… I…"

I turn and walk back toward Icicle, who I realize still has the camera trained on me.

"What are you doing?" I ask.

"I thought it might be a story," he says. "I thought you might be a hero."

"I will never be a hero," I say.

I take off running, my shoes throwing snow, and I don't stop until I reach the van.

chapter 8

"I made you a little hot chocolate."

"Thanks, Mom."

She hands me a cute mug that features a graphic of Michigan as a winter mitten, and I take a sip.

I nearly do a spit take. My eyes grow wide as saucers.

"What the hell is in this, Mother?"

"A little something 'extra,'" she says, using her fingers around the word "extra," before doing it again. "A little 'warmth.'"

"Would you stop with the quote marks," I say.

My mom laughs and then winks a perfectly mascaraed eye on her perfectly made-up face. "You're going ice fishing this morning. Believe me, you need a little something-something in your coffee. Or else."

"Or else what?"

"You might not make it back here with all your wits. Much less all your fingers and toes."

I stare at her and then take another drink.

"Is it really that bad?" I ask. "I've forgotten. I just remember dad going and loving it."

"Let me just say this. Your father used to always have a cup of my hot chocolate before he went ice fishing." She stops. "Or two." She stops again. "And he'd take a thermos."

I take an even bigger sip.

"Do you like it?" she asks.

"It tastes like white lightning. Are you running some sort of bootleg moonshine operation up here with the northern Golden Girls?"

She laughs again, harder.

"You've gone soft. Sun-kissed highlights and tanned skin in January? Rosé by the pool? Your skin should be pasty right now, and you should be wearing big sweaters and thermal underwear."

"Then explain how you look so good?"

"I'm three-quarters of a century old, sweetheart. You do your hair and put on a little lipstick and the whole world thinks you're Jane Fonda because you've made an effort." She pauses. "You know better than anyone. What you endured in your job is worthy of a lawsuit. Men continue to treat women like objects. And women continue to play the game." My mom pours herself a cup of coffee and continues. "Do you know your father never saw me without makeup?"

"*I* never saw you without makeup."

"My mother taught me it was what women did. 'Wait for your husband to fall asleep before you remove your makeup. Put it on before he wakes.' Did you know I did that for decades? I'd wait until your father fell asleep, and then I'd sneak to the bathroom and take off my makeup. I trained myself to wake up at 4:30 in the morning so I could slink out of bed and put on my face."

She opens the refrigerator and pours a few drops of cream into her cup before continuing.

"When your father was ill, he couldn't sleep. I was so exhausted and depressed, and yet I was still sneaking away to put on my face. He was awake one morning, watching me. He said, 'I never knew you did that.' I said, 'I did it for you.' Do you know what he said?" My mom stops and shuts her eyes, remembering. "He said, 'Do you know when I fell in love with you? When I saw you at the lake, and you'd just emerged from the water. You didn't have a stitch of makeup on, but you were the most beautiful woman I'd ever seen. It was like there was a glow around you, as if you were in a spotlight, meant for me to notice.'" My mom opens her eyes and looks at me. "Society places such unjust expectations on women to attain perfection."

"You've always looked beautiful, Mom."

"And so have you," she says. "I don't know how you do your job. It must be tough to know you're good at your job and yet be expected to look a certain way."

"It is," I nod. "It's like a facade."

"Same for me," she says. "When will society learn it's not our looks that make women such powerful creatures, it's our minds, hearts and souls?"

"Never?" I offer.

My mom shakes her head and leans against the counter. Though my mother is in scrubs, her body is lean and tight, her forearms muscled. I'm amazed, even shocked, at the incredible shape in which she remains.

"I got in good shape for your father," she says, noticing me staring. "A good caretaker must be strong, not only physically, but also mentally and spiritually to care for those who need their strength. More often than not, caretakers get sick or injured. I vowed that wouldn't happen. And now my patients rely on that strength. It keeps me balanced."

"I rely on your strength, too, Mom."

She blows me a kiss. "Drink up, sweetie."

I take another sip from my mug.

"I think I'm already buzzed."

"Ha," my mom says, her laughter echoing in the kitchen. "You're a West Coast transplant who doesn't wear shoes all winter. You're going to be miserable ice fishing if you're not at least warm inside. And ice fishing is boring. You gotta pass the time. Hooch helps."

She continues. "You know, I used to go with your father and his friends before I knew better. It ain't a day by the pool, my dear. You've forgotten all about Michigan winter traditions. We don't play bridge and go to the club in Michigan. We play euchre, we drink and we ice fish."

I laugh. "I feel like my life is a little bit like a winter version of *Survivor* right now. Cardboard sledding, now Lisa wants me to ice fish. What's next?"

"Why is the station having you do all this?"

"Ratings." I sigh. "They're doing a whole winter-long segment called Sonny in the Winter to introduce me to viewers. It's sort of like *Candid Camera*. Get me in the wild and hope that I'll say or do something that will make news. Maybe even have another meltdown."

"Well, that's just cruel!" my mom exclaims.

"Welcome to television, Mom." I stop. "I kind of think Lisa actually *wants* me to have another meltdown. We have a very strange relationship. Sort of like frenemies."

"Why?"

"We just never clicked in college," I say. "I think part of it was me and part of it was her."

"Are you sure it wasn't more one-sided?" my mother asks. "Your side?"

"Thank you, Mother," I say. "Yes, actually, I'm starting to realize I wasn't a very nice person to her."

"Go on," my mother prompts.

"I know she's trying to resurrect the station, and I know she's trying to resurrect my career, but I kind of feel like she's getting a really big kick out of all this winter torture."

"Revenge is a dish best served cold."

"You're a regular Philip Marlowe, Mother."

"Thank you."

"She *knows* I need this job, and I *know* she needs me. It's a very unhealthy relationship."

"Perfect for you then," my mom says.

"Ha-ha."

"I think she always believed in you," my mom says. "I think she saw a great talent in you as well as a soft side you refused to show to the world. Give her the benefit of the doubt this time."

I nod.

"I miss this," my mom continues. "Mornings with you. Our banter. You've always been the one to make me laugh, the one to debate with me, the one to get me into a little bit of trouble."

She looks at me for the longest time. "It's nice. My daughter back home."

"I'm fifty, Mom. It's a little weird."

"I like weird," my mom says.

"Me, too." I reach out, take her hand and give it a mighty squeeze. "Well, I best get going. Icicle is taking me to meet Mason and some ice fishing locals at Bear Lake."

My mother laughs. "*That* is a sentence I never thought I would hear you say in my entire life. But that's not why I'm laughing. Um, what are you wearing?"

"This."

"Take another drink, sweetheart." She eyes my outfit. I'm wearing dark slacks and a turtleneck. "*That* will not keep you alive."

"I want to look good taping my segments. I don't want to go overboard like I did when I went sledding, but I also don't want to wear Lisa's hand-me-downs. I thought this was a perfect balance." I look at my outfit. "I'm planning to take a coat, too."

"Oh, that'll do it," she says in a sarcastic tone. My mother walks around the counter and makes me stand. "Think about it. You're going to be sitting in shanty with a fishing pole stuck into a hole in the ice. It's not just I'm-gonna-grab-a-Starbucks-to-warm-up cold out there, it's bone-aching, heart-stopping, can't-feel-my-hands cold. You don't need to look nice. You need to look like a local."

"But I'm on TV. I'm new. I'm Sonny Dunes. It's my thing."

"Well, your next TV gig will be playing a corpse on *CSI* if you wear that." She looks at me. "What were we just talking about? Wear some camouflage. Maybe show your viewers that you understand what you're doing so it doesn't come off like a joke. Embrace the culture. Don't embarrass it. Or yourself."

"Ouch."

"Better to say that now than when you get frostbite and lose a toe in those shoes. Come with me. Let me help you get dressed.

"Oh, but take another drink first. Ice fishing is like watching paint dry. In Antarctica. Naked."

"Can't wait," I say.

My mother takes my hand. She actually skips as we make our way upstairs.

I remember Bear Lake in the summer. When the beaches at Lake Michigan were too packed, or the water too choppy, my parents would often take Joncee and me inland to Bear Lake where we could float all day long without a worry.

Bear Lake is an *On Golden Pond*-y type lake—serene, filled with reeds, white swans and mournful loons—a perfect complement to Lake Michigan, which sits not too far away. In the summer, the lake is filled with kayaks and Jet Skis, the edges lined with fishermen, quaint cottages tucked into the tree-covered shoreline.

Icicle parks, and I step out of the van.

This is *not* summer.

In the winter, the summer charm of the lake has been replaced with more of a *Game of Thrones* vibe.

The wind slaps me, hard, and I shiver. The windchill is roughly the equivalent of a toddler's age. My eyes water, and the inside of my nostrils freeze. I stare across the icy water, the lake indistinguishable from the land and the horizon. Big, thick flakes of snow fall.

Icicle and I begin to make our way across the lake. I am leery, but he assures me it's safe even though I have already checked the depth of ice on the lake.

"Frozen over solid," he says. "Trust me."

My mind floats back to Lisa and Northwestern.

Ice-fishing shanties and pop-ups dot the ice. It's like a bottle brush village come to life on the frozen lake.

"Where are we going?" I ask. "Everything looks the same."

No one is out. It looks desolate, save for the shanties, some of which have puffs of smoke emerging from them.

"Ice fishing has probably changed a lot since you were young," Icicle says. "Like everything else."

He realizes what he's just said, and catches himself, albeit too late. "I'm sorry. I didn't mean that you were old or anything. But you didn't have cell phones or anything like that, right?"

I nod. "We had rotary phones. I used to write directions down. Google was known as a dictionary."

He laughs. "I just meant even the shanties have changed." Icicle points at one as we pass. "See?"

He's right. Many resemble tiny homes, complete with fireplaces. I can see lights flicker inside some.

"TV?" I blurt.

"Yep."

My heart lifts. *Maybe my day won't be so awful, Mother,* I think.

"Over here!"

I turn, squinting to see where Mason's voice is coming from.

My heart drops.

Tiny home, this ain't.

Mason's shanty is more of a lean-to, that actually leans in the stiff northerly breeze, much like I am doing.

"Well, aren't you a sight to see," Mason says with a hearty laugh, which echoes across the barren lake.

"I'm surprised you can even see me," I say. "I'm camouflaged."

He laughs again, a laugh that is like sunshine. I feel immediately warmed to see this man I barely know.

"Looks like somebody got the memo about what to wear." He stops and looks me over. "Well, almost."

My mother dressed me in a full-on *Apocalypse Now* thermal snowsuit.

"Doesn't it come in another pattern besides camo?" I had asked my mom.

"Yeah, honey," she'd replied. "Plaid."

I opted for camouflage because it was easier to accessorize.

"I added this scarf for a pop," I say. "It looks like Burberry, but it's fake. Got it at the outlet mall," I say in a stage whisper. "And I thought the fur-lined Russian cap would set off my earrings. See? They're fish."

"Well, you're ready for… I don't know what, but you're ready for something," Mason says. "This way, ma'am."

Mason laughs again. "That is, if you can move."

My mother has dressed me in so many layers—moisture-wicking thermal underwear, and waterproof, insulated socks and boots—that I move like Violet in *Willy Wonka and the Chocolate Factory* when she turns into a blueberry.

"Shut up," I say.

I waddle into the shanty, which is only slightly warmer than being outside.

"What do you think?" Mason asks.

"It's like *The Shining*, but less cheery," I say.

"Amberrose?"

I jump.

There's a man—well, at least I think it's a man based on the timbre of his voice—perched on a stool in the middle of the shanty. All I can see through his knit balaclava are two brown eyes and a mouth with chapped lips. He pulls off his full winter face mask. A distinguished looking man with hair as silver as the dimes my grampa used to collect is standing before me. He has a kind face with cheeks as rosy as Santa's.

"Amberrose Murphy? How long has it been?"

"I'm sorry?" I ask, struggling to place this man in my old life.

"Art Vanderberg. I worked with your father at the bank. Boy, oh, boy, talk about salt of the earth. That man was Traverse City before there was a Traverse City. He was on every committee and council in the county. He built that bank. He didn't just loan people money, he loaned people his heart and faith. How's your mom? I know it's been tough for her after his passing, you being so far away and, well…" He looks at me and lets his sentence trail off.

I don't know what to say. I have been gone so long, away from people who knew me, my family and our history, that I could pretend my former life was fiction.

I can hear the ice creak, the lake moan, the wind whistling across the shanty.

"I thought Lisa would have told you that Art was joining us," Mason jumps in. "She thought it would be a good idea for you to talk to a local about the beauty of ice fishing. And there's no one more local than Art."

"Is that a compliment?" Art says.

I laugh.

"Sorry," I finally say. "I think I'm still drunk. My mother put a lot of liquor in my hot chocolate this morning. Said I'd need it to stay warm."

"Smart woman!" Art says. "Good woman. I think Patty Rose's helped half the county pass on to our Creator peacefully."

I nod.

"Ready to hit the hard water?" Art asks.

"What?"

"The ice," he says. "That's what we call it."

He gestures to a group of folding stools he has placed in front of two perfectly round holes in the ice. The shanty is one of the new-fangled ones, shockingly big and rather roomy, not like the ones I grew up with that were claustrophobically tiny. I take a seat. Not without effort, mind you, considering how inflexible my body is in so many layers.

"What are you catching?" I ask.

"A cold," Art says.

Icicle starts to giggle, almost like a kid. He's been so quiet I forgot he was here. He mics me up, and then holds up the camera. "I'm going to start filming to get all this, okay?"

"Good man, Icicle," I say.

"You can catch brown trout, rainbow trout, perch and walleye during ice fishing season," Art says.

"What do you use for bait?"

Art pulls a flask from his jacket. "This."

Icicle giggles again.

"You're a regular Johnny Carson, Art," I say. "You and my mom would get along swimmingly."

"Good one," Mason says, taking a seat beside me.

"I still prefer to use live bait in the winter," Art says. "Minnows, or worms with a lead sinker. Let me do the honors."

He pulls a live minnow from a bait bucket and puts it on a hook. He hands me the pole.

"What do I do now?" I ask.

"Drop it in the hole and wait," he says. "And drink."

I drop the minnow into the hole, and it disappears beneath the ice. Art and Mason follow suit.

"Tell me about your life, Amberrose," Art says. "I mean, Sonny. Sorry. I'll never get used to that."

It's still hard for me to see people I knew growing up. When they see me, I believe they can still only see the pain our family suffered. I think they see the story of my life in caps, just like we use on the news: TRAGEDY! So many childhood friends, like Icicle's mom, have tried to reach out to me, but I've yet to return their calls, just like the ones I've yet to return to Cliff and Eva asking how I'm doing. I hide when I see people around town that I used to know. I act like I don't hear their voices when they call my name. I'm still hiding in plain daylight.

"TV," I finally say, trying to sound chipper. "They change everything."

I glance at Mason. He gives me a slight smile as if he knows I am lying.

TV didn't change you. You changed you, his look seems to say.

I revert to journalist mode to cover my emotions—the beauty of journalism, all facts, no emotion—by asking Art about the "art" of ice fishing and why he loves it so much.

He talks a bit more about what bait he uses, how to know when a fish is biting and the beauty of patience.

"Your father and I used to solve the world's problems out here without ever saying a word," Art says with a big smile. "It was good for him. Companionship with a good dose of silence. He just needed a little peace after all he went through. He just wanted the world to stop spinning for a little while."

My heart leaps into my throat. I wasn't expecting Art to get so real. I know I am going to cry.

"Here," I say, standing abruptly, handing my pole to Mason. "I need some air."

I race out of the shanty and into the frozen tundra. Icicle follows. "Want to tape your forecast now?" he asks.

I shake my head.

"Are you okay?"

Mason pops out of the shanty.

I shake my head again.

He looks at me and gives the sweetest, saddest smile. His eyes stand out in all the white, like blue sky amid all the clouds.

"Why don't you go talk to Art?" Mason says to Icicle. "Interview him about some of his most memorable catches."

"Good idea," Icicle says, popping back into the shanty.

"Here's the deal about ice fishing," Mason says, putting his hand on my shoulder. "It's not really about the fishing, as Art said. It's about the companionship. It's about the solitude. It's about idling for a while in the middle of winter in the middle of a frozen lake." He stops. "It's about not thinking for once. Just being."

Mason scans the lake. "You sit, in the freezing cold atop a frozen lake, dangling bait into a hole in the ice. The endgame is to catch something you can't see. Crazy, right? But we all try to control life. Bend it to suit us. Try to reimagine the past, or alter the future. We're rarely in the moment."

I shut my eyes. And then I open them.

It is otherworldly on the lake. A frozen ghost town. I miss the sun and the warmth.

Or do I miss being out of the glare of people I knew? The anonymity?

I scan the lake again, and there is a surreal beauty to this frozen wonderland. Smoke puffs from shanty chimneys and the little cottages surrounding the lake. The sun peeks out briefly amid the thick cloud cover, and everything sparkles. I am in a real-life snow globe.

"Wanna give it another shot?" he asks.

I nod. "It's probably easier than trying to go to the bathroom in all this gear," I say. "My mother didn't think about that."

He laughs and leads me back inside.

I grab my pole and angle it into the ice. Oh, how Joncee used to love to fish in the summer with our father. They would head out before dawn the two of them—thick as thieves—whispering and giggling, a real-life Opie and Andy Taylor with poles slung over their shoulders. They would take the johnboat out onto the lake, or sit on the dock, all morning long, eating egg sandwiches. I had no interest in fishing. I was a bit too girly and a bit too old, but Joncee and my dad? It was their thing. They'd show me and mom their catch for the day and then set off to clean it. My mom would fry fish all weekend long. Half of our stairwell is filled with pictures of the two of them holding fish in midair, some of them longer than Joncee's tiny body.

I look over at Art and imagine my father sitting here with him.

Did he talk about Joncee? Did he tell Art about how much he hurt? Or what I did? Did he discuss his marriage? Or did he just sit here and be at peace for once in his life?

Yes, as Mason said, this a strange sport, ice fishing. Here you sit, in the freezing cold atop a frozen lake, dangling bait into a hole in the ice. The endgame is to catch something you have to trust is there.

Is it pure luck? Is it fate? Is it out of our control?

Or does it just force us to stop? Stop thinking. Stop controlling. Stop everything. Just stop.

What would it be like if we were just able to cut a little hole in our frozen, damaged exteriors and let life—and all those memories—hook us once again?

The tip of my pole bobs and then grows taut.

"You got one!" Art says in a stage whisper. "Stand up!"

I stand, and Art moves behind me. "Mind if I help?"

"Please."

He places his hands around mine on the pole, tilts it closer to the ice and then pulls up on it. I can feel the weight of the fish.

"He's a fighter!" Art says. "Give him a little slack." He releases a little line, and I can feel the fish try to dart away. "Pull!"

We pull the pole into the air. "Start reeling, hard!" Art says.

I reel until I'm out of breath, until I'm sweating. I pull off my fur cap and toss it aside.

A fish about the size of Moby Dick appears in the hole.

I keep reeling, and Art grabs a net.

Pa-loop!

The fish flies through the hole and begins flopping around on the ice.

"It's a winter walleye!" Art yelps.

He nets it quickly and removes the hook.

The walleye is golden, the color of sunshine in Joncee's flaxen hair.

"Wow!" I say, completely out of breath.

"You did it!" Mason cheers.

I look at him, and his face is emblazoned with pride. I smile.

"Got it all!" Icicle says, peering through the camera.

I'd forgotten he was here again.

"That's great," I say.

I look at my fish, its eyes as wide as mine.

The wind whistles across the shanty, but I swear it sounds like Joncee's infectious giggles.

Ya did it, Amberrose! Ya did it! I can hear her say. *I knew ya could! I just knew it!*

"Are you okay?" Mason asks.

I shrug because I don't know, and it's the truth, something I am wholly unfamiliar with.

"Can you take a picture?" I ask, reaching for the fish.

Mason grabs his cell, and Icicle refocuses the camera.

I hold up the walleye and smile.

"That's a framer," Art says.

"I think you're right, sir," I say.

All of a sudden, I lean down and drop the fish back through the hole. It stops for a split second, shocked, and looks at me with what I swear is a look of gratitude before swimming away.

"Why'd you do that?" Art cries.

I stare into the hole for what seems like forever.

"It needed a second chance, too," I say.

chapter 9

"Great work!"

I wait. Lisa beams.

"And?" I prompt.

"Oh," she laughs, waving her hands, "that's it. No enemy fire today. And ratings are still going up. If this trend continues, then we'll know it's baked in and not just a blip."

"I feel the pressure," I say without any hint of a joke.

"Good," Lisa says. "By the way, I took a look at the suggestions you sent me before you started. We're going to revamp our graphics, make them a bit more current and polished. I want strong graphics that mimic the strength of our team and our news, but ones that are easily understandable for our older viewers. Icicle is going to work with you on them."

This time I beam.

"Really?"

"Sonny, you've been in this business as long as I have. And you've worked at stations much bigger than ours. I respect you."

"Thank you," I say. "That means the world."

The room goes silent, and the quiet hum of her ceiling lights suddenly begins to sound like a helicopter taking flight.

Lisa shakes her head. Her smile fades, her cheeks droop and her eyes turn from me to the wall.

"What?" I ask. "What is it?"

"It's nothing," she says.

"No, what is it, Lisa?"

"You didn't say you respected me, too."

Her words hit like a missile.

"And that's what it's always come to between us," Lisa says. "College, career, life. You've always thought you were better than me."

"No," I start. "That's not true."

"That's bull, Sonny, and you know it." Lisa stands and points at the picture of us in her collage. "I bet you don't even remember this picture."

I look at her, but I don't have a chance to answer.

"I do," she continues. "And you want to know why? Because it was the first and last day I felt like I was part of a group of friends. We all ate pizza as we set up our dorm rooms. We all hung out that first week like we were equals, the new girls on campus. We were going to take over Northwestern and then the world." Lisa stops, and her voice quivers ever so slightly. "And then it was over. You and your friends joined sororities. And do you know who was left all alone? Me! All alone in a dorm with undergrads the rest of college. You never invited me to be a part of your group. You never invited me to do anything. It was like I didn't exist." Without warning, Lisa slams her hand down on her desk. "And I was stupid enough to believe you liked me again."

The photo collage behind her shakes.

"I'm so sorry, Lisa," I say. "It wasn't you." I take a deep breath.

Tell her, Sonny. Tell her why you ran away from Michigan. How she reminded you of your sister. Why you built a wall around yourself. Why you don't have many friends today. Why you aren't married. Why you don't have a family. Tell her, Sonny.

"It was…" The word "me" never gets out of my mouth, as Lisa's office door bursts open.

"There's a fire at a historic cottage on the bay!" a reporter shouts.

Lisa starts to rush past me but stops.

I look at her, expecting a truce. My heart lifts.

"You're meeting Mason at eight. You're a judge for the Traverse City Restaurant Association's winter chili cook-off. You'll be doing your forecasts live from TC Brew Co. on Front Street." She turns. "I'm a judge, too. But we don't have to sit by one another. I trust that, even if we can never be friends, we can be colleagues."

The door slams.

Good job, Sonny.

I scan all of Lisa's Northwestern memorabilia. Back then, we were a college football laughingstock. We'd go to games knowing we would lose, but we'd chant, *That's all right, that's okay, you will work for us one day!*

All we wanted to do was go to the Rose Bowl. It was a dream for every Northwestern student. The purple among the roses.

I look at the photo of all of us from college. I barely recognize those young girls.

I pick up the framed picture and look between me and Lisa.

The ironic thing is Lisa is the one whose face is filled with confidence. Mine is all pretend, an act to distract.

I didn't even know who I was, and I still truly don't because I'm alone, and I've chosen to be alone. I didn't tell anyone at college about Joncee. I just wanted to forget. I just wanted to be a new person. I just wanted a new life and a new start. I just wanted to run.

I just wanted, literally, the world to be sunny and new again.

And if I couldn't ever have it that way again in my life, I could at least have a job and live in a place that would make it seem that way.

I had forgotten the way that the earth takes on another form in winter. It pulls out a coat of white from its seasonal closet to beautify its wardrobe. But winter is smart. It is actually distracting us, glossing over the truth: it is simply protecting itself from the bitter cold of the world.

I pull my own coat tighter around me and survey the terrain.

I used to sled these hills with Joncee long before they were vineyards, when this was rural land, open and free to the local kids to roam. Now it's a fancy winery. A beautiful stone fireplace roars in the corner, and floor-to-ceiling windows provide a view all the way from the vineyard to the bay.

I'm unsure as to why Mason invited me to lunch. I'm unsure as to why I said yes. But I'm slowly learning that running isn't solving any of my issues.

A host appears on the steps leading to the dining room, and I turn expecting Mason to be behind him.

No!

My heart leaps, and I grab my menu and place it in front of my face.

"Amberrose Murphy?"

Too late.

I slowly drop the menu as if I'm doing a facial striptease.

"Tammy Lynn? Becky Jo? And Jenny? Oh, my gosh! It's so good to see you!"

When in doubt, I use my news voice.

The three give me a once-over. They were my BFFs all the way from grade school. We were cheerleaders. We knew everything about each other. We were babysitters for each other's younger siblings.

"I heard you were back," Tammy Lynn says.

"Heard?" I joke to cover my emotions. "You better be watching! Helps the ratings."

"We're CHRY gals," Becky Jo says. "Younger demo."

"I'm changing that."

"Speaking of changing," Jenny says. "You haven't. At all. Do we hate her, girls?"

They laugh and nod, and I can't help but smile.

They are ghosts of who they used to be. And yet they haven't changed at all, and I feel jealous of their banter, their ease with one another, the fact that so little in their lives seems to have changed. My mom has told me they have families of their own, and their parents and siblings are doing well.

They are blessed.

"Well, we heard about what happened in California with your…" Tammy Lynn stops.

"Breakdown," I finish. "You can say it. It happened. Live."

They laugh, and the tension breaks.

"I would have done the exact same thing," Becky Jo says.

I laugh.

"Well, we all thought you were ghosting us just like you did after you left," Jenny says. "Haven't returned our calls since you've been back. Never reached out when you came home to visit." Jenny was the head cheerleader, always energetic, always peppy, always smiling. "That kinda hurt, Amberrose."

I look at them. "I'm so sorry. I work such strange hours. I'm always a day late and a dollar short."

They nod understandingly.

"Well, you have our numbers, and we'll call you to have drinks with us, and you *will* say yes, got it?" Jenny says.

"Got it."

Jenny turns. The host is still waiting patiently.

"Well, we better skedaddle," she says.

They wave, but at the last second, Tammy Lynn turns and leans toward my table, hands around her mouth, whispering as if she's just uncovered the biggest secret of her life and can't contain it any longer.

"You know, we still talk about what happened to Joncee. Such a tragedy. You know you had nothing to do with that, right? Just a crazy accident." She straightens up. "Welcome home, Amberrose."

Jenny elbows Tammy Lynn.

"Sorry. Sonny. Welcome home, Sonny."

I wave, but I can feel my chin tremble.

And there it is: the reason why I left. Why I didn't want to return. Why I don't reach out to former friends. Why winter is so hard.

My sister may be dead, but her ghost lives on in this town, and when people see me, they see her.

And the memory of that night haunts me.

"Sorry I'm late."

I jump in my seat.

"Sorry to scare you."

So many meanings.

"It's good to see you," Mason says. "And it was rather hard to see you the other day when you were dressed completely in camouflage."

His humor disarms me, and I feel immediately…not so scared.

I stand, and he gives me a big, warm hug.

"You look great," Mason continues.

Mason is wearing a dark suit with a crisp white shirt and polka-dot bow tie. "So do you," I say.

"I had board meetings this morning. Gotta look the part."

"I know all about that," I say.

"Isn't this place amazing?"

"We used to sled these hills as a kid," I say. "They sloped and dipped, so you gained just enough speed but were never out of control, like a Slip 'N Slide over a hilly backyard."

"I did the same," he says. "Then Freckles Williams bought the land and turned it into a successful winery."

"The former TV kid actor?"

"Yep," Mason says. "And the wine and food is stellar."

The waiter arrives with two glasses of wine and a charcuterie board.

"I ordered ahead," Mason continues. "Wanted to surprise you. Cheers."

We toast and take in the scenery for a moment.

"I loved how you gave that fish a second chance the other day," Mason says as he reaches for a chunk of blue cheese.

"It deserved it."

"So do you."

I drop the fig I'm holding.

"Listen, I know a little about your sister. I've heard. People talk."

"I can't do this today," I say. "I've already been down this road." I nod at my friends at a table across the room. "That road is closed. If that's why you asked me here today..."

"I asked you here today because I like you, Sonny. A lot. And I want to get to know you better."

I look at him, eyes wide. "We just met."

"I know. That's what everyone says, 'We just met. It's too soon.' I get it. Defense mechanism. You don't want to get hurt. I don't want to get hurt. No one wants to get hurt." Mason takes a sip of his wine. "But I'm not a kid anymore. I'm in my fifties, I've loved and lost, and I've lived a lot of life in those years. My heart knows when it knows. And it knows you're special. If I put my heart out there, then I'm going to put it out there. No games."

I take a sip of my wine. Is this really happening?

"So I'm putting it out there. If it's too soon, then so be it."

He looks into the fire.

"Andi and I used to have a dog, Lucky. Found him in the woods, near death. Saw a flash of blue in the dark. Lucky's eyes were sky blue, Andi's favorite color. 'Meant to be,' she always said. Andi took Lucky home and nurtured him back to life. Slept with him by the fire to keep it warm and safe. She loved that dog, and that dog loved her. When Andi died, Lucky looked and looked for her around the house. For weeks. It just broke my heart. One day, I let him out to do his business, and Lucky ran. I looked for him for days, put out flyers, offered a reward." Mason stops. "I found that dog laying by Andi's gravestone. He found her. He died with her." Mason stops. His lip quivers. A tear forms in the corners of my eyes. "Do you know how many times I thought of running away, giving up? I wanted to die from heartbreak and loneliness, too, just like Lucky. Guilt ate me alive. I mean, my kids left here, and I get it." He stops. "But running doesn't solve anything. It's just a defense mechanism. It just distances you from the love we all deserve."

Mason continues. "Life's short, Sonny. And it's hard. So, so hard. None of us know how much time we have, but we all need love. We all need a second chance. Me, you, Lucky, that fish…it's okay to forgive yourself. I guess… I guess I just don't want you to be a runner your whole life."

My gut tells me to stand and run, not just from Mason, but from my childhood friends, my hometown, my state, winter, everything.

Instead, I nod at Mason and then finally remove my coat.

Who knew that tasting chili could be so, well, chilly?

And I'm not talking about the weather, although right now—according to the current conditions on my laptop—it is seventeen degrees and a steady snow is falling.

The brew pub is packed, and that's certainly made it feel warmer, but it's still downright brisk inside the drafty restaurant, and there's no doubt the tiff Lisa and I had earlier is only making things colder.

Mason is seated between the two of us, a literal buffer.

"How's it feel to be Switzerland?" I ask.

"I can sense the iciness," he whispers. "And it's not the weather. What's going on?"

He notices Lisa watching.

"What do you think of Front Street?" Mason asks me, a bit too loudly and cheerfully, in an effort to cover. "Changed, huh?"

TC Brew Co. is housed in an old brick, two-story building with arched windows. Front Street, the main street in Traverse City, is filled with historic buildings, and the beautiful Boardman River meanders just across the way, before spilling into the West Arm of Grand Traverse Bay. The entire downtown has experienced a major transformation. Every building has been restored, and the area is filled with topnotch restaurants, wine bars, brew pubs, and high-end clothing, retail and flower shops. Old-fashioned lampposts dot the streets, and lights twinkle in the snowy branches of the barren trees. Across the street, a line of people snake down the sidewalk, waiting to enter State Theatre, the beautiful, old movie house that filmmaker and activist Michael Moore renovated and relaunched, which is the center of the city's annual Traverse City Film Festival, now one of the most respected film festivals in the world.

"In the summer, the town bustles with tourists, but there's something about it in the winter," Mason says. "It becomes our town again. The locals' town. It's like a town right out of a Currier and Ives painting."

Mason is wearing a heathery blue turtleneck today. The lighter flecks bring out the color of his eyes and the darker hues make his silvery hair shimmer. I can't help but notice the way the turtleneck emphasizes his angular jaw and five-o'clock shadow as he talks.

"Michael Moore really helped reenergize the city with the

theater in 2007. Today, we have a mix of young liberals and older conservatives. The town is a political fulcrum, new and old."

"Which are you?"

"The perfect balance of both," Mason says with a wink.

"Perfect answer for a chamber guy," I say.

"But I'm definitely old-fashioned when it comes to my chili."

I laugh and blow on my hands to keep them warm.

"Tell me more."

"I used to make chili for my family all the time," Mason says. "My wife would often go weeks when she'd stay in bed. She couldn't shower or dress much less cook or care for the kids, so I'd make chili. I knew it was full of protein and the kids liked it. It would last for days. I'd freeze it, so we could eat it for a quick lunch or dinner. And it made the house smell like a home. My kids despise chili now. They ate so much of it growing up that they just can't stomach it," Mason muses. "But I think it's the memory of chili they don't like. Those memories can affect not only how we remember things but also how we see things today."

He looks at me, and it's as if he's a spotlight illuminating my soul.

"Have you always been this honest?" I say.

"About what?"

"About everything."

Mason nods. "I've learned to be. It's such a healthier way to live. I mean, who's the person we lie to most often?"

I look at him, shrugging.

"Ourselves. I heaped so much blame on myself. But I realized there are some things you just can't change, no matter how much you want it or how hard you try. And you sure can't change the past."

"But what if you could have?"

"Sonny," he says, "you're a woman of science. You darn well know you can't change a forecast even if you wanted to, right?

You may want the weekend to be sunny and beautiful, but if it's going to rain it's going to rain. And you have to be honest about that."

"Life isn't a forecast, though, Mason," I say, my voice low.

"No, it's not, but you can predict the weather a whole lot more accurately than you can predict life," he says. Mason looks at me for the longest time. "Why don't you try living for once the same way that you approach your forecasts: just take it a day, or a week, at a time. See how that goes."

I look out the windows. "It's snowing," I say in a deadpan.

"Perfect time to see that snow in a new light then."

I change the subject. "So, what's Mason's perfect chili?" I ask. "Not a lot of chili in the desert. It's not your go-to meal when it's a hundred degrees."

"Funny you should say that because I call it Mason's Hot and Bothered."

"You do not!" I laugh.

"I do, too, and it's a guarded secret. I can't tell you. I could make it for you, though, if I respect your judging skills tonight."

"Challenge accepted," I say.

A young man with a hipster beard in a TC Brew Co. hoodie jumps on the bar with a mic. "Welcome to the Twelfth Annual Traverse City Winter Chili Cook-off!" People stop sipping their beers and look up.

"I'm Trav Charles, this is my restaurant—get it? TC for me and Traverse City? I'm so clever—and these are my rules," he says to laughter. "Actually, the rules are set by my man Mason, who's right over there. Mason, give a wave."

Mason stands and salutes the crowd.

"Mason is the head of the chamber around here, and he's the man that organizes all the winter activities we love that keep us sane," Trav says. "He's also one of the judges, and *he* set the rules, so any problems you have with the final results, talk to him, not me."

I laugh, and Mason points at me.

"Or you can blame Sonny Dunes, the new meteorologist at TRVC-8."

People cheer me with their beers.

"But don't make her mad," Trav continues. "You've all probably seen the viral video of what happens when you do."

The crowd goes crazy.

"And if Sonny goes funny then blame her boss, TRVC news director and longtime Traverse resident Lisa Kirk."

The crowd applauds.

Servers bring out trays of chili in ramekins, along with glasses of beer. In front of each ramekin is a number. A scoring sheet and pencil are handed out to the judges.

"Each restaurant has paired a beer to go along with its chili," Trav announces. "That is part of the overall presentation. Most points will be awarded for taste, followed by overall presentation: how the chili looks and smells, how it is—or how it's not—garnished, and how the beer pairs with each dish. While the judges eat and drink, so will you! Belly up to the bar!"

People crowd forward for bowls of chili, and I look at Mason as trays of ramekins are set down in front of us.

He lifts his glass and his spoon. "Cheers!" he says to me and Lisa, tapping our glasses with his, before doing the same with his spoon. He looks at us as if we are going to reciprocate his gesture with one another. We do not.

I eye the tiny bowls of chili before me. They are as different in color as the beers.

"Number one," I say out loud. "Here we go!"

I lift my spoon and taste. "Oh, my gosh. This is delicious." I look at Mason, my eyes grow wide, and my tongue feels as if it's on fire. My eyes water, and I reach for the beer. I down it in one gulp, and I hear cheers. I look up, and a group of young adults is recording me, laughing hard at my reaction.

"Hotter than the weather," I say.

"This is a five-alarm chili," Mason says. "Some call it Dragon's Breath Chili or Hellfire Chili, but it's made with habaneros, and it is H-O-T hot."

"Just like me," I joke, winking at him.

Mason looks at me. "You beat me to the punch."

My eyes grow wide and continue to water. "No need to cry about it," Mason says, matching my wink.

I progress through each bowl of chili, Mason knowing exactly what we're tasting without a name or recipe in front of us.

"Chili con carne, or Texas Red," Mason comments on the next one. "Chunks of beef, cumin-spiked sauce made from red chilies. Oh, and this is Cincinnati-style chili. We serve this type of chili a lot on our Coneys in Michigan, especially in Detroit. This is Chili Four-Ways—chili over spaghetti with cheese and onions."

We continue through a white chili, a tomatillo-y chili verde, a vegetarian chili, and a chili with so many beans, I bloat like a balloon immediately. I realize that by the end of our tasting, I've drank nearly every beer accompanying the chili.

"I have to do a live broadcast," I say out loud. "Am I slurring?"

"No more than usual," Mason says. "What was your favorite?"

"Secret ballot," I say, before leaning over to whisper, "Chili verde for me."

"Good choice," he says. "I think I can have you over for dinner. Real date. At night. At my house."

"Which did you choose?" I ask.

"The habanero," he says, his voice huskier than normal. "I like it hot."

My face flushes when he looks into my eyes, and all of a sudden I want to dive into his blue, blue eyes to cool off. Instead, I say, "Then you're in the wrong state."

He laughs.

Deflection, my old friend.

"What about you?"

I lean forward on the table to engage Lisa. I can feel the beer coursing through my bloodstream.

"I probably like the one you despise," Lisa says.

Mason makes a face and mouths, *Ouch*.

"I doubt that," I say to her. "We have more in common than you know."

I lean back in my chair and hand Trav my tally sheet when he comes by to collect them. He sets down yet another beer in front of me.

"It's called Sunny Days," he says. "It's blonde but has a punch to it. Like you."

Mason laughs.

"If you enjoy it, I might rename it Sonny Dunes."

I take a sip, and my face lights up. "I think we have a deal."

Icicle approaches and says, "I'm set up outside for our live shot at nine. You ready?"

I take another sip of my beer. "Now I am."

I stand, grabbing the beer and a half-eaten ramekin of chili, and Lisa waits a beat before she stands up and follows me outside. Icicle has the camera focused on the open door of TC Brew Co. I take a look through the lens. The restaurant, bright and happy, bustles in the background while snow falls steadily on the street. A huge billboard announcing the *12th Annual Traverse City Winter Chili Cook-off!* is in the corner of the shot.

"Nice, Ice," I say.

"Thanks, Sonny."

Lisa is on her cell. "We'll be ready to go in about a minute."

Some people spill onto the street and some cross over from the theater. People are fascinated by TV cameras. They flock to them like moths to a flame, and yet they mostly act like fools in front of them, waving, smiling, shouting to their moms or girlfriends, or—too often today—screaming at us.

I take my position in front of the restaurant, position the beer and chili just-so in front of my body and wait for Icicle to give me a count. When he points at me, I become Sonny, even in the snow.

"Hi, northern Michigan, this is Sonny Dunes coming live to you tonight from Front Street and TC Brew Co. where—as you can see behind me—it's packed for the Twelfth Annual Winter Chili Cook-off. This is another segment of Sonny in the Winter and, although it may be cold outside tonight, it's warm in there, and in my tummy. Thank goodness, I have something cool to wash it all down." I hold up my beer and take a sip, and people clap behind me. "If you're out and about, come on down and join us. I'll be here, and after a few more of these, which TC Brew Co. has now named after yours truly, I might just make my own pot of chili. Wanna help me stir the pot? My snowy, seven-day forecast coming up in fifteen minutes. Back to you in the studio!"

"And we're clear," Icicle calls.

I take off my mic and remove the clip on the waistband of my slacks, and hand them to Icicle.

"Nice," Lisa says, her voice colder than the temperature.

"Thanks," I say, turning to head back inside to get warm.

"Did you believe a word you were saying?"

I turn to look at Lisa.

"Look," I start.

"Watch it," Icicle says, gesturing around with his head. People are holding their phones, beginning to record our tiff.

I smile and mouth, *Thanks.*

We head back inside and take a seat. Within minutes, Trav jumps back up on the bar and hushes the crowd. "We have our results! It was a very close contest, but I can now announce that the winner is the Chili Verde from Tres Hermanos here on Front Street! Congrats!" Trav holds up a trophy of a giant bowl with a spoon sticking out from it, and an older man comes forward to grab the trophy. He holds it up as the crowd whoops and applauds, and high-fives people as he returns to celebrate at a table serving his chili in the back.

I turn to look at Mason. "I got outvoted, it seems," he says.

I look at Lisa. "Good taste," I say.

"In most things," she responds. "Lisa, I think we need to talk." I stop. "No, I want to talk to you, okay?"

She nods, barely.

Icicle appears again. "Time for your forecast."

We all head back out once again, and I position myself in front of the restaurant.

A crowd gathers yet again, but this time, I notice, there are more people. Some are tittering, some pointing at me, most looking at their cells and then looking at me.

"That's her," a woman in a North Face jacket says. "You should be ashamed of yourself."

"For what?" I ask.

That's when I hear my voice coming from the phone.

"What is that?"

The man she is with holds out his cell.

"Don't ever do that again!" I am yelling at the two little girls I saw while snowshoeing with Icicle. "Ever!"

The little girl who played the trick on her sister begins to cry.

"What are you doing?" the mom says, pulling her scared, little girl into her arms.

"I will never be a hero," I say.

The video has been edited, just like the one that circulated when I was cardboard sledding.

The next clip makes it look as if I've stolen Art's prized fish—the one I caught—and released it without his permission. His kind face looks shocked. "Why'd you do that?" he asks. And then there is footage of me racing out of the shanty as if I'm fleeing the scene of a crime.

I look at Icicle. "Did you do this?"

"No!" he says, his expression serious. "I would never do that, Sonny."

"What about you?" I turn to Lisa.

"Sonny, we may have our differences, but my job is on the line here. I would never do this to you."

"I can't trust anyone around here." I turn and look at the crowd. "What are you all looking at?"

Cell phones are trained on me. No one moves.

Icicle's eyes are wide. He is pointing at me. I realize too late we're live.

"You all want Sonny to lose it on air again, don't you?" I say to the camera. I look around at the bystanders. "Don't you?" The crowd goes quiet. Cell phones—like the camera itself—are pointed directly at me. For a moment, I'm a kid again, and I'm on summer vacation with my family in Florida. I feel like Lucy, the dolphin I saw at a water park as a girl. Lucy performed when asked, and her sweet little face looked so happy, but when I took a picture with her and stared into her beautiful eyes, she looked so sad. And when I gave her a treat and she spoke to me as cameras flashed, I could swear she said, "I don't belong here."

I take a deep breath and look into the camera.

"What do any of you actually know about me? What do you know about anyone who's on TV? You have a perception of who we are based on what you see on a screen in your living room. But that's only a fragment of who we are. You don't know anything about me. What I've experienced in my life. You see what you want to see. You believe what you want to believe. And I will never be able to change your mind."

All around me, people are watching, taping, gaping. Some giggle, some stand in silence. My eyes veer to a woman who is playing the viral videos of me to her friends. I walk over to her.

"Do you want to know why I went to journalism school and became a meteorologist?" I ask this stranger. "Because I thought

I could save someone's life. Because it used to be the news was all based on fact. Now, we're obsessed with social media that's neither social nor media. We believe what 'influencers' tell us to believe and no longer think critically for ourselves. It's not only sad, it's a shame. What you're seeing is a lie."

I turn back to the camera.

"What do you believe, folks?" I stare into the camera. "And, big surprise, it's going to snow for the next seven days. Until we meet again, have a Sonny day, northern Michigan!"

I pull off my mic. Icicle is staring at me openmouthed. Lisa is just behind him, her face whiter than the falling snow. I walk away. My walk turns into a jog, which turns into a full-out sprint.

"Sonny!"

Mason's voice shatters the cold silence.

"Don't run!" he yells, his voice filled with emotion. "Please!"

I don't turn around.

I'm an expert at running away.

chapter 10

FEBRUARY 2022

I am the only one wearing a winter coat as I emerge from the plane in Palm Springs.

The outdoor airport is one of the most beautiful in the world, lined with palm trees, wall-to-wall sunshine, the mountains hugging you as you walk out of the terminal. I shed my coat and tie it around my waist. I lift my face to the sun.

"I've missed you," I say. "I'm home."

I rent a car and drive to my house. The couple renting my home arrive in a few days, so I have little time to make hard and fast decisions.

Should I stay? Should I go?

Why are the biggest decisions in my life always reduced to '80s songs?

I stop at Ralph's on the way and pick up a few groceries. When I walk into my house, it is a bit musty. It smells like someone else's house, so I begin opening windows to air out that "shut up" scent. I immediately change into my bathing suit, check all my plants—the gardeners have been doing a wonderful job—and head to the pool, which I've not heated. I dip a toe in—much too cold, especially with the nights turning chillier—and head for the hot tub. I turn on the jets and immerse myself in the hot, bubbling water.

It is surreal to go from gray skies to blue, from cold to warm, from northern Michigan to Southern California, from new life to old life in the blink of an eye.

I shut my eyes, and the image of the sun remains, floating. Slowly, it breaks apart, into a million tiny dots.

I see snow falling.

I emerge from the spa, towel off and take a seat on a recliner. I turned off my phone immediately after showing my boarding pass at the airport in Traverse City. I take a big drink of water, a deep breath and turn on my cell.

My screen is filled with text messages.

Mason, Lisa, Icicle, and, of course, my mom.

I called her last night after I reached the airport and left her a voice mail. When she called, over and over, I refused to answer. I listen to her voice mail now.

I take it you're back in the desert. I hope the sun brings clarity. Ultimately, though, I know it won't bring happiness, honey. When will you stop running away? You're such a fighter at heart. Even last night, watching you on the news, you were fiery and real, and that's why people love you. Because you're like all of us. We try to do our best every day, but sometimes we screw up. Some days, we take two big steps forward, and the next we take a big one back. But you know what I always preach as a hospice nurse, honey: don't live with regret. And you're filled with it. Your bucket is overflowing. And your reactions—both personally and professionally—are proof of that.

I blink away tears.

Do you know who was the bravest of all? Your father. He visited Joncee's grave every single week. On Memorial Day, he planted peonies. In the summer, he brought her ice cream. In the fall, he raked leaves and jumped in the pile just like she used to do. And in the winter, he made snowmen with big happy charcoal smiles. He honored her memory; he didn't run away from it. And that's what I try to do. I know every one of your quirks, honey: touching light switches, door handles and seat buckles, air-braking in the car on snowy drives. I've watched you do it ever since you arrived home again. In the morning. Before bed. When I leave. But none of those things will bring your sister back. And they won't keep you safe. I can't even do that. I wish I could roll back time for you, for me, for all of us, but I can't. None of us can. I have to believe there's a reason God challenged our family in this way. I used to think it was so we could give a bit more of ourselves to the world, touch people in our own way to make them feel better even for just a moment. I can hear her hold back her tears. *But now I think it was so maybe, one day, we could give a bit more of ourselves to each other. I love you to the Mackinac Bridge and back, sweetheart. And I want you to love yourself that much, too.*

I hit end and sob until I am gasping for air.

I stand and walk around my house, a total wreck at the thought of abandoning my mother.

Again.

I think of her alone, and I begin unconsciously counting, touching, doing the obsessive things to cope I always did at home.

It doesn't matter how far, fast or much you run, Sonny. You can never escape what happened.

And then I go to bed and fall asleep and dream of my mom and dad, of Joncee, and of snowmen that smile forever and never melt.

I am Dorothy in *The Wizard of Oz*. Except it's me—not Judy Garland—and Toto is Joncee, who follows me around like I know where I am going. There is a Yellow Brick Road, but it's in the snow. The skies are bright blue but snowflakes still fall, and they look like glitter. Joncee and I jump in a toboggan and ride it to a dune overlooking Lake Michigan. The water is gold, and the horizon as pink as Joncee's coat and cap.

I want to see what's on the other side of the horizon, Joncee says. She takes off running. She is fast as a racehorse.

Before I can even yell to stop her, Joncee is gone. I pull the toboggan up the dune, ride it over the edge and land in the water, sliding all the way to the horizon.

Joncee! I call. *Come back! Please! Come back!*

I stand. The water is solid like the ground. I tap on the horizon, but it's a wall—a theatrical set—that separates my world from the other side. There is no door. I knock again.

Hello? Hello? I call. *Joncee!*

A voice from somewhere says, *You're just seeing what you want to see. You're not seeing reality. Go home!*

I grab the toboggan and pull it all the way across Lake Michigan and back to the shoreline. When I reach it, the world turns black-and-white. The snow is no longer magical. The sky is gray. The horizon clouded.

Ding-Dong!

I hear Munchkins singing around me.

Ding-Dong!

I wake with a start.

It's the doorbell, Sonny.

Bleary and exhausted, I stumble toward the front door, half of me lost in the in-between, between the dream world and the real world, part of me still in Michigan navigating my mother's house.

I open the front door, and the glare blinds me. A delivery driver in a brown uniform stands before me.

"Sign here, ma'am."

He holds out an electronic pad, and I scrawl something with my finger. As he hands me a package, he looks at me closely for the first time and says, "Don't tell me. You're that woman, right? The one on TV."

"Yes," I say, too tired to lie.

Then he does a hammy double take. "I knew it," he says, laughing. "You're that chick who totally lost it on TV, like a hundred times, right. You're in the new *People* magazine. My girlfriend loves that magazine. You're famous, lady. No, actually, you're infamous." He points at me, covering his mouth. "Wow. My girl will totally freak. Can I get a selfie with you?"

I start to say no, but his cell is out and his arm is already in the air. "Smile," he says. "No. On second thought, look angry." He snaps the picture. "That'll do, I guess," he says, sounding disappointed. "You just look sort of confused."

He disappears through the gate, and I sleepwalk into the living room and open the package. An envelope with *Sonny* written on it is taped to the top of a gift-wrapped box.

I open the envelope. It is a handwritten letter. I don't recognize the handwriting.

Dear Sonny,

I know this is an odd way of reaching out, but it's the only way I know I can get out everything I want to say.

I put my heart on the line the other day. I asked you to give yourself a second chance. I hoped you wouldn't run away…again. It's been a very long time since I've felt this strongly about someone, and it's been a long time since I've dated, so I really don't know what I'm doing or how to do it. Maybe I'm just old-fashioned. Being honest. Writing letters. Maybe I like them because I know the recipient will have something to keep forever. It won't be erased like a text message or deleted like an email.

First, I'm sorry for what's happening to you. I don't know who's doing this, or why, but I believe bad people aren't just mean they're also dumb, and they will get caught sooner or later. I also believe that you're a good person who's experienced a lot of bad in your life. We're all tested. Sometimes, I believe, it's for a reason. So we can be better people, better teachers, better friends, better spouses, better period.

I spoke to your mother. She gave me your address. She's worried about you. So am I. Talking about death is never easy. Sometimes, we don't just bury those we love, we bury our pain and ourselves right along with them. They die, and a big piece of us does, as well.

I live with pain and regret, too. Every day. What more could I have done? What more should I have done? Did I get so lost in Andi's pain that I couldn't see the world in the right light any longer?

Before Andi took her life, she woke up early one pretty winter's day, made pancakes in the shape of snowmen for the kids, and then we all went skiing. Lucky, too. That night, when we returned home and put the kids to bed, I walked out of the shower to find Andi sitting on the bed with all her jewelry spread out before her. When I asked her what she was doing, she said, "Making plans for the future." She had Post-its with names written on them attached to different pieces of her favorite jewelry. The pearls her parents had gotten her after her college graduation were to go to her sister. The diamond earrings I had bought her for our first wedding anniversary were to go to our daughter. An onyx ring was marked for my son to give to his future wife. Every piece that held a special memory was earmarked for someone she loved. Except for two pieces: her wedding ring, and a necklace of Leland Blue that I bought for her at Becky Thatcher Designs when we had a staycation and spent a week traveling around our own area. "My wedding ring stays with me," she said. "And this necklace is for you." When I asked her why, she said because it tells a story that someone will need to hear. She said I needed to be prepared for one day a long time in the future.

She was so happy, better than she had been in months. I actually I thought she was at a turning point. I never put two-and-two together.

She took her own life the next day. I buried her with her wedding ring. I kept the necklace.

I thought of all this when I returned home after you left.

Do you know the story of Leland Blue? To me, nothing is more representative of northern Michigan than this stone. It's beauti-

ful, hard to find, rare and fragile, just like love and life. Actually, it's not a stone—just like love and life are never what they appear to be on the surface. Leland Blue is slag, a byproduct of smelting iron ore. During a short period of time in the late 1800s, iron ore was mined in northern Michigan, and shipped to a smelting plant near Leland, Michigan. During the smelting process, the iron ore was heated in huge furnaces to separate iron from the byproducts, poured into molds and shipped south to the steel mills in Pennsylvania and Ohio. The byproduct was dumped into Lake Michigan. The waves and the sand polished the slag into beautiful stones. These stones occur in as many shades of blue as the summer sky in Michigan: Arctic blue, cerulean, sapphire and sky blue. Some are streaked with shades of greens and grays.

A therapist once suggested that Andi focus her attention on something that got her outside, grounded her, allowed her to lose herself for a while. She became obsessed with collecting stones. Most people focus on fossils or Petoskey stones, but she loved Leland Blue. She walked the shoreline for hours. After a while, she knew where to look. The reflection of the sunlight off the rocks under the water brought the stone's blue hues to her attention. She began to wear waders, carry a walking stick and a strainer, with a pouch for the rocks tied around her waist like an apron.

Sometimes, I'd have to go find her and tell her it was time to come home. She loved late fall and winter most, when the locals owned the beach again.

Andi was truly connected to that stone. She loved that Leland Blue captured all the natural beauty of Michigan: the color of the water and the texture of the sand. When we found that necklace on vacation, Andi cried, like all those days she'd spent searching had led her here to discover her greatest find: a necklace filled with Leland Blue.

Becky Thatcher herself told Andi that the stone's color and brushlike marks reminded her of Van Gogh's skies, like in Starry Night. *She also said that the stone was not easy to work with because the stone is porous, pitted from air bubbles, often dull and fractures easily. The beauty, of course—be it in a stone or a person—lies in the imperfections. The magic is found in our foibles and fragility. The fractured are the most interesting because our lines, wrinkles, breaks, fault lines and holes—be they on our souls, hearts or bodies—tell a story.*

The summer day Andi and I bought that necklace was spectacular. The temperatures were in the upper seventies, the breeze smelled like the lake, and the sky was, literally, Leland Blue. We went to the beach and walked the shoreline. People stopped us left and right to admire her necklace. We walked forever, and suddenly, right in front of Andi, was a huge piece of Leland Blue, the biggest she'd ever seen or found. She pulled it from the water.

"Why can't life always be this easy?" she marveled.

"It can," I told her. "It can."

You ask why I speak so openly about my late wife? It's so I will remember. So others will feel more open to discuss their own grief and loss. So we can see what a blessing simply being alive is.

Sometimes, you have to search a long time to find what you're looking for. Sometimes, the answer lies right in front of your eyes, like that stone. Sadly, we too often don't see it because we're blinded by our sorrow.

I've always wondered why I kept this necklace, but it's as if Andi knew you would come into my life and need to hear the story.

When I see you, I see blue.

I know you see it, too: in the desert sky, Lake Michigan, the color of the ice on the bay.

But I want you to see that color without feeling *blue.*

No matter what life throws at you, never forget you are loved, that your life matters, and that your impact on others can never be measured but can always be felt when it's removed.

Take care of yourself, Sonny.

I've enclosed some Blue for You… I know it's a big, ole personal gift from a relative stranger, but my heart is in this letter, in

this blue and already a part of you. Be still. Stop running. Find peace. Be sunny, Sonny.
Mason

I am crying before I even open the box. The necklace is spectacular.

I put it around my neck and suddenly the world comes into focus, like a crystal clear, summer sky in Michigan, one that is so, so blue it makes your heart ache and also makes you realize that this very moment is an incredible gift.

And, for a moment, your own blues fade away.

chapter 11

"I like your necklace."

"This old thing?" I smile. "I felt like I needed a little extra protection." I touch the Leland Blues. "And, well, the fractured are the most interesting, right?"

Mason smiles and open his arms. He hugs me, and I hold on. He doesn't release me until I pull back.

"Let's just blame all those fault lines on the San Andreas, okay?" he asks. "You can do that. You're a California girl." He stops and tilts his head. "I mean, are you? Or should I be using past tense?"

"Don't know," I say. "Maybe I was just California dreamin' on a winter's day."

Mason smiles.

"It's still winter here, you know."

"I know," I say. I look at this man I barely know who I suddenly feel like I've known forever. He makes me feel like I'm home. Is that what it feels like to open your heart, let down your guard, allow people to see the real you? "Thanks for picking me up. I didn't want to bother my mom this late. I couldn't call Lisa or Icicle. I was hesitant to call my old girlfriends I've avoided like the plague. I didn't know who else to call."

"Gee, thanks," Mason says.

"That didn't come out right. I just meant…thank you. Truly."

Even at midnight, he looks good. No, scratch that. *Great*. Like Tom Brady after a game. He looks like, as my grandma used to say, good looks grew on a tree.

Mason puts his hand on my back to guide me through the airport to the luggage claim, exerting enough pressure to make me feel calm and safe but not enough to make it feel uncomfortable. *Ever the gentleman.*

As we walk, I'm captured by the quaintness of Cherry Capital Airport. While arriving in Palm Springs feels like you're on a tropical vacation, Traverse City's airport truly capture's the state's natural beauty. It's like a Pure Michigan hug.

The terminal is akin to walking into a Frank Lloyd Wright home. The Arts and Crafts interior is the antithesis to most airport designs, meant to parallel the natural beauty of the Grand Traverse region. The overall feel is that of an Up North lodge, with its stone fireplace, cherrywood, copper fixtures and stained glass.

When I hurriedly hightailed it from Michigan, I sneaked into my mother's house, while she snoozed soundly in front of a blaring TV and roaring fire, and packed as if I were never coming back. I felt like the Grinch stealing everyone's Christmas as the happy family slept. I took everything, even the funny Michigan gifts she got me for Christmas. And now I'm hauling it all back like, well, the psychotic meteorologist I am.

"Nice vacation?"

Mason asks this loudly. I jump and immediately begin to scan the group around me, worried that someone might recognize me or be filming me on the down low yet again. But there are only about a dozen people, and everyone is bleary-eyed from the late flight.

"I'm teasing you, Ginger Zee," Mason says, referring to my meteorology hero from ABC news. "No paparazzi around right now."

"I'm not worried about *Hollywood Gossip* or *People* magazine," I say. "I'm worried about whoever is doctoring videos to make me look bad." I look at Mason and scrunch my face. "I guess I'm already doing a good enough job of that without anyone's help."

We gather my luggage and head to his SUV. Though we landed in a near-blizzard, *nothing* shuts down an airport in Michigan. Palm Springs would have canceled flights for a decade with this weather. The cold smacks my face outside, and I'm suddenly slapped back into the reality of living in northern Michigan instead of Southern California.

No hot tub tonight, Sonny, I think. *No pool in your future.*

And yet there is a stunning beauty to this winter world. The snow is falling in big, wet heaps, and the world—even at the airport—is hushed. Mason and I drive in silence until he pulls onto the highway.

"So, what are they saying about me?" I finally ask in the dark.

"You didn't look?" he asks.

"I couldn't."

He glances at me as if I were lying.

"I couldn't, for my own sanity. It was just too much. I only turned my cell on to listen to my mom's messages."

"The station didn't call?"

"They did. I didn't call back."

"Well," he starts, "the station stated publicly that you were taking a short leave of absence in order to deal with some personal family issues."

"That sounds crafted by an attorney and publicist," I laugh.

"And what are people saying about that? That Sonny is funny in the head?"

Mason is silent for too long. "Well?" I ask.

"The local press is having a field day. Social media is worried about your mental health. The other stations are saying you aren't a true Michigander. Polly Sue is filling in for you, and…" Mason stops.

"And?"

"And I noticed last night her graphic stated 'TRVC Chief Meteorologist.'"

"What?" I say, too loudly. My voice echoes in the quiet. "Sorry. I'm just wondering if that means I'm fired, replaced, demoted, demonized, defeated…" I stop. "Should I go on?"

"I think you've covered the bases," Mason says.

The wipers can barely keep up with the snow, and I can't even see a road in front of us. I grip the handle on the passenger door, and push my feet hard into the floorboard. Mason glances over but doesn't say a word.

"I've driven in the snow my whole life," he finally says.

"That doesn't matter," I whisper.

"I know," he says. "And I'm so sorry."

We drive in silence for a long time, M-22 meandering out of town and along the water. The snow refuses to slow.

"I'm happy you're wearing the necklace," Mason says. "And I hope my note didn't cross any lines."

I glance over at him. "I know it must have been hard to write. I know it must have been hard to give me something that meant so much to you and your wife." I wait until he catches my eyes. "But I'm glad you did. It was sweet, heartfelt and courageous, and it actually made me see things a bit more clearly."

"I was worried the gift was a bit too odd," he says. "It's not every day a fella gives a girl a necklace from his dead wife."

I don't laugh.

"Supposed to be a joke," he says, squinting out at the road.

"I know it's a strange thing to send you. I know there's a lot of history. I know I probably shouldn't have sent it, but I also knew that if I never saw you again, that necklace would have a new life." He stops. "Maybe even save one." His voice breaks and there is silence for a long while, only the *clop-clop* of the wipers. Finally, Mason whispers, "I like you, Sonny. A whole lot."

My heart is thumping, but I'm so, so exhausted. I can't find any words, much less the right words.

"Okay then," he says softly. "I'll shut up now."

"I like the necklace, Mason," I say. "I do. You know, I used to wear a lot of my sister's jewelry, and I turned my dad's rings into earrings and some of his tie tacks into a bracelet. I like when things tell a story." I stop. "I like you, too, Mason. A lot, I think."

I realize I am touching the necklace. Mason looks over, sees that I am and beams.

"Well, I'm glad you're home," he says. "Michigan needs some sun."

As we near the house, Mason asks, "What are you going to say to your mom?"

"I have no idea." I sigh. "I just pray she's sound asleep, so I can sneak in and get some rest before we talk. Otherwise…" My voice drifts off.

"She loves you," he says. "More than anyone else in this world. Just remember that."

"What did she tell you?" I ask. "About me. About Joncee. About what happened."

"She told me you're still haunted," he said. "I just wanted to know you were okay." Mason pulls into the driveway. "I want you to tell me in your own words what happened to your sister when you're ready. Talking about it is important. Believe me."

I don't answer.

"Thank you for the letter, for the necklace, for the ride…for pretty much everything since I've arrived. I may need your help finding a new job."

"You won't need my help." I open the door. "Let me help you with your luggage."

Mason drags my bags through the snow and onto the front porch. I find the key and ever so slowly and quietly as possible unlock the door.

"I'm like a cat burglar," I whisper. "And there's a big dog waiting for me inside." I stop and put my hand on Mason's arm. "Thank you again."

I begin to turn but Mason says, "Would you like to go out on Thursday? It's Valentine's Day."

"It is?"

"It is. I was thinking I might cook for you."

"Embarrassed to be seen with me in public?"

"Do you want to be seen in public?"

I shake my head.

"That's what I thought," he said. "So, is it a date?"

My heart skips.

A proper date? I want to ask. *An old-fashioned date? What's that?*

"Yes," I say.

"Great! I can pick you up at seven."

"I can drive," I say. Mason looks skeptically at me. "I can. My mom put snow tires on my car."

He laughs.

"And seven is perfect," I continue.

"What do you like to eat?"

"Surprise me," I say. "But not chili. It's sort of left a bad taste in my mouth."

Mason chuckles. "No chili."

"Good wine," I say. "And I don't share dessert."

"A woman after my own heart," he says.

Mason leans in and kisses me lightly on the cheek. "I can't

wait." He walks down the snowy steps before turning. "Get some rest, Sonny. And good luck."

"I'm going to need big doses of both."

I watch him drive away. Before I head inside, I turn and see our footsteps in the newly fallen snow.

Like me, I can't tell if they are coming or going.

The house is dark, save for the roughly hundred night-lights my mother has plugged in. My childhood home has always resembled, ironically, an airport runway. My mother, ever the nurse, used to regale us with horror stories about household accidents.

"People trip in the dark, or fall down the stairs," my mom used to tell us after a day at the hospital. "All they wanted was a glass of water, and next thing they know they're in the emergency room with a broken leg or a candlestick that got lodged in an unsavory location."

My mom took every necessary precaution, and it still wasn't enough.

I silence an emerging grunt as I—gingerly as possible—lug my luggage across the bumpy threshold and park it atop the big rug in the foyer.

What will you think when you see this in the morning, Mom? Happy? Sad? Hopeful? Mad?

I tiptoe up the stairs holding my breath. My mother has always been a light sleeper, so I'm still amazed I could make it out of the house when I was on the lam without her hearing me. She must have been so exhausted. Growing up, my mom could sense when Joncee was a having a nightmare before she even yelled for her. The roar of the wind across the bay kept her awake. It was only when it snowed and the world was silent did my mother's mind quiet.

She and Joncee always loved snow. Winter was their favorite season.

Squeak!

Dammit! I forgot the seventh step always squeaks when you're moving slowly.

I used to joke that my parents built this house just to torture me. Their bedroom was just off the top of the stairs, which made it impossible for me to sneak in or out, much less even slink down for a piece of cherry pie in the middle of the night. And the seventh step squeaked. I truly believe that—right before the carpet was installed—my mom and dad removed a nail in this stair to make it squeak. It was their secret children alarm, their auditory Bat-Signal.

I realize I am still paralyzed, one leg hiked above the stair in midair like a frightened flamingo. I hold my breath. And wait.

Nothing.

I finally exhale in silence. I can see that my mother's door is wide open. I hit the ground and crawl the last few steps and then into my bedroom. I slide my door shut, an inch at a time, while still seated on the floor. When it finally closes, I stand, grab my cell and turn on the flashlight.

This is ridiculous, I think.

A fifty-year-old woman sneaking into the childhood home she ran away from only to return—her life in shambles—terrified to wake up her mother. I want to laugh at the absurdity of it all, but it's just too darn sad. I feel dirty from the flight and desperately want to shower, or at least wash my face, but I know the sound of a running faucet—much less a single drip of water—would wake Sleeping Beauty and cause a scene that I am just too exhausted to deal with right now.

I pull back the covers and begin to crawl into bed but think of Mason and his winding, dark drive home in the snow. I tiptoe to my window and look out. Even in the middle of the night and heavy snow, the icy bay shimmers. I scan the road left and right. I shut my eyes, count to fifty and visualize Mason arriving home safely. I then rub the lock on the windowsill ten times.

You can't, I think. *You'll wake her up.*

I try to get in bed without finishing my routine, but I can't. I walk to the light switch and turn it on and off twenty-five times and then touch every object on my dresser.

Finally, I feel safe.

"You're home."

I scream.

"What are you doing? You scared the wits out of me! Are you insane?"

The lights come back on in my room. My mother, who looks great, mind you, in the middle of the night, lifts a brow and gives me a look that says, *Do you really want to go there with that question?*

"It's my house, remember?" she says.

I crawl into bed.

"I didn't mean to wake you," I say. "I'm sorry. Can we talk in the morning? I'm bone tired."

My mom is leaning against the door frame, arms crossed. She is wearing navy blue flannel pajamas with big white snowflakes on them.

The irony is literally too much to bear.

"Sorry, but I need to talk about this," she says. "You scared me when you left without telling me. I mean, you sneaked into my home and left without even talking to me. You only left me a very panicked message from the airport and then you didn't return any of my calls. I was worried sick. I was scared you might hurt yourself. I…" She stops and doesn't just close her eyes, she squeezes them shut. When she finally reopens them, they are wet with tears. "…am your mom. Why would you do that to me?"

She takes a seat on the edge of my bed.

"You're not the only one who lives with pain, my dear," she continues. "I am haunted every single day of my life. Do you know how much effort it takes just to push away all of that anguish and all of those memories? You don't think I worry about you every second of every day? And then to be treated as if I don't matter?"

I look at her. My heart shatters.

Have I been only so focused on my own pain that I've forgotten about the woman who lost her daughter?

"I know how hard it is for you to be back here," she says, her expression still pained. There are shadows under her eyes. She doesn't just look tired, I realize, she looks utterly exhausted. "Not just back in Michigan but back home." She takes a big breath. "I told you, I know all about your routine, honey. The counting and touching and clicking. I've secretly watched you do it for decades, after Joncee died, when you'd return home to visit, after your father passed. It rips me apart inside. I think of everything I should have done. We should have gone to therapy. We should have talked about it more as a family. That's why I try to be so open. I wanted you to open up to me. I know that's why you moved so far away. You wanted to be as far away from those memories as possible." She stops. "But none of that—the rituals or the running away—will bring your sister back. It won't protect those who are still here. And it won't help you heal."

I cannot hold my emotions inside any longer. I am raw and exhausted. I bawl, heaving waves of tears, as if I'm a spring thunderstorm releasing a torrent upon the earth.

"How do you do it?" I finally ask. "How have you been able to go on?"

"Because I have you!" Her voice rises with each word. *"You!"*

I sob anew, holding on to my mother with all of my might.

"You're my only daughter. You're my entire world. You're my everything. My whole life centers on you, don't you know that? I am strong for you. I am funny for you. I get up every day and do my damnedest to be happy and make the world a better place because of *you*. You're all I have left. I—" My mom stops and begins to sob as loudly as I did. "I love you so much my heart aches. I love you so much that I never wanted to guilt you into moving back to Michigan to be close to me."

I look at my mom as if for the first time, as if I've never seen her before. I feel a mix of guilt and relief, as if my soul has released a sigh it's been holding forever.

She continues. "It's not like you were just down the block, and I could check on you every day. I had to let you live. Do you know how hard that is for a mother? To let their only surviving daughter just go? You lived across the country. I worried about you every minute." My mom sighs. "I don't want anything else in this world except for you to be happy. That's all I've ever wanted. And not just happy or at peace, sweetheart, but blissfully, insanely happy. I know you act the part—Sonny the meteorologist, bright and bubbly—but you're not. Stop acting. You deserve every ounce of happiness in this world. You do. I want you to hear me. You had nothing to do with Joncee's death."

"I did, Mom. It's my fault."

"No, it's not. Stop it. It's not. It was just an accident. You were sixteen. You were a kid. I wish we could erase everything that happened that night, but we can't. And we never will. But how long are you going to punish yourself?"

"I'm scared, Mom," I say. "Of losing you, of losing someone else I love. I… I… I don't know if I could actually go on living if that were to happen again."

"I know, angel. Life is so hard. And losing someone you love is the hardest part. When your father got sick, I was so angry at God. I asked Him how He could do this to me, someone who had so much faith, someone who helps so many other people." My mom looks out the window at the snow falling. "I finally realized I had to stop viewing it as a punishment. I had to view it as a blessing."

I shake my head. "I don't understand what you're saying."

"I watch someone die every week," she explains. "I actually prepare them and their families for death. None of us gets out of here alive, honey. Some are taken way too soon, and that pain—that searing hole in our souls—never goes away because it's just not fair. But each life is a gift, especially to those who remain. We are forever touched by someone else. That changes us. That is such a grand blessing."

She stops and wills herself not to cry.

"But too many of us, I've learned as a hospice nurse, live as though we're dying. We're trapped in fear. We let that define us. But our lives should be defined by our joy, passion and happiness. One day, very soon, you will look in the mirror and be my age, and I beg of you right now to promise yourself that you will not be trapped in regret like too many of my dying patients are." She inhales deeply. "No, I want you to promise *me*. Promise me you won't regret not falling in love, you won't regret not finding joy, you won't regret..."

She stops. Her chin is shaking, and her lips are quivering.

"...not forgiving yourself."

"How do I do that, Mom?"

"You say, despite all the pain, 'Thank you, God, for blessing me with the best sister I ever could have had. I would not be the person I am without her. I would not be doing what I do without her.' You are *you* largely because of her. You don't want to erase that or forget that, do you? No! You want to celebrate that."

I reach out my arms, and my mother holds me, rocks me until my sobs subside. "And I would strongly urge you to continue the counseling you once said you were getting in California here in Michigan. I can refer you to one of the best, a dear friend of mine. I send families to her every week. You need to heal. And you can't do that alone. No one can."

"Thank you, Mom. I will do that."

She stands. "I better let you get some rest. I'm glad we were able to talk...*really* talk...for once."

"Mom?"

She turns.

"Would you stay?"

She smiles the saddest, sweetest smile I've ever seen, turns off the light and crawls into bed next to me. I put my head on her shoulder, and she strokes my hair. Her breathing slows, and, eventually, she begins to sleep.

I look out the window at the snow falling. The world is quiet, and, for once in my life, my mind is, too. Stillness settles over my body as it has over the world outside. I begin to drift off, my mother holding me, and I can feel my sister on the other side of me, just like we used to do when it was snowing and my mom would read to us in bed.

For the first time in a long time, I feel safe.

I am home.

"You look beautiful, sweetheart."

"Thank you."

"That red dress is just magnificent," my mother says. "Where did you get it?"

"From your closet, Mother. Very funny."

My mother laughs, and I do, too. It feels good to laugh. It feels good to have a home filled with laughter.

"You've always looked beautiful in red. Joncee always looked best in blue."

"And you in anything," I say.

"Thank you," my mom says. "Oh, here."

She hands me a glass of red wine from out of nowhere, and I give her a look. "You're like a drunk magician," I joke.

"When was the last time you had a proper date?" she asks.

I stare at her like a ventriloquist's dummy. "Well..." I start.

How many relationships have I sabotaged for fear that—if I fell too deeply in love—I might lose them as I lost my sister? How many men have I dated who were threatened by my success? How many men have I dated that were just plain losers?

I got sick of setups by my friends with money-driven men from LA who owned second homes in Palm Springs and came into town looking to party like teenage boys. I never clicked with the younger Silicon Valley men who worked so many hours that, even at dinner, they couldn't look up from their cell phones and after a few dates couldn't bother to call even though their entire life was spent on their cells.

I think of the horrors of online dating, swiping left and right, men looking only to hook up, sending—*ahem*—dick pics before we'd even exchanged a hello. And how many times did my friends and I head out of Palm Springs to go "Down Valley"—to ritzy Rancho Mirage or placid Palm Desert—to restaurants and clubs populated by ninety-year-old men who would intentionally trip you with their walkers as you made your way to the bar and then—while you were still sprawled across the floor—ask you to come back to their place?

My career was my partner, and it sustained me for a very long time. I didn't have much time to think about being alone. And then…and then I became comfortable with my aloneness. Sonny was all Amberrose needed.

Until Mason.

"Your silence speaks volumes," my mother says. "Drink up."

"I have to drive in a near-blizzard *and* be semicoherent for my romantic dinner," I say.

"Oh, honey. I'm driving you."

"My mother can't drive me to a date on Valentine's Day!"

"Watch me. I know how much you hate to drive in the snow. And until you earn back that powder confidence, I don't trust you driving. And, most importantly, you don't trust yourself driving. I don't want to worry tonight, okay? I've done enough worrying of late."

"So do I have to call you when I'm ready to come home? Or will you be picking me up at a certain time? This is just weird, Mother."

"I just assumed you'd be staying the night."

"Oh, my Lord, Mom." I grab the glass of wine and take a healthy sip. "I'm not that easy."

"Keep drinking," she says with a wink. "Don't worry. We'll work it out."

I peek out the window. The snow hasn't slowed. "You know, I haven't looked at a weather forecast in days. It's the longest stretch I've gone in my career."

"What is Lisa saying?" my mom asks.

"I'm meeting with her this weekend."

"Keep drinking."

I finish getting ready, opting to wear a cute—albeit slippery—pair of ankle boots to keep my feet from freezing but to show off my legs. On the drive, my mother asks, "Want to hear about my most romantic Valentine's date?"

"I love a good dad story," I say.

"Wasn't with your father," my mom says.

My body springs upright like a human jack-in-the-box. "What? Do tell."

"Jimmy Reed. He was my college boyfriend. So handsome. He looked like Tab Hunter."

"Who?"

"You should know that! You lived in Palm Springs!" My mother rolls her eyes at me and focuses on the road ahead and her memories. "Never mind," she says. "He took my breath away."

"Was he more handsome than dad?"

"Much," she says.

"Mother!"

"I'm being honest." She shrugs. "He was a lifeguard, he worked out every day and he looked like a California surfer. Anyway, he knew someone who worked for the state of Michigan who oversaw the Mission Point Lighthouse, which was deactivated a long time ago."

"The wooden one with black trim and the tower on top at

the end of Old Mission Peninsula?" I ask. "We went on a field trip there in school once."

"Yep," my mom nods. "It has the most stunning views. Well, Jimmy arranged the most romantic dinner for me in that lighthouse. Just the two of us in the middle of a snow squall. Candlelight, chocolates, pizza. I felt like I was in a movie. Jimmy told me that the lighthouse stood just a few hundred yards south of the forty-fifth parallel north, halfway between the North Pole and the equator. He said that was why the light was so stunningly beautiful in this part of Michigan, as if golden gauze had been draped over the world." My mom stops. "And then he looked at me and said, 'But you outshine the light here,' and he kissed me."

"That *is* romantic," I gush. "Why didn't you end up with him?"

"I met your father," she says, "and something just clicked."

"But Jimmy was better looking, right? And I know dad wasn't the most romantic man in the world."

She smiles. "I knew immediately about your father. Jimmy had to work to take my breath away, but your father did it without trying. It's like I was complete as a person, but there was a missing puzzle piece without your father. And when I met him, I could actually hear it."

"Hear what?"

"My soul click into place with his." She snaps her fingers. *Click!* "It's not about looks, or money, or dinners in lighthouses, it's that your dad made me a better person. I wanted to be a better person because of him. He believed in me and supported me. He respected me. He wanted me to succeed in my career." My mother looks out at the headlights beaming through the snow. "And his soul radiated light, brighter than any lighthouse, more beautiful than any forty-fifth parallel. In my eyes, he was the most beautiful man I'd ever seen because I could see his soul.

And he still is." My mom glances over at me. "You'll know when it happens. Ope! We're here!"

Mason steps onto the front porch and waves.

"He's *so* good-looking," my mother says, her body bent over the steering wheel, staring. "And what a nice house."

"I thought you said none of that mattered, Mother."

"It doesn't," she says. "But it doesn't hurt, either."

I shake my head.

"How do I look?"

My mom gives me a close once-over. "Perfect." She stops. "Like you're ready to play seven minutes in heaven. Remember?"

"Ugh, Mother. You're like an elephant with your memory."

"Well, I will never forget opening the pantry to find you kissing Bobby Montgomery. You used to take baths with him. It was very disturbing."

I open the car door. "Goodbye, Mom. I'll call Lyft if I need a ride."

My mother roars. "Lyft? In northern Michigan? In February? In a snowstorm? Good luck with that. I'm your Lyft."

I start to shut the door.

"And don't get anything on my dress," she adds.

"And, the mood is officially killed. I might as well become a nun."

"No, honey, nuns now have social media, so you'd still be in the same place you are now." She begins to reverse but stops to open the passenger window. "You didn't tip me."

"I'll give you a tip," I say. "Stop annoying me."

I hear laughter as her car pulls away. "Be careful," I whisper as I watch until her headlights are gone. I remember our conversation from last night and that calms me.

When I turn, Mason is behind me.

"Your mother drove you?"

He says this slowly as if he's just uncovered a devastating state secret.

"No," I say with a straight face. "I took a Lyft. Driven by a woman who looks just like my mom in a car that looks just like my mom's."

"You must have felt comfortable then," Mason says. "I've never sat in the front seat before."

"You really have to look at the driver's photo closely. You'd be surprised at how many look like seventy-five-year-old women."

Mason laughs and takes my hand. "Stairs are slick. Snow's really coming down."

He guides me inside, which is toasty warm, takes my coat and scarf and then whistles like a teakettle. "You look amazing."

"This old thing," I joke, thankful my face is already red from the cold and not his compliment.

"And that necklace," he adds. "Where did you get it?"

"Old friend," I say. I smile and touch the necklace. "Thank you. And thank you for having me over for…" The words just stop when I look around his home.

"Dinner?" he offers. "Valentine's?" Mason mimics a drum roll. "A date?"

"Everything," I say. "Sorry. It's just…you have such a beautiful home."

"Thank you. Helped design and build it myself. I needed a new start—a new home—after Andi. And I always wanted a true Michigan cabin."

Mason's "cabin" is all knotty pine with vaulted ceilings and massive windows overlooking Omena Bay. It's cute as a button with oodles of charm and old-school nostalgia: a lakestone fireplace soars to the rafters, a vintage farm sink centers the kitchen along with open cabinetry covered with burlap curtains, and the dining room lights are made from weathered orchard baskets. There is an open loft with a ladder, and the appliances are the aqua color of my mom's beloved McCoy vases.

"Are those old?" I ask, walking toward his kitchen.

"New, but look old." Mason opens the refrigerator and then the oven. "See? Aren't they cool?"

"I love them," I say.

"And the floors were salvaged from old barns on Old Mission Peninsula. Look at the character."

I reach down and touch the dark floors. "You even used square nails," I say.

"If I do it, I do it right."

His voice is husky. I stand and Mason is inches from my body. It finally dawns on me that Tom Brady attended the University of Michigan and that maybe, unbeknownst to everyone, he ran away from the NFL and left Gisele to escape back to his beloved college state to start over.

With me.

Mason might be even better looking the more I get to know him. A man with a good career who built his own house and can cook. It's like finding a pot of gold at the end of the rainbow, and the leprechaun turns out to be superhot.

My breath hitches in my throat. My legs feel as if they are made of candlewax, and Mason is a blowtorch. He leans toward me.

"What's cooking?" I ask, taking a sidestep. "Smells amazing."

You idiot. Why didn't you let him kiss you?

I mean, you're wearing your mother's clothing, likely unemployed, unable to drive in the winter and still too many years away from Social Security. You need something exciting in your life right now.

I U-turn and bend over the stove, waving the aroma toward my nose. I realize too late I probably resemble a witch over a cauldron.

"It's not chili," I say, even though there's not a pot on the stove. "Thank goodness."

"Ina Garten's roasted chicken," Mason says. "With honey-roasted carrots and roasted potatoes."

"You like to roast?" I say.

You sound like an idiot, Sonny. You like to roast?

"Speaking of which..." he says, not making fun of me. Mason points to the roaring fire. I notice there is a bottle of wine, two glasses and a platter of appetizers on an oversize birch leg table. "Follow me. Let's roast in front of the fire for a bit."

We take a seat, and he pours a glass of wine.

"I hope you like it," he says. "It's a Michigan white burgundy, perfect for the roast chicken and the cheese and whitefish dip."

I swirl my glass and sniff, and then swirl some more. I lift the glass and take a sip.

"Amazing," I say. I grab a plate and a few nibbles of cheese. I taste the smoked dip, rich and flavorful. I gesture around his home. "Everything is..." I stop. "I'd forgotten."

"Forgotten what?" Mason asks next to me on the sofa.

"How much character Michigan has: the wine, the food, the homes, the water. Everything." I take a sip of wine and look around. "Living in Palm Springs was like living in a Sinatra song. The architecture, the midcentury vibe, the palm trees, the sunshine, martinis by the mountain." I stop. "There's an iconic Slim Aarons photograph called *Poolside Gossip* that defines the midcentury mystique of Palm Springs."

"I've not heard of it," Mason says.

"It shows California society women—dressed in midcentury fashion—locked in conversation, cocktails in hand, by a sparkling turquoise pool, with the idyllic mountains hovering in the background. It depicts everything I love about Palm Springs." I stop again. "I'd erased my mental picture of Michigan." I look out Mason's windows. Snow falls on the bay, the wind and the churning of the water a melodramatic soundtrack. Pines draped in snow flank the windows. The stunning stone fireplace heats the cabin.

"Fireside Gossip?" Mason asks. *"Snowy Secrets?"*

I laugh. "You do run the chamber, don't you?" I look at him. "I'd forgotten Michigan's majesty."

"*You* should run the chamber," he says.

A buzzer goes off in the kitchen, and Mason stands. I turn and watch him pull the chicken from the oven, followed by the carrots and potatoes. He carves the chicken, and then heads to the dining room table to light the candles.

"Can I help?"

"Bring yourself and the wine," he says. "The two most important things here."

He makes two plates and brings them to the table.

"Cheers," Mason says, lifting his glass after he takes a seat. He cocks his head as if he's thinking. He looks at me, his blue eyes sparkling next to his wineglass. "To creating your own brand-new picture of Michigan."

"Cheers," I say, clinking his glass. "That's lovely."

I take a bite of chicken. It is beyond incredible. "Wow."

"It's all Ina," he says. "She changed my life with this recipe. So easy. You just season up a bird, put some herbs, onion and lemon inside, and stick it in the oven. Makes great leftovers, too."

"You're a Renaissance Man," I say. I look at his plate. "And a leg man."

"Yes, I am," Mason says, his voice husky once again.

My face flushes, and I scan the room rather than look Mason in the eye. I chuckle, covering my mouth as I do.

"Okay," I ask, pointing toward the fireplace. "How did I not notice the picture of the dog wearing the crown over the mantel. What's the story?"

Mason laughs and wipes his mouth. "That's the former mayor of Omena," he says.

"What?"

"Mayor Doris," he says. "For over the last decade, Omena has elected an animal as mayor. We've had dogs, cats, chickens, goats and horses. My Doris won seven years ago and served for two. Omena residents pay a buck to take part in the special election, with all the proceeds going to the historical society. Nearly ten thousand votes were cast in the last election, and Sweet Tart, a cat, won. All the candidates have a platform. After Andi died, I went on one of our favorite hikes, the one where we found Lucky. Well, as luck would have it, I found Doris abandoned in an old barn. I felt like it was a miracle, as if God and Andi were talking to me through this dog. Took me weeks to convince her to eat. A few more to convince her to trust me. She was all bones. Barely alive. Her nails were so long they were growing back into her paws. She had chewed through the rope to set herself free, and it was embedded in the skin around her neck. I didn't know if she'd survive. Best dog I ever had. Saved me after I lost Andi. I felt I had to save something in this world." Mason stops. "Doris ran for mayor and won. Her story resonated with folks around here, many of whom moved to this small town of three hundred to be left alone much of the year. Towns like Mayberry. I call it Bay-berry. Anyway, Doris raised money for the local shelters. She campaigned on equal rights for humans and animals. She passed away two years ago. Her picture just sums up the best of us, doesn't it? All we need is love to survive the worst in life. Just takes someone to give a damn to make a difference."

I clench my teeth in order to will myself not to cry.

Is he speaking about Doris? Or me?

"Cheers to Doris," I finally say, lifting my glass to the picture and then to Mason.

After dinner, we take the remaining bottle of wine back to the sofa and have some chocolate-dipped strawberries. Mason turns on some music.

"Frank Sinatra," I say. "How appropriate."

He smiles. Without warning, he holds out his hand.

"Would you like to dance?"

He pulls me off the sofa and into his arms, and we sway to Sinatra for the longest time.

"Tell me about that scar on your forehead," I say. "It must tell a story. Old sports injury? Do something heroic?"

He chuckles and touches it.

"I tripped over Doris in the dark when she was sleeping in middle of the room. Fell right into the fireplace and cracked my head. Passed out. Doris licked me awake. Required a few stitches. Ironically, it's in almost the same spot where I fell into the hearth as a kid." He looks at me. "Sorry it's not a legendary story."

"It's a sweet one," I say. "And that's even better."

After a few songs, Mason holds me at arm's length and asks, "Have you ever danced in the snow?"

"What? No, it's freezing."

He looks at me. "You need a new memory of winter. You need a new picture of Michigan."

He grabs my coat and hands me some of his boots. "They're too big, but they'll do," he says.

Mason leads me out the French doors to his patio overlooking the bay. The snow reaches my shins. Mason pulls me close.

"Don't we need music?" I ask.

"We have it," he says. "The water. The hiss of the snow. Our heartbeats. That's our music."

We sway for a bit, and I watch lights from cottages around the bay illuminate the water. I think of when Joncee and I would wrap ourselves up and go sit on the frozen shore in the middle of winter. We'd hold hands and make up stories about what everyone was doing in the cottages around the bay.

It's like living in the middle of a real-life snow globe, isn't it, Amberrose? she'd ask, giggling, her breath coming out in little puffs that hung in the air. *And what's more beautiful than that?*

And then we'd make up stories about what winter would be like when we were older.

One day, we'll both stand in the snow and boys will kiss us! We might even dance and twirl like those people do when they kiss in that snow globe Mommy puts out every Christmas.

Without warning, I start to cry. Mason doesn't say a word, he just pulls me close, close, closer, until I am one with him.

"Do you want to tell me about what happened?" he finally asks.

My heart is beating so rapidly, I feel dizzy. We stand in the snow, and I hold on to him.

"I was sixteen. I'd just gotten my driver's license on my birthday in March. I'd picked up some of my girlfriends, and some boys were coming over to my house for a secret party. My parents were at some fundraiser. I had just started to date Jasper Kingston, our high school quarterback. Joncee was at a friend's house having a slumber party. She got spooked, which she often did, and wanted to come home. I told her she was fine and not to ruin my night. She kept calling, saying they'd watched a scary movie, and she swore Freddy Krueger was in her friend's house. She begged me to come get her, but I hung up on her." I shake my head. "It had started snowing. It was a surprise storm that came in off the lake, one of those wet snows, and then the temperature dropped and the roads iced over. Joncee annoyed her friend's brother so much that he ended up driving her home. He hit a patch of black ice outside of town, lost control of the car and it slid into the bay. He got out, but he couldn't save Joncee. It was my fault she died. My fault. If I'd gone to pick her up like she asked, she would be here right now. If I'd just been a good sister, she would be alive. And I will never forgive myself."

I am sobbing uncontrollably, and Mason holds me until I stop.

"It wasn't your fault, Sonny. It was a tragic accident. You can blame yourself forever, like I did. It won't change a thing. It won't bring her back." He stops and cups my face in his palms. He runs a finger on my cheeks to dry them.

"How do I forgive myself? How?"

"You just do," he says. "You realize you both loved each

other more than anything in this world, and that you will see her again one day. As she was. As she always will be. Your little sister who loved you—and winter—so much."

He holds me. "Maybe," Mason says, "all of this snow is a sign from her."

"A sign?"

"Maybe she's saying, 'Welcome home. Embrace winter. Like we used to do. Remember who you were.'"

Mason looks down at me. "She's the reason you became a meteorologist, isn't she?"

I nod.

"So maybe you could save someone?"

I nod, tearing up again.

"Have you ever thought about how many lives you might have saved by your forecasts, your predictions, your warnings?"

I shake my head.

"You'll never know, but you have. You can never measure the impact that your sister continues to have on everyone, including you. That's an amazing legacy."

"Thank you." I sniffle. "I'm sorry to ruin Valentine's."

"You didn't ruin it, Sonny. You're actually shoveling out your heart after all these years. And what better day than today to do that?"

We stand in the snow, and then I lean in and kiss Mason for even longer, until snow collects on our noses. A sound makes me stop, and I turn toward the bay, my head cocked, a hand around my ear.

"Did you hear that?" I ask.

"Hear what?"

"A loud crack or something."

"I didn't," he says. "I'm an expert at identifying winter noises around here. Could be a raccoon. A pine tree snapping in the wind. Or ice on the bay even."

I look at him but don't say a word. The sound, I finally realize, was a click. Like a puzzle piece.

"Never mind," I say, and smile.

This time, he leans in and kisses me, and we twirl in the falling snow, like beautiful ice dancers in a snow globe.

And this time, I do hear music.

chapter 12

"You look remarkably—" Lisa searches for the right word, tugging her sweater around her tightly as if to pop out the correct one "—relaxed."

My head spins. How could she know about last night? Or do I seem different? I certainly feel different.

"Time away must have been good for you," she says.

"Look—" I start.

She cuts me off. "Wasn't good for the station."

"I'm sorry about everything, Lisa. I'm sorry I blew up on air. I'm sorry about our fight. I'm sorry I ran away."

"No, you're just sorry you might have ended your career for the last time."

Her voice is roughly the decibel level of a flyover by the Blue Angels. She gets up to shut her office door. A crowd of weekend staff has already gathered to witness the commotion.

The scariest thing about Lisa's tone is that although it's loud, it's largely without emotion.

Lisa takes a seat behind her desk and checks her cell.

She's done, I think. *With me. With everything.*

"No, I really am sorry, Lisa. Truly. I hurt you. I hurt the station. I hurt my coworkers. I hurt my anchors. I hurt Icicle. I hurt my mom." I look at her. My lips begin to quiver. "I just hurt, Lisa. And I have for a very long time."

I take a deep breath and become a verbal blizzard.

"My little sister died in a tragic accident when she was still a kid," I say.

"Oh, Sonny!"

"I loved her more than anything. I still do. Joncee adored everything about winter. She was pure light and goodness. How do you go on when your little sister is taken? When her life is stolen before it's even started? When you blame yourself?"

Lisa reaches out and takes my hand.

I continue, head down. "The only way I could was to put a wall around myself, to distance myself from those who wanted to get too close. I did that in college, Lisa, because you reminded me of my sister: all energy and sweetness and love of winter. I don't think I could have gone on, so I just lashed out, or kept people at bay. All I wanted was to be someone new, someone different, someone who didn't have to talk about her sister."

"You became Sonny?"

I nod. When I am finally able to look at her, tears are welled up in her eyes.

"I'm so, so sorry, Sonny," she finally says. "My heart breaks for you. I wish I would have known. I wish you would have confided in me. Thank you for sharing. And what a huge compliment. I reminded you of your sister." Lisa begins to cry. I grip her hand tightly and give it a shake. There is a long silence, and then Lisa continues. "Better yet, why didn't I know this? I run a news station in a small city. I should have done better research."

I smile.

"You really hurt me in college, and that stayed with me for a very long time. I know I come on too strong. I…" Lisa stops, unable to finish her thought. I finish for her.

"I should have been a better colleague. I should have been a better friend."

The last word hangs in the air.

"So?" I continue. "Am I fired?"

Lisa laughs a hard, staccato laugh that takes me by surprise.

"Oh, you're not getting off that easy," she says. "I can't just fire you and eat your contract. That lion you call an agent negotiated too well: you actually get a bonus if you're fired. Yep, I'm the idiot who agreed to that. And you get paid for a full year."

"She's good."

"She's evil," Lisa laughs. "We need all the help we can get around here anyway. Staff is too small, and budget is too tight. So, you stay. But with changes."

I take a sharp breath.

"I'm demoting you."

"What? My contract allows that?"

"I'm a lion, too," Lisa says, sitting straighter in her chair, very proud of herself. "There's been a push among the staff and reporters to make Polly Sue the interim chief meteorologist."

"She doesn't know a high pressure system from a Big Mac. She's not a meteorologist, Lisa. From what I've heard, she was the traffic girl who Mighty Merle the Meteorologist, shall we say, took under his wing."

Lisa sighs. "I'm not going to get into office gossip, but I am going to give the job to her—"

"Lisa, no."

"—temporarily," she adds.

"What about me?"

"You'll be helping Polly Sue prepare her forecasts and—" Lisa stops and actually winces "—doing weekends for a while."

"Are you kidding me with this? I'm fifty and doing weekends again?"

"You've had two on-air episodes, Sonny. The local media and other stations are having a field day with this. Viewers are loving what a good sport you've been on air, but I have to be careful. It's a news station, but I can't have a news station without advertisers. And they're a little touchy right now, to be honest. I'm sorry."

"What's next? Are you making me do the weather from used-car lots on Saturdays?"

Lisa winces again.

"You're going to run the Frostbite Marathon next weekend."

"A marathon? In this weather? Are you nuts?"

"It's a relay, Sonny. You're doing the next-to-last leg. Polly Sue will run the last few miles. Consider it team building. And I still want you out and about in the winter. I still want you to do live shots. And I still want you to be part of the team. But you have to *try* to be part of the team, okay? Then, we'll see what happens."

"What happens is that I'm going to end up going stir-crazy and living all alone in a cave somewhere in the snow like the Grinch."

"I think that's already happened," Lisa says.

I take a deep breath and knock.

Polly Sue looks up and sees me through the window on the door. She doesn't respond. I knock again.

She rolls her eyes and waves me in.

"Can we talk?"

"I'm super busy," she says. "You know, now that I'm the chief meteorologist."

Interim! I want to scream. *And you're not a meteorologist.*

"I'd like to talk." I nearly choke on the next words. "Please, Polly Sue."

She sighs with great drama. "Yeah?"

"I wanted to apologize for my recent actions. I didn't mean to leave you, Lisa and the station in the lurch." I pause. "I'd also like to apologize to you personally. I didn't mean for our relationship to get off to such a rocky start."

"Shut the door," she says.

I look at her.

"I won't ask again, and I won't say please."

I shut the door.

"Let me be clear, *Amberrose.* This was supposed to be *my* gig all along. Now it is. And I plan on keeping it. You're unstable. You're a hot mess. You're an outsider." She stops and eyes me from head to toe. "Also, you're getting a little long in the tooth."

You little…

"Let me repeat the words you said to me when we first met, just so we're clear: *you* work for *me.*"

I think of my conversation with Lisa and take a deep breath to steady my rising emotions. "I've certainly not acted like the professional I am, and for that I apologize. This station deserves better. You deserve better. I deserve better. I blame myself for what's transpired, and I just want you to know that I plan to help you in any way I can," I say.

"Oh, you do, do you? Well, I don't need any help. I can see a snowstorm coming from Saskatchewan." She stops. "And the viewers like me. They trust me. They've already soured on you because—like me—they can spot a fraud."

From underneath her desk, she produces a pointing stick.

"Surprise! I got you one, too! Consider it a little gift from me. And I'd love for you to use it." She smiles like she just got goosed. "All the time."

I'm out, I think. *I can just as easily do radio somewhere.* I consider that thought. *No, I can't. I can't do radio.*

"Take it," she says.

I reach for it, and she waves the pointer up and down my body.

"PS. I'm going to suggest to Lisa that you change your hair

color. That blonde is a bit harsh. Maybe go naturally gray. It's all the rage right now. Or, red like me. But mine's natural, so…"

Polly Sue stands, her polyester dress making all kinds of noise.

You're going to rustle on air in that thing when you move, I don't tell her. *And the color is not flattering at all.* And then I shake my head. *You brought a lot of this on yourself, Sonny. Walking out. Pulling rank. Acting irrational on air. Stay calm. As my mother always says, "This, too, shall pass."*

"Better practice." She stops and lifts her own pointer. "Here, I'll show you." Polly Sue taps me on the head with it. "I wish you'd disappear." She laughs. "It's working!"

I grip my pointer so tightly that I nearly break it into two.

I smile.

Polly Sue swishes to the door and heads off down the hall.

I raise the pointer over my head as if I'm going to whack her with it.

I see Icicle at his desk out of the corner of my eye. His eyes are wide. He shakes his head at me.

I lower it for a moment and then lift it again, as if it's a sword. I pantomime impaling her.

Icicle stifles a laugh.

No, he mouths.

Polly Sue turns suddenly.

"Already feels good in my hand," I say with a smile.

She rolls her eyes and strides away, her dress making an irritating scritching sound

I walk over to Icicle.

"Can I buy you a cup of coffee?"

He looks at me and continues to edit footage.

"Or else," I say, lifting the pointer.

"Okay," he says.

"I'm still mad at you."

Icicle's voice sounds like that of a hurt little boy.

He takes a bite of the blueberry streusel muffin I bought him and looks out the window of the coffee shop in The Commons. He can't even look at me. He has *yet* to look at me.

I nervously glance around at the happy Michiganders in their winter coats, bulky sweaters and cute boots sipping coffee and happily embracing winter. An open fireplace flickers in the middle of the café. I remember when I would depart Palm Springs to head to Big Bear to ski with my girlfriends. I loved that girls' getaway. I loved shooshing down the trails, playing in the snow, drinking wine in the hot tub while flakes fell.

It was because my distance from here allowed me to distance the memories.

But the winter joy, deep down, was still the same.

"Iced coffee in the winter?" I ask Icicle.

"You get used to it," he says, his statement an indictment. He tilts his eyes somewhat in my direction at the table. "I'm not laughing at your jokes, either."

Icicle looks so sad and so much like a little kid that got his feelings hurt that I just want to erase all of his pain.

And that's when I understand: Icicle and I are similar in many ways. We both have bad memories from our childhoods. I lost my sister. He was an unpopular misfit. Neither of us can let go of our painful pasts. We try. We try so hard, and yet everywhere we turn, the memories remain. Everywhere we run, we see ourselves. We can't escape the fun house mirrors of our youth.

"I'm sorry," I say. "I've said that to everyone today, but..." I stop. "Icicle, please look at me. Please."

He turns a few millimeters and then slowly lifts his eyes to meet mine.

"But know how much I really mean it when I say it to you. I am so sorry. I didn't mean to blame you for the videos. I didn't mean to run away. I didn't mean to break our trust. We were becoming friends."

"We were?"

"Yes, we were." I stop. "We *are*."

His tall, lanky body deflates, like a pool float with a fast leak.

"I *thought* you were my friend, Sonny," he says, his voice barely a whisper. "And then you accused me of something really bad." His voice warbles. "I don't have any friends, Sonny."

I shake my head and clench my jaw, but a tear still pops into the corner of my eye.

"I don't either."

He looks at me with those puppy-dog eyes.

"Allergies," I say with a wink.

"It's February," Icicle says. "No allergies. You should know that better than anyone." He stops. "And I thought you had lots of friends."

I reach out and grab his hand. I give it a big squeeze.

"I know all about what happened to your sister," he says. "My mom told me a long time ago. I'm really sorry."

I nod, clenching my jaw even tighter. "Thank you."

"Do you know, I used to watch all of your forecasts on my laptop? I studied your on-air persona but also the accuracy of your forecasts. Everyone saw Sonny the sunny news personality, but I saw Sonny the meteorologist." He looks me square in the eye. "And you deserved that Emmy for how you handled the 1994 earthquake. You saved so many lives, Sonny, before and after. Your aftershock warnings..." Icicle stops. "No one will ever understand the hours you worked to help your community. You're a role model to me. To call you a friend is something I never imagined."

"Icicle—" I start.

"But if we're friends, then don't friends share what's hurting them? Don't friends trust each other? Aren't friends always there for each other, no matter what?"

I look at him, searching for an answer.

"I don't think I've ever had a friend like that," I finally say. "I have had people who wanted to be friends, but I've kept them as acquaintances because I've been too scared to share everything about my life. I've been too scared to get hurt again. I've been too scared to lose someone again."

Icicle smiles a smile so much older than his years.

"Take it from someone who nearly died, Sonny. No one wants to think about death. No one wants to consider how short our lives really are. But I do. And I want my life to matter. But I'm stuck, Sonny, halfway between living and dying, and there's no worse place to be. Remember when we talked about zombies? That's what I feel like a lot of the time."

"Oh, Icicle."

"You didn't let your past define you."

"Yes, I did."

"But at least you did something with all your pain. I don't even have the courage to run away."

"It doesn't take courage to run away. It takes courage to stay."

"I just want to prove to people around here—my parents, everyone—that I'm not just a shocking story in a *Weird Michigan* book or a punch line to a winter joke. I want people to see me in a new light. I want that light to thaw Icicle. Forever."

My heart aches for him.

"How do we do that?" Icicle asks.

"I don't know yet," I say. "But friends can do anything, right?"

"Are you my friend? Friends don't accuse friends of doing bad things."

"Yes, I'm your friend, Icicle. Are you mine?"

He looks at me but doesn't answer immediately. "Yes," he finally says.

I look outside, and a little girl with skates slung over her shoulder catches my eye. She waves. I wave back.

"Want to go ice-skating?" I ask out of the blue.

"What about work?" he asks.

"You're running with a rebel now," I say. "I'll tell Lisa we're working on a story."

Icicle laughs. "Okay!"

We head to a rink with a stunning view of the bay. As I'm lacing up my skates, I say, "You're going to have to help me. Weak ankles."

"I don't think so," Icicle says. "Not with some of the shoes I've seen you wear."

I laugh, and we head out into snow and skate under the winter sky. In the distance, the bay churns angrily in the wind. Icicle grabs me and spins me.

But the cold of the world can't hurt me today.

"Whoo!" Icicle yelps.

Because I'm with a friend.

I think of Joncee and the snow globe. As I come to a stop, dizzy from spinning and laughing, Icicle comes into focus. He is wearing a green sweater, and his emerald eyes sparkle. This kid is sensitive, smart, funny and deep. I finally see him, as if for the first time. Not just see the way he looks, but inside of him, the clarity of his soul, the size of his heart, the brightness of his being.

It's as if Joncee's soul has taken up residence in Icicle's body.

"What are you looking at?" he asks. "Did my face freeze in a weird way?"

Joncee would have said exactly the same thing.

"No." I point behind us. "Look," I say. "Our tracks on the ice disappear so quickly."

"Ice-skaters apply a huge amount of pressure on the surface of the ice," Icicle says, "which causes it to melt super-fast and become slippery, which is best for ice-skating. But when we skate away..." Icicle suddenly spins in a circle and points at the ice "...there's no longer pressure on the surface, and it freezes over again. That entire process happens in the blink of an eye, and that's why you don't see any tracks on the ice."

I stare at him. "Wow," I say. "That would make a fascinating segment. Something for kids that interests them in science and meteorology perhaps. Take a fun winter activity and explain the science behind it. Maybe we can work on something. Goodness knows, I have the time now."

Icicle's green eyes grow large. "Could I help?"

"It could be your thing," I say. "I'd help *you*."

"What about Polly Sue?" he asks.

"Polly who?"

As we leave the ice, I turn around again. A beautiful pattern may not remain on the ice, but it does in my heart.

"Her hair color's not even real, Mom."

My mother grabs the end of my hair and gives it a slight tug. "Glass houses, honey."

"Thanks for the confidence boost, Mother."

She laughs. My mother truly thinks she is Nora Ephron and Leanne Morgan all rolled into one seventy-five-year-old woman's body.

"When was the last time you ran this far?" my mom asks. "And I don't mean away from home."

"You're on a roll today, aren't you?"

My mom pops her hip out and slaps her own rump. "I'm feelin' it."

"I hiked a lot in the desert, and I got in a few miles every week running," I say. "I'm in great shape for my age."

"You are. But I know how much you hate running in the cold."

"Okay, Mom. I just got demoted. I'm literally running behind Polly Sue today and handing her the 'virtual' baton, the personal and professional symbolism of which is so rich I can barely take it."

"I hate to repeat what your agent told you, but..."

"Keep my mouth shut and just do my job?" I finish. "I hear you. I'm trying. I'm good at doing my job. I'm not so good at keeping my mouth shut."

"The world is nodding its head in agreement, my dear," my mom says. "Now, are you sure you can actually run in all of that stuff, Frosty?"

I finish lacing my tennis shoes and look down at myself. I'm wearing two long-sleeve tech shirts, running tights, shorts, running gloves, a headband, a windproof jacket, tech fabric running socks and new running shoes with a good sole. My mother is right: I hate running in the cold. I love running when it's ninety degrees.

"Oh, and this! I forgot!"

I grab another long-sleeve T-shirt from the stool beside me in the kitchen and hold it up.

Reading from the front, I say, "'2022 Frostbite Marathon! BRRRR by the Bay!'" I flip the shirt around and continue reading. "'Team TRVC! Sonny Dunes!'"

"I can't tell you how much I love this," my mother says, her voice dripping in sarcasm. "Here, let me help you put it on."

My mom yanks it over my head and forces it over my body. My arms stick out beside me like a fat snowman. "You look adorable," my mother says. "Let me see you run!"

I take off and jog through the living room. My mother is nearly hysterical when I return. "I may not have grandchildren, but this makes up for it in so many ways."

"Okay, Erma Bombeck," I say. "Let's go."

My mother grabs her coat from the foyer, and strides past me toward the garage.

"Grab your purse and keys," she says. "You're driving."

"Excuse me?"

"If you can run in that gear, you can drive in it." She puts her hand on my shoulder and gives it a shake, as usual. "You need the experience. You have a car. I can't be driving you to work and on dates all the time. You're nearly my age after all."

I don't move. "I can't."

"You can, and you will." My mother cocks her head and gives

me the look, that look that mothers always use on their children when they're making a stand. I'd like to have met the mother who invented that look. If she had patented it, she would be very, very rich today.

"Mom," I start. "The snow. The road. The memory. Everything." I stop. "How can you pass by the same place every day where she died without thinking about it."

"I do think about it, honey. Every single time. In the winter, I watch kids slide across that bay on skates. In the summer, I watch them tube behind a boat. That very same spot where your sister died is a spot that brings so much joy to kids to this day. The irony used to be too much for your father and I to take sometimes. We'd drive the opposite way, add twenty minutes to the drive just to avoid the memory. But, one day, I drove to the spot where Joncee died and just sat on the beach sobbing. When I looked into the water, the sun was illuminating it. It sparkled and shimmered, and I swear I could hear your sister giggling in delight. That spot is such a parable for life: we must somehow allow the light to shine so we can erase the darkness."

I look at my mom. So strong. All alone and yet surrounded by friends. And…light.

"You know the irony of ironies, don't you?" my mom asks. "The fact you left Michigan and changed your name to Sonny. That always astounded me. It always made me smile."

"Why?"

"You chose light in your life, honey. Can't you see that? Despite running away from everything, despite going to the other side of the country to escape, you changed your name to reflect optimism and hope to people. But we both know you didn't do it for your viewers, you did it for yourself, right?"

I look at her, dumbfounded, shaking my head.

"Must be nice to wake up and look in the mirror every morning and say, 'Hi, Sonny!' Must make you feel really good inside."

I throw my arms around my mom.

"And if my girl is strong and brave enough to wake up every day with such hope—much less to start over and establish a wonderful career—and then face all her demons and return home, well, it just reinforces what I've always known." My mom puts her hand under my chin and looks me right in the face. "You've always been a bright light. And nothing can dim that. Nothing. Now you get behind that wheel, and you run your own race, and you set your own course, do you hear me?" She gives my head a little shake.

"Are you ever going to stop shaking one of my body parts?" I ask with a laugh.

"Never."

I grab my keys and get behind the wheel of my SUV. I open the garage door. It is snowing heavily. I back out and brake too quickly in the driveway, fishtailing slightly. I can feel my heart pulsing in my head. I am filled with panic. I put my head on the wheel and then lift it to look at my mother in the passenger seat.

"I can't do it, Mom."

"Sonny..."

She is singing.

"'Yesterday my life was filled with rain.'"

I look at her, confused.

"That old song 'Sunny' by Bobby Hebb," she explains, "the one your father used to dance to with Joncee when she was little, remember? She would stand on top of his shoes, and they'd dance while it snowed. Sunshine in the winter. Forever love. Constant warmth." My mom looks at me. "But you knew that, didn't you? That's one of the reasons why you chose that new name, wasn't it, Sonny? It wasn't just because you heard it in Palm Springs, it's because you never forgot, did you, my sweet little girl? You just chose to remember in a way that only you would understand."

Fat tears waver in my eyes and plop on my T-shirt.

"Ready?" my mom asks with a big wink.

I nod my head, back out of the driveway and point my car down M-22. When I pass the part of the bay where Joncee died, I look. Kids are playing in the snow. I grip the steering wheel tightly and keep heading the car—and my life—in the right direction.

You know how your mouth feels when you eat an ice cream cone too quickly? Painfully frozen? That dull ache that forces you to stop for a second no matter how much you just want to continue?

Well, that's how my lungs feel right now. They burn. And I want to stop running.

There is just something about running in the cold and snow that's not right. My eyes water. My snot freezes. My knees ache. The wind burns my cheeks. I feel like a hot ember that's been tossed into a deep freeze. My insides are burning. My exterior is a sheet of ice.

There is a big crowd gathered to watch the annual Frostbite Marathon. They are the smart ones—drinking warm coffee, taking nips from flasks, eating piping hot doughnuts—cheering on their idiot friends.

I was chosen to run the third of the four legs, the six miles that go directly along the shore. More accurately, I was chosen to freeze to death and then hand off, literally, to Polly Sue, who will finish the race and receive all the glory, TV interviews and photo ops.

These are all the things than run through your mind when you're mentally and physically exhausted and running in a windchill that is actually less than the number of miles you're completing.

I hear a roar. My heart lifts.

People are cheering for me!

I feel invigorated and pick up my pace.

I look up. People are holding up signs saying, Run, Tim

Allen, Run! You'll Be The Last Man Standing! and School 'Em, Toolman!

I'd forgotten the actor has a home in northern Michigan and loves to support local causes. My heart drops.

"Sonny!"

I look up.

A group of people are waving signs in my direction.

You Will Never Be A Hero!

Sonny's Funny… In the Head!

Today's Forecast: Crazy

I stop, as if I'm stuck in quicksand. But then I hear "Sonny!" again and look up.

My mom is standing next to Mason. They are holding up signs that read, For Joncee! and Sonny Skies Ahead!

I smile, jumpstart myself and start running, faster and faster. I pass Tim Allen. I pass about twenty other runners as I finish my leg of the race. I turn to head toward town where I can see the final group of runners waiting to run the last leg of the race.

I will show everyone my strength. I will show Lisa that I will run toward this opportunity rather than away from it. I may not finish this race, but I will win the biggest race of them all and reclaim my job.

I see Polly Sue waiting in the zone sectioned off to the side of the race route called the relay exchange corral. When I cross the line in the corral, I must touch Polly Sue so she can start her leg.

Polly Sue looks like she just came from a department store makeover. Her hair, like her lips, is flame red in the snow. She turns away from me to scan the road ahead of her. That's when I notice that emblazoned beneath her name on the back of her shirt are the words *Chief Meteorologist*.

The world spins for a second, and when she turns back, I trip. I go down like a house of cards.

That is, if the cards were made of concrete.

Somehow, I stumble-fall across the line. Polly Sue leans down and smacks me on the head to signal to the judges—in her own lovely way—that we've officially touched.

"God, you're pathetic," she says before taking off.

And then she's gone. Like my career.

I feel like crying. I feel like running away yet again.

When I start to get up, a hand appears in front of me.

Icicle, camera perched on his shoulder, is waiting to help me off the ground.

chapter 13

"Do you want to get a cup of coffee?"

"Nah."

I don't lift my head to look at Icicle.

"You sure?"

"Yeah."

I hear the door shut, and I sigh.

I am hunched over a computer in "the cave," my term for the dark, tiny room where the weather team is housed. I am as bleak as the weather. I have taken my agent's advice to heart: just keep my mouth shut and do my job.

I hear the door squeak open again.

"Are you okay?"

"I'm fine!"

There is silence for a second, before Icicle says, "You don't *sound* fine."

I spin in my chair, and Icicle's eyes grow big as a satellite dish. I take a deep breath and say as calmly as possible, "I said I'm fine."

He looks at me. "You don't *look* fine."

"Sit."

He does.

"You wanna know something? The snowplow guy came before dawn this morning, and I got out of bed to watch him. It's something my sister and I used to do."

"How old is he?" Icicle asks.

"It's a mystery," I say. "His name is Phil, and I realized this morning that he's been doing his job without much praise his whole life. No matter the weather, he shows up and performs. And when he's done, I—like so many other people he'll never really know—will be able to go on with my day. It finally dawned on me that my job is a lot like his. And that I should be like Phil. Show up. Shut up. Do my job. Help as needed. Go on with my day. Sonny got used to having a lot of attention and celebrity. Sonny got used to great ratings and big bonuses. Maybe Sonny needed to learn a lesson and grow up."

Icicle narrows his eyes and scrunches his face. "Why are you talking about yourself in third person? It's kinda weird." He stops and looks at me, his face now serious. "You tripped at the end of the race." Icicle shrugs. "You were tired. It was an accident. It happens."

"Have you seen the viral videos lately?" I grab my cell. "Here's one titled 'How Far Can Sonny Fall?' Here's one that shows me falling that's set to music: 'Free Fallin'' by Tom Petty. And this one? 'Fallin'' by Alicia Keys. Oh, and this one to that '80s song 'Catch Me I'm Falling' already has over a hundred thousand views. They added a sound effect at the end when Polly Sue hits me on the head that makes it sound as if she's thumping a bad melon."

I hit play. Icicle laughs. Hard.

"Yeah, that was a good one," he says, before putting a hand over his mouth. "Sorry."

I play it again.

"It *is* funny."

I put my cell down and look at Icicle. He's all dressed up for the weekend shift—in a cute, skinny 1950s tie and tie clip and a vest, looking very Fred MacMurray, though he wouldn't have any clue who that is—although there's only a winter skeleton crew here covering local-yokel news of fundraisers and council meetings.

I'm part of that crew. Over a quarter century of experience, and I'm working Saturdays again. I might as well be at the Gap.

"You want to know the really funny thing, Icicle? I'm pretty sure I didn't trip. I don't know what happened. I was running really well. I felt strong. There was nothing in my way."

"Maybe someone dropped something on the ground over where you had to tag Polly Sue?"

I shake my head. "I was so focused. I mean I can still picture the road in front of me. It was clear as a bell."

"I would tell you to shake it off, but my dad always says that to me, and I hate it," he says. "I guess it's what athletes say to one another, but it's really just a way of saying, 'Ignore what you feel. Bury your emotions. Keep going for the sake of the team.'" Icicle looks at me. "I was never really part of a team. Until now."

I smile. "You're a good person, you know that?"

He shakes his head as if he either can't believe it, or has rarely heard it. "You are," I say. "Believe that."

He looks away. "Thanks, Sonny. Are you sure you don't want a coffee?"

"You twisted my leg," I say. "Which is already twisted from my fall. Make it my usual, with an extra shot. Long day here alone. Thanks."

"Back in a sec," he says.

I spin around in my chair and return to the tools of my trade: radar images, monitoring weather patterns, checking out NASA satellite images.

Winter pattern. Same ole, same ole.

I yawn. I pick up my cell to check how many views the viral videos have gotten—being a meteorologist, it just seems right to put a number to my humiliation—when I notice something from NASA. I look again. My heart races. I lean closer to the screen.

No! Could that be a polar vortex forming?

What most people don't realize is that there is always a polar vortex. Actually two of them, one in each hemisphere, north and south.

I close my eyes. After going to Northwestern and working in Chicago, I can actually quote The National Weather Service's definition of a polar vortex word for word, even after all these years away because I was still fascinated by the winter weather in Michigan even though I lived on the other side of the country. I pull up the NWS site and smile. They explain it so perfectly to laymen, which is how I must do it for viewers.

"One polar vortex exists in the lowest layer of the atmosphere, the troposphere, which is where we live and where the weather happens. The other exists in the second-lowest, called the stratosphere, a shroud of thin air that gets warmer at higher altitudes.

"The polar vortex is a large area of low pressure and cold air surrounding both of the Earth's poles. It weakens in summer and strengthens in winter. The term 'vortex' refers to the counterclockwise flow of air that helps keep the colder air near the Poles. Many times during winter in the northern hemisphere, the polar vortex will expand, sending cold air southward with the jet stream, something that often occurs during wintertime and is often associated with large outbreaks of arctic air in the United States."

I click on my computer to pull up the radar again. I bend even closer to study it.

If both of these polar vortexes align, Michigan—and much of the U.S.—will be akin to that forgotten bag of ice-covered peas you discover in the back of the freezer in the garage, covered in layers of impenetrable cold.

I bend even lower.

The windchill in northern Canada is currently seventy below zero.

I sit up. I check the area's record low temperatures.

I sit up even straighter.

If that were to come here, we could be looking at the coldest temperatures in history. And not just here, but as far south as St. Louis and Indianapolis.

My heart is thumping in my chest. On the palpitation level, I'm somewhere between personal panic of what this could mean for Michigan and meteorological excitement for possibly discovering something that has yet to be discovered.

I search my laptop, looking to see if anyone has yet to predict this.

Nothing.

My heart beats even faster.

"Here's your coffee."

"Come here!"

"Your mood has changed, and you haven't even had any caffeine."

"Look! What do you see?"

Icicle hands me my coffee and then leans over to look at the screens.

"Polar vortex?"

"Yes!"

"Are you sure?"

"I think so," I say. "A huge one. My mentor, who spent his career working for WGN in Chicago, explained a mega polar vortex event to me this way, which I saw explained the same way in a recent Washington Post article. He always said to imagine the tropospheric polar vortex as a backyard full of dogs, and the jet stream is a fence. The dogs are always trying to escape through gaps in the fence. Sometimes, a few of them manage to get out and cause a little damage, like when they get into your garbage can, a couple of days of very cold weather. But on occasion, the fence collapses and the dogs run wild. That is when historic cold occurs. The entire fence is collapsing, Icicle. And these puppies aren't just cold, they're historically cold."

He looks at me. "What if you're wrong?"

"What if I'm right?" I ask. "That's the challenge of being a good meteorologist. Matching science with your hunches. What if I don't forecast this, and it happens? Think of the good people around here, their homes and animals. Think of our farmers, their crops and livestock. Think of the orchards and their fruit. Think about towns like Leland and its Fishtown shanties along the water, and what a massive buildup of ice coupled with the winds could do to those historic structures." I stop. "My career is pretty much in shambles already. I'd rather be wrong than risk not being right."

"*You're* a good person, Sonny," he says, echoing what I said earlier. "Believe that."

I smile.

"You always wanted to be a weatherman, right?"

He nods excitedly.

"Study this. Find out everything you can. I'm going to talk to Lisa."

"You two are talking?"

"We actually resolved our issues, I think. I decided to be honest."

"Honesty is the best policy," he says.

"Did you just come up with that?"

We laugh, and then I pick up the phone to call Lisa.

★★★

The Big M, where Lisa has asked to meet me, is a Michigan sports bar filled with U of M and State memorabilia and fans. I spot Lisa already at a table for two and take the seat opposite her.

"Hey!" I say.

"Same ole, same ole," Lisa says, shaking her head at the large screen TV behind us. Northwestern is playing Michigan State in basketball. The Wildcats are being mauled by the Spartans.

A waitress comes by to take our order. She is young and peppy. I feel old and tired. I think of what my father used to say: "I'm sick and tired of feeling sick and tired."

"I think you're the only Northwestern fan in here," she says to Lisa, who is dressed from head to toe in purple.

"Make it two," I say. "I went to Northwestern, as well."

The waitress is wearing a formfitting, green long-sleeve T-shirt with the image of an angry-looking Spartan on the front.

"Oh, my gosh. You're Sonny Dunes, aren't you?" She looks at me like she has just been slapped. "You're famous."

"You mean infamous, right?"

"No," she gushes. "Not at all! My grandma and grampa live in Palm Springs. They adored you when you were there. Watched you every night. Said you were the best weather person they'd ever seen. And they've lived in New York, LA, Dallas, Detroit. I started watching you when you came here. They will absolutely die when I tell them I met you. Can I get a selfie with you?"

I nod my head, and the waitress grabs the cell from the pocket of an apron tied around her waist. She leans in and snaps a photo.

"What can I get you?" she asks. "On the house."

"Surprise me," I say. "And if it's on the house, make it a double."

She laughs. "Back in a sec."

I look at Lisa. "That's the type of reaction I was hoping for a couple of months ago." She scans the bar. People are looking at our table. Some are whispering. Some are taking photos. "Not that." I pause. "As I mentioned, I need to talk to you about something important."

"I'm so thankful you were able to share so much with me the other day, and I'm beyond grateful we resolved our personal differences, but I just want you to know right here and now that I cannot give you your job back, Sonny. You're still on thin ice with the advertisers." She winces. "And, yes, I know that was a terrible analogy for this time of year."

I smile. Lisa does, too.

"At least that broke the ice," I say.

"Ha-ha." She takes a sip of her very dark beer.

"But that's not what I wanted to discuss, if you can believe it."

"Oh, really? Now I'm intrigued. You know, that's why I asked you to a public place. I knew you couldn't cause a scene if you asked for your job back, and I declined."

"Sneaky," I say. "It's like breaking up with someone. You do it in a public place to minimize the potential drama."

She nods. "I've been broken up with a lot in my life."

My heart sinks for her. It has to be hard to be that girl who always tries so hard to be liked and yet friendships never come naturally or easily. The more certain people try, the more those around them sense it and turn away from them. It reeks of desperation. I've seen it my entire life, from grade school to the news station. The strong avoid the weak. The pretty stick with the pretty. The jocks stick with the jocks. We stick with those most like us, not because they necessarily make the best friends, but because we don't want to give any indication to others that we may be weak or vulnerable, too.

"Here you go."

I look up, and our waitress is holding a glass filled nearly to the brim with red wine.

"Now that's a big pour," I say.

"I called my grandparents in Palm Springs just now, and they told me they remembered how much you liked good wine," the waitress says. She looks around and then leans down and whispers, "We're not really known for our wine at this bar, but my boss does keep a few really good bottles hidden in the back for special guests."

I try it. My eyes widen.

The waitress looks as if she's holding her breath.

"It's really good," I say.

"Whew." She sighs. "I'm so glad. The rest of the bottle's for you."

I look at my glass. "There's some left?"

She laughs.

"I don't want you to get into any trouble," I say.

"It's fine," she says, wiping her hands on her apron. "I'm moving to Chicago in the spring for a new job. My parents and grandparents would kill me if they sent me to college and I spent my life serving beer and wings."

"Casey!"

The waitress turns when she hears her name. "Gotta go."

I take a sip from my overflowing glass before holding it up toward Lisa. "Cheers!"

She clinks my glass. "Now please tell me what we're cheering."

"I think we're going to have a record-shattering polar vortex."

Lisa looks at me. "That's something to celebrate? What? When?"

"Within the next few weeks," I say. "I was studying the radar today, and I can see it happening, Lisa. It's going to be bigger, longer and colder than anything we've seen in decades." I stop. "And no one is forecasting this yet."

Lisa narrows her eyes at me. "Is this your way of fooling me into giving you your job back?"

"No! No!" I realize I am shouting, and people are looking over. I think whenever anyone looks at me anymore, they think, "Here she goes again!" I lower my voice. "Lisa, I honestly don't care who the chief meteorologist is right now. I don't even care if Polly Sue gets all the credit for this. I just want to be sure people have time to protect their families, farms, orchards, homes and towns." I reach into my purse for the printouts and forecasts I've already developed.

"Wow," Lisa says, looking them over. "You've done your homework." She looks up at me. "This is why I really hired you, you know? There's no better meteorologist than you." She takes a drink of her beer. "But—let me just throw this out there for your sake—what if you're wrong? This could be your last straw in management's eyes."

"I'm not wrong. And what have I got to lose?"

"But the station's reputation is on the line. *My* reputation is on the line."

"Just blame me if I blow it, Lisa. You can say you fired me for..." I stop and laugh. "I think you already have a laundry list of reasons."

"And if you get it right?"

"I just want to do my job, Lisa. This is making me remember why I got into doing this in the first place." I stop. "If I can save one person from losing a life..."

"Like your sister?" she asks.

I nod.

"I'll talk to the station manager, and I'll talk to Polly Sue."

"Thank you, Lisa."

Lisa polishes off her beer, glances at the score of the game—which is not good for Northwestern—signals the waitress for the check and pushes her chair back as if she's ready to leave.

"Tell me about your childhood, Lisa. Tell me about your life." I look at her. "I mean, if you want and have the time." I look away nervously. "I shared a lot the other day. And I know I should have asked a long time ago."

Lisa looks into her empty glass. "Thank you," she says, finally looking up at me. "For asking." And then she pulls up her chair again, points at her glass and yells, "Casey! I'm gonna need another beer, and she's gonna need the rest of the bottle."

When her beer arrives, Lisa takes a sip and says, "I was best friends with my father growing up. We were each other's worlds. When I was ten, my parents told me they were getting divorced, and I was devastated. Less than a year later, my dad married the woman he was having an affair with, and they started a new family. They had three children in four years, and it was like I didn't even exist anymore. My whole life has been spent wondering what I did wrong, why my father didn't love me, and how could I earn his love back. I did everything right, Sonny. Everything. I was top of my class in high school. I was top of my class at Northwestern. I run my own news station. And it's still like I'm a ghost, like my father's life before his new family was a mirage."

Suddenly, everything falls into place. The desperation I sensed in Lisa was all because of her father.

I reach out and take Lisa's hand. "I'm so sorry I never asked you. I'm so sorry for all you went through. And I'm so sorry for how I treated you in school. I only saw my own pain, no one else's, and that was very selfish on my part. You didn't cause your parents' divorce or your father's abandonment. We both just have to learn to forgive ourselves." I shake Lisa's hand like my mother does mine. "You didn't do anything wrong. And you never have."

"Thank you for listening," she says. "You're so good with people." Lisa takes another drink of beer. "Well, most of the time."

She laughs for way too long.

"Okay," I say. "That's enough laughing."

"Even our waitress. People are drawn to you, Sonny. They always have been, even in college."

"You know, it was a facade I perfected. If I could ingratiate myself to people, then they were more likely to take me at face value and less likely to go deeper. My friends were too often props in my life and too often not people I needed to help me. Coming back home has taught me a lot."

"Thank you for sharing that," Lisa says. "Thank you for sharing so much lately."

"Took a while."

"Well, you should teach me some of those skills," Lisa says. "Even the way you stand up to people. It may drive me nuts as your boss, but I have to admit I respect your gumption on a personal level. You're a fighter. People respect that."

"Northwestern sucks!"

A drunk man with a Grizzly Adams beard stops a few feet from our table. He wobbles on his feet.

"Northwestern sucks!'" He points at the television. "Scoreboard!"

Lisa looks at me. Her eyes are wide. She looks as though she wants to flee.

I wink at her. "You got this one."

"Did you play ball at State?" Lisa asks.

"Huh?" the man asks.

"I didn't think so. See, I went to Northwestern for the education. It's one of the world's top universities. I went to study with the best professors, the smartest, most diverse student body, in the most current facilities, with the most incredible job opportunities and networking. I didn't go there for the sports programs, though I am proud of what Pat Fitzgerald and Chris Collins have done to turn around the football and basketball programs. Northwestern doesn't suck. Your childish behavior does."

The man gives Lisa the finger and yells, "Scoreboard!"

"That's all right, that's okay, you will work for us one day!" we both chant, our hands in the air.

"Well, not you," Lisa yells, turning toward the man. "I would never hire you!"

We high-five.

I point. People are recording Lisa's outburst.

"Well done," I say. "And welcome to the club."

chapter 14

"This is more exciting than *90 Day Fiancé*."

My mother is curled up under a quilt on the end of the couch beside me.

"That begs a lot of questions, Mother, none of which I want answered right now."

She sips her hot chocolate. "Did I give you enough mini marshmallows on yours?" she asks. "I know this is a tough night. I want to make it as sweet as possible."

I look at my mug. The top is thick with marshmallows, mounded high. "I think you gave me enough," I say.

It's Monday night, and we're waiting as anxiously for the TRVC news to start as many do the Super Bowl. Lisa spoke with Polly Sue, who refused to meet with me or have me co-host the special weather report that will air as breaking news at the top of the newscast. Icicle and I provided Polly Sue with state-of-the-art graphics, the latest radar images and a detailed report of how the polar vortex is developing, when it will arrive and what it will mean for viewers. I suggested that the segment be broken into two halves, the first on the polar vortex and the second on how to prepare for it. I have provided Polly Sue with a solid seven minutes of reporting, and I feel buoyed that Lisa agreed to give the segment so much time, coverage and importance.

The station's music begins, the anchors come on air and there is immediately the dramatic music that accompanies the breaking news segment.

I sit up, my heart beating rapidly, and inhale a swath of melting marshmallows.

"Breaking news at the top of the hour," says Stan Stevens, the anchor with white hair and whiter teeth who looks like a snowman's grandfather. "Chief Meteorologist Polly Sue Van Kampen joins us for the latest. Polly Sue, what's going on?"

"It is snowing like, well, northern Michigan in February," Polly Sue says with a laugh. She gestures to the green screen behind her with her stupid pointer. "I think we'll see up to four inches overnight in the counties nearer the water and up to eight in our more inland counties. The reason? The winds will be picking up overnight and shifting to the south. Snow will become a bit thicker, so if your kiddos aren't going to school tomorrow morning, then it will be the perfect day to build a snowman with all that heavy, wet snow." Polly Sue turns toward the camera. She is wearing a bright red dress that is way too short for the nightly news.

"She looks like a fire hydrant," my mother says. "Or like she'd be working next to one on a street corner."

"Mother!" I say. "I think I love you even more!" I glance at her and then back to the TV. "She must be leading up to the big news."

"On a personal note, I would like to thank all of you—" Polly Sue spreads her arms open wide in front of the camera "—for your support. I'm honored to have been named TRVC's chief meteorologist, and I wanted to show a clip of this little, local gal's rise from intern to a key member of your nightly news team. I'm proud to say I've helped our ratings nearly double since the start of the year."

"What the hell!" I scream, sitting up and sloshing hot chocolate over the front of my hoodie. "What is she doing?"

A video montage of Polly Sue's life—*Glamour shots and prom photos?*—set to cheesy music, one like you might see at a high school graduation or wedding reception, begins to air.

"Sshhh!" my mother says, teasing. "This is big news!"

I am so furious, my entire body is trembling. I text Icicle.

What is going on?

She's gone rogue, Icicle texts back. No one knows what to do.

I text Lisa.

What the ???

Nothing from Lisa.

I watch the TV. Nothing there, as well.

None of my forecasts, graphics, information, or predictions. None of my hard work. I feel as if I'm standing in the eye of a hurricane, and the entire world is being obliterated around me. And I can do nothing to stop the mayhem.

"Stop her!" I finally scream.

As if the television hears my demands, the station suddenly cuts back to Stan, who acts as if nothing has happened. "Our top story tonight!" he says. "A fire at the boat storage facility at Bayside Marina..."

My phone trills.

Lisa is laying into Polly Sue right now. Hold on...

I wait and wait as the little bubbles under Icicle's last text continue to dance.

Polly Sue apologized. Said it was a mix-up. They're just going to get through the rest of the broadcast and deal with it tomorrow.

I text Lisa.

You know this wasn't a mix-up, right?

She sends a brief reply.

Talk tomorrow, okay?

My mom and I watch the rest of the news in silence. There is no mention of the polar vortex and no apology from Polly Sue.

"That little redhead really is the devil," my mother says. "Watch your back. And your front. And your side."

"I get it, Mother," I say. "What do I do?"

"You've been professional," my mother says. "Maybe it's time to be a human polar vortex, and you don't stop until that little fire hydrant is frozen solid."

My mother nudges me with her feet.

"Why are your feet always so cold, Mom?"

"I have a lot of polar vortex in me, too," she says with a wink.

I wake early, unable to sleep. The sun has briefly broken through the clouds over the bay. Snow covers the land. Everything sparkles as if the world has been dusted in sugar. My mom's birdbaths are now vanilla cupcakes, the front yard and its bushes a beautiful wedding cake. There is something hopeful about a newly fallen snow on which no one has yet to tread. It makes you feel as though anything is possible, that perhaps you can leave a path for others to follow or create one that no one has taken before.

I know what I must do.

I wash my face and pull on some warm clothes. I head downstairs, make some coffee and then begin pulling things from the fridge.

"Are you making a salad for breakfast?"

My mother looks at me confused.

"I'm making a snowman."

"Have you had your coffee yet?" my mom asks. "And your meds?"

I chuckle and resume foraging through the refrigerator. I pull out some cherry tomatoes to add to the carrots and parsnips I have placed on the island.

"Okay, what's going on?" my mom asks as she pours a cup of coffee.

I stand. "Remember what Joncee used to say when it snowed? 'It's a perfect day to build a snowman.'" I grab my mug of coffee and take a sip. "I'm beginning to realize—ever so slowly—that I can't control the world like I've always wanted to do. I can't run from reality. What did you tell me a while back? Life involves loss, grief and setbacks. How we choose to deal with all of that is living. I woke up, and I choose to just live in the moment today."

My mom looks at me.

"Joncee had it all figured out before we all did," I say. "That's the beauty of being a kid. You live in the moment. You can be happy with what surrounds you. You don't overthink. And, for today, I can't overthink a thing anymore, or I'll explode. I just want to be. And that means building a snowman. Wanna help?"

My mom glances at the clock on the microwave. "I have an appointment at noon, so we have a few hours, don't we?"

I nod.

My mom gets dressed and meets me in the front yard. It is

one of those magical winter days along the lake where it is simultaneously sunny and snowing.

I stop and look around at the birds perched in the pines, squirrels running up trees and knocking the snow free, rabbits sitting still, their noses twitching in the cold, deer walking along the frozen shore. I—none of us—do this often enough: stop and look around. Take note of our surroundings. Slow to notice the world without rushing to the next place.

"Remember all of Joncee's rules for building snowmen?" my mom asks.

I laugh, and my breath puffs in front of my face.

"I know the first one—know your snow," I say.

My mom laughs.

"Had to be just right," I continue. "Not too powdery, not too slushy."

"She liked snow that felt like glue, whatever that meant," my mom says.

"You know what? I think she'd approve of this snowfall."

I pick up a handful and toss it into the air.

It is ideal snow for building a snowman: wet and compact, so it sticks together and doesn't fall apart.

"Where should he go?" I ask.

"Joncee's second rule," my mom says. "Somewhere flat and shady, faced away from any sun, so that he will live a long time."

I point to an area in the front yard overlooking the bay. "How about there? It's under that big pine on a level area where people driving by can see him."

"Perfect!"

"Ready?" I ask my mom.

I begin to push snow together to form the base of the snowman, and I can hear Joncee laughing beside me, reciting her rules.

No, Amberrose! Do it this way! she'd say. Joncee always started with a big snowball in her hands, which she'd place on the ground and roll around until it reached the size she wanted. Then she would brace the area around it by packing extra snow, so the wind wouldn't knock it over.

Flatten it! she'd tell me next, reminding me to flatten the top of the snowman's foundational snowball so the next one would be more secure and the entire structure would have stability.

Three-two-one, Amberrose! Remember before you start the next snowball! she'd continue, letting me know the snowman should look proportional, its head smaller than the middle snowball, which should be smaller than the bottom one.

"Aren't you hot?" I ask my mom, a half hour into our work. In fact, I am sweating so much that—despite the cold—I remove my puffy coat.

"You're a true Michigander now!" yells Mason. "No coat! I knew this day would come!"

I jump. I didn't even hear him pull up in the snow.

"Michiganian," my mom corrects him. "I'm not a goose. Michigander is just plain wrong."

"Michigan legislature voted Michigander as the way to refer to its people," Mason says, getting out of his SUV.

"What do they know?" my mom says with a laugh.

"You're a true Michigander-anian," Mason says.

My mom releases a big whoop that echoes across the silent bay.

"Need some help?" Mason asks.

He begins pushing snow together for the middle of the snowman.

"What prompted this today?" he asks. "If you don't mind me asking."

"Seemed like a snowman kind of morning," I say. "What prompted you stopping by today?" I look at him. "If you don't mind me asking."

"I missed you," he says.

My mom bolts upright. A big smile covers her face. Her nose is as red as the berries on the holly bush in front of the house.

"I missed you, too," I say.

"And I saw the news," he continues. "I just wanted to make sure you were okay."

"No work chatter right now," I say. "Just build."

We work in silence. I huff and puff as I make perfectly round balls of snow. The sound of my breathing—through my earmuffs and the scarf around my neck—makes me feel like a little girl trapped in an adult body.

Once we have the body built, I take a step back and cross my arms.

"What do you want him or her to look like?" I ask.

My mom crosses her arms, too, and considers the snowy body. "You mean, not a regular ole Frosty?"

"It can be anything," I say. "Right?"

"You know, I'm sort of a snowman expert," Mason says. "A Frosty historian, if you will."

"Do tell," I say.

"In my job with the chamber and my job as a father, I've built hundreds of snowmen. And in my job promoting winter festivals and writing winter reports for my kids, I've uncovered a lot of fascinating facts."

"Such as?" my mother prompts.

"Well, did you know the earliest photo of a snowman dates all the way to the 1800s?"

"Wow," my mom says. "What else?"

"Snowmen are considered one of humanity's earliest forms of folk art," he continues. "They were a phenomenon in the Middle Ages and were constructed with incredible skill and thought. This was a time of limited means of expression and money, so snow was like free art supplies being dropped from the heavens. One of the most popular activities of that time was for couples to stroll through town to view the works of art. When Michelangelo was nineteen, he was commissioned by the ruler of Florence to sculpt a snowman in his mansion's courtyard." Mason stops and turns to me. "And I know this is a bit too parallel to what you're forecasting, but in Brussels they endured six weeks of subzero temperatures. It was called the Winter of Death, but the citizens turned it into what would be known as The Miracle of 1511 in which the entire city was filled with snowmen, many of which told a story of family, politics, church or hope. Historians say it was their Woodstock, a defining moment of artistic freedom."

My mother and I are staring at this man, his face ruddy from the wind, his handsome face like a boy's. He's like a walking winter encyclopedia of fun facts, delivering them all in a giddy rush like a kid giving a report at the science fair.

"You know your snow," my mom says. "Just like Joncee used to, right?"

I smile and nod.

"Thank you," he says. "I do love snow." Mason looks at me. "I'm thinking you're learning to like it, too."

"I am," I say.

I think of what Mason just said about artistic freedom, as if he were channeling Joncee's final rule for building snowmen, and a sense of peace falls over me. I scan the scene. I can see my entire family—old and new, present and past—here in the front yard building a snowman. Together.

"And I think I have an idea, too. Follow my lead."

I instruct Mason and my mom to gather a variety of items, from inside and outside, many of which elicit double takes, eye rolls and shrugs.

I place my items as if I were a fashion designer dressing a model, tweaking, culling, adding as I go.

When I'm finished, I take a few big steps back, the crunching of my boots in the snow my theme music as if I were on *Project Runway.*

Satisfied, I finally exclaim, "Ta-da!"

"What is it?" my mother asks.

Mason looks at her and bursts out laughing.

"It's us!" I say. "All of us!"

I continue. "Joncee used to always say, 'Why does a snowman always have to be a man? Why can't it be me? Or you? Shouldn't they be whatever we want them to be?' I was thinking of that this morning, and, Mason, when you were talking about the history of snowmen, it dawned on me that we don't have to limit ourselves. Not only in making a snowman but in our own lives. I don't have to limit myself in terms of career, or relationship or happiness." I look at my mother. "Why do women have to choose so often, Mom? Career or family? Personal or professional fulfillment?" I stop. "Winter or summer?"

I admire my creation. Its curved stick arms reach into the air. From a distance, my snowman resembles a saguaro cactus.

"When I ran away to Palm Springs, it finally dawned on me why I loved the desert so much: it reminded me of Joncee. I may have tried to leave all of Joncee's memories behind, but I couldn't. You were right, Mom. I always remembered. The cactus always seemed to resemble a little kid to me, solitary and all alone. But when I'd see them, they would come to life for me, arms up, ready to hug me. I felt surrounded by Joncee's presence in the desert. But when I was leaving this last time, it hit me—I always thought those cacti were greeting me home but maybe they were always trying to wave goodbye. Maybe they came into my life for a reason. Maybe, like a snowman, they were a symbol, a marker, a placeholder for Joncee. But not the real thing. And maybe it's okay to forgive myself and finally say goodbye." I look around at the winter beauty. "Because I'm not cold anymore."

My mother comes rushing over and hugs me. "Oh, honey. You've never been cold. You just froze from the inside out to protect yourself."

Mason walks over and holds his arms open, too. "You're one of the warmest people I've ever met," he whispers.

We all look at our creation.

"The golf club in the snowman's hand reminds me of dad," I say. "The pink scarf with the caduceus nursing pin is for you, Mom. Mason, the blue necklace made from beach glass is in memory of Andi, and the abominable snowman stuffed animal I bought at the Yeti Festival is for you. And the patchwork star on top of its head is for me and Joncee."

"It's beautiful," Mason says.

"I wouldn't go *that* far," my mom says. She laughs. "But I do think it's my favorite snowman-person-cactus-creation-thing I've ever built in my life. Who has their phone? We need a picture."

"I do," Mason says.

The three of us gather around the memories of those we lost and those who remain, and smile.

"Perfect," Mason says, showing us the photo.

And, despite all the imperfections, it is.

The knot in my stomach doesn't tighten—not even driving snow-packed M-22—until I arrive at work. I head to Lisa's office and knock.

"Shut the door," she says, ushering me in.

I take a seat.

"So?" I ask.

Lisa sighs. My expectations deflate along with her body. I already know the answer.

"I talked to my bosses, and then I talked to Polly Sue. While we didn't like the stunt she pulled, Polly Sue did make the point that she is currently the chief meteorologist..."

"Interim!" I say.

"*Interim* chief meteorologist, and as such, she disagreed with your forecast. She stated that she believed you were in error with your prediction, and she didn't want to alarm viewers for no reason."

"No reason! Did she give you a scientific reason why she disagreed with my forecast? Or did she just disagree with it because she hates me? I mean, that has to be the reason because The Weather Channel is now forecasting it! I was right!"

"Sonny." Lisa starts calmly, talking like any boss would to an employee who's about to cause a scene.

"She didn't give you a reason because she doesn't know a low pressure system from a can of beans." I stop. I realize I sound just like my father. What other gems are next out of my mouth to confront Lisa? *Were you raised in a barn? If you keep making that face, it will freeze that way? Don't make me turn this car around?*

"We did give her a warning. Management agreed."

"That's not enough. We need to get this on air now, so at least we're first with the forecast here."

Lisa walks around her desk and takes a seat beside me.

"I believe you, Sonny," Lisa says gently. "I do."

"Then overrule this. Do something."

"My hands are tied."

I look at her, shaking my head.

"Do you want to know something I finally realized?" I ask. "I haven't done anything wrong."

A surprised look covers Lisa's face. "Now Sonny..."

"I haven't. Could I have acted like I'm supposed to act? Act like 'an adult' is supposed to act? Act like I've done my whole life? Which means running from situations, hiding my emotions and acting like everything is okay?" I look at Lisa and take a deep breath. "I think that's the reason I'm here right now, sitting beside you. Because, for once, I confronted what is in front of me. I addressed the internal and external conflicts in my life." I turn to face Lisa. "I was an integral part of the number one news team in Palm Springs and was replaced by a computer-generated Barbie doll simply because I was a woman of a certain age making too much money. I was fired by a rich, spoiled brat who knew nothing about the news but wanted to play news director. Why? Because he was running from his past, too. I ask you this—why *shouldn't* I have gotten mad and done what I did? Stand up for myself? Cause a scene? Men do it all the time and are praised for it. I got ostracized. And then I come here and am suddenly the victim of vicious online slander. Has that happened to any of the men who came here before me?"

Lisa shakes her head.

"Why would someone do that to me? And who did it? What is so wrong with getting angry about the injustice and confronting it? Who's going to stand up for me if I don't stand up for myself? It's like putting a popcorn kernel into hot oil and not expecting it to explode."

I continue. "I'm so sorry for the trouble I've caused you. I didn't intend to do that. But I'm no longer sorry for defending myself. I haven't been too good at that my whole life, and I'm kind of learning to love it."

A tiny smile cracks Lisa's face.

"I will honor my contract, do what I can to help you and the station, and then I will leave."

"Sonny!"

"It's okay. Maybe I'll work for the state, or a university. Do research. I've actually remembered why I wanted to become a meteorologist in the first place, and I have you to thank for that."

Lisa takes my hand and squeezes it. "You're not going anywhere, Sonny. I want you here. Got it?"

"Then my upcoming forecasts have to include my prediction about a polar vortex because I know I'm doing the right thing. And I'm sick of second-guessing myself."

I get up and walk to the door.

When I pull it open, Polly Sue is standing just outside, her head near the frame, a hand around her ear.

"Hi, Mrs. Kravitz," I say. "Eavesdropping again?"

"Who?" she says, literally laughing in my face. "You wish you were that important in my life, Amberrose. Lisa wanted to talk to me. Probably about dropping the 'interim' from my title."

I start to say something, but shut my mouth. It isn't worth it.

"Oh, Amberrose," she says. "Make sure to use your pointer on the air to point out that nonexistent polar vortex."

I start to tell her she's going to need a search party to find that pointer when I'm done with her, but then I see Icicle down the hallway waving madly as if he's trying to flag down a taxi in the first rainstorm of the year in Palm Springs.

"Have a lovely day," I say instead.

"You should sit down for this."

"I am sitting. Are you okay?"

Icicle is nervous. As nervous as a dorky kid working up the nerve to ask the prettiest girl in school to prom.

He takes a seat next to me. He's sweating profusely. Even though it is chilly in the station—it is always chilly in a TV news station, downright cold on set so that we don't perspire—his white shirt is stuck to him and his hair is slicked across his forehead.

"I feel like I'm in *Mission: Impossible* and you know there's a bomb strapped to me that's going to detonate in a matter of minutes," I say.

He doesn't laugh. "Something like that," he says, his voice thick with panic.

"Stop it right now," I say. "Tell me what's going on. Out with it. Why have you whisked me away to the broom closet turned green room where we only send guests who train wild animals?"

"I have something to show you," he says.

"You are totally freaking me out right now," I say.

He cracks the door, peeks outside, craning his long neck left and right, then locks the door and turns out the light.

"So," Icicle finally says in a barely audible whisper. "I couldn't come to grips as to why Polly Sue didn't use the news segment last night to talk about the polar vortex. I mean, you're handing her a gift. I watched her yesterday, and she didn't do any additional research on her own. I asked if she needed help fine-tuning the graphics we provided or needed additional assistance, and she just waved me off. Then when I watched her last night, I knew."

"Knew what?" I ask.

"I ran for student council treasurer my junior year in high school," he says. "I ran against a really popular guy, Ramey Johnson. He was a football player, everyone loved him even though he was as smart as a rock. I mean, a regular, old rock was smarter than him."

"Okay, where are you going with this?" I ask.

"I promise this will make sense."

I nod.

"So anyway, I knew I was going to lose to Ramey, but I still ran because my parents pushed me to do it. I also knew that even though this was an important position—I mean, Ramey managing a budget? He used to make bets to see how many hot dogs he could cram in his mouth!—high school was all a popularity contest. I put up posters like everyone else, and the week before the election, some of them were defaced. 'Ron Lanier for Treasurer' was Magic Markered to read 'Ron is Lame for Treasurer.' Not real clever, but it hurt. So I hid in a custodial closet one night and waited. Sure enough, I saw Ramey defacing my posters, or pulling them down."

I sigh with all the patience I can muster. "Where are you going with this, Icicle?"

"Oh, yeah," he says. "I thought, why would he do this? He knows he's going to win anyway. What's the point of hurting me? I went home and tossed and turned all night. I woke up at dawn, and it hit me: Ramey was the one who was scared. He knew, deep down, he shouldn't be treasurer. He knew, deep down, he didn't even deserve the status he had. Ramey knew all of this would come crashing down on him after high school because he didn't have the smarts, talent or drive to make something of himself. It was all handed to him simply because he could throw a football. And Ramey believed the only way to keep his status was to cheat."

"Icicle, I have to get ready for my segment."

"I'm about done, I promise," he whispers, his voice shaking. "I stayed here late last night after everyone left, just like I did in high school because I knew."

"Knew what?"

Icicle pulls out his cell, and the light illuminates his face. It is pained.

"Everything clicked," he whispers, as if to himself. "I went back through all the footage I shot of you when you first arrived, from when you went cardboard sledding to when you went snowshoeing. Hours and hours of footage that we edited for your Sonny in the Winter segments. Then I checked my browser history. All of those files had been forwarded to Polly Sue."

Icicle plays the viral videos of me cardboard sledding and yelling at the family.

"Polly Sue is the one who edited that footage and sent them out to everyone," he says. "Polly Sue has fake social media accounts where this all started, and I can trace them all back to her because they were started under Magic Merle's old accounts here. And I also called my friend Bill, who runs the security firm that has all the cameras around here. He sent me hours and hours of video. It shows Polly Sue stealing the footage. Includes some great audio, too." He stops. "Do you get it now? Polly Sue is Ramey. She's scared. She knows everything has been handed to her and she doesn't deserve it. And she'll do anything to protect her status."

My mind shifts back in time to what *Hollywood Gossip* did with that footage of me in Palm Springs.

Why didn't I think of this?

I stand and hug Icicle with all my might.

When I let him go, he says, "What do we do?"

"I already have a plan," I say. "Just act cool for a while."

He shifts his body, and the light from his cell again illuminates his face. He looks pasty and panicked.

"You're going to need a way better poker face than that, though," I say.

"I didn't think you'd show," Lisa says.

"I'm part of the team," I say with a big smile.

Lisa gives me a wary glance.

"Well, I'm glad you're here," she says. "We've never won the Annual Snowball Fight before. Big competition this year, not only from the other stations but also from all the restaurants and shops in town."

"I bet you're going to be good at this."

I turn. Mason walks up with a big smile.

"You have no idea," I say. "A few unresolved issues and a touch of hostility make me throw a snowball a lot harder than normal." Lisa eyes me. I raise my hands as if I'm surrendering. "All good. You just have no idea how much I want to beat those other stations. They haven't particularly been nice to me since I arrived in Michigan." I flex my muscles, hidden under a fitted running shirt and zip-up jacket along with about two pounds of my mother's home cooking. "These arms are ready for business."

We are standing in the middle of the high school's football stadium. It is bigger than I remember any high school football stadium being. State-of-the-art scoreboards flank the end zones and flash the logo for the Annual Snowball Fight.

"So, how does this work?" I ask.

"This is my pride and joy," Mason says. "It's sort of like dodgeball in the winter."

I think back to my days of dodgeball and grimace. I was not

the most agile at ducking out of the way of those hard dodgeballs or throwing one with enough power and arc to strike someone on the fly. I could cheer, yes, but agility, no. I think of falling in the snow here over and over again.

"I was always great at dodgeball," I lie.

"Really?" Mason asks.

"You sound shocked."

"Just surprised," he says with a smile. "So, each team gets a turn throwing snowballs at the other team. Each team picks a person to start, and everyone gets a chance to throw and be thrown at, until the teams of four have each had a chance to go. The team being thrown at has a one-foot snow wall to duck behind. Gives them a little better chance and makes it a little harder for the throwing team. Each person must be standing when the snowball is thrown, but they can dive, go low, juke, dart, run, whatever, to avoid a snowball, just like in dodgeball. Winner moves on to face the winner of the next bracket. I have it set up as TV versus TV, restaurant versus restaurant, retail versus retail, school versus school in the beginning, sort of like regions in the NCAA tournament. Then winners of those divisions meet until there is a snowball champion."

"Wow. Impressive," I say.

"We've never made it past our region," Lisa says. "We always lose to the Channel 2 News Team because they stack their team with former athletes. All of their reporters played baseball or football."

"Where's the rest of our team?" I ask. My heart is already beating rapidly.

"They're coming," Lisa says, her voice ominous.

I turn.

Polly Sue strides across the field, hair ablaze, wearing all red.

Beside her is Chance LaChance, a name even more invented than Sonny Dunes. He is already a main nightly news reporter who is salivating—and publicly campaigning—to be a weekend anchor. At the ripe old age of twenty-three.

"Sonny," Chance greets me, saying my name slowly like an evil cartoon cat toying with a fish in a bowl.

"Chance," I mimic.

"I'm surprised to see you today," he says.

"Oh, I'm full of surprises today," I say with a big smile. "I wouldn't miss this for the world!"

Polly Sue ignores me.

"Would you help me with my coat, Chancey?" she purrs.

Chance helps her remove her red coat, and then the two kiss.

Well, *kiss* is the PG word one might use. *Make out* would be another. *Put your tongues away* might even be more appropriate.

And now it makes sense. He's using her. She's using him. I'm being used. It's like *Guiding Light* meets *Wings* meets *Murphy Brown.*

After the PDA, Polly Sue begins stretching dramatically, arcing her back toward the gray, snowy sky. That's when I see it. The back of her bright red long-sleeve shirt screams in giant, white letters, *Polly Sue, TRVC Chief Meteorologist.*

I look at Lisa. Who looks at me. Her eyes are wide. *Don't,* she mouths. *Please.*

"Like my shirt?" Polly Sue asks innocently. The question is asked in general although I know it is directed at me.

"So hot, babe," Chance says.

I keep myself from rolling my eyes.

"Okay, okay," Lisa says, ever the team leader. "Let's direct all that passion toward the other teams. I want to win for once." She looks at me. "We're taking on Channel 13 first. You especially should want to get even with them for what they did to you."

"Oh, I want to get even," I say.

I hear Mason's voice blare over the speaker system.

"Let's get ready to ruuummmmbbbleee!" he says, imitating

the announcers from World Wrestling. "Teams, take your positions!"

Figures scramble around the snow-covered field like toy soldiers. Mason has set the field up so four fights can take place at once: one in each end zone, and one each around the thirty-yard line.

We are stationed in the end zone where the wind is swirling. I feel like I'm about to take part in one of those classic football games in the snow. Bears vs. Packers. Winner take all.

My dad would be so proud of me for thinking like this.

We take on Channel 13 first. Channel 13 doesn't have an anchor or reporter on staff under the age of 108. Palm Springs used to be known as "Heaven's Waiting Room" before a youthful resurgence—from Coachella to the Kardashians—changed the community's demographic. Channel 13 is "Heaven's Living Room." It's the station that plays in every doctor's waiting room. Every other commercial is for a cataract operation or walk-in tub. The anchors, like Rocky Gibraltar—real name, mind you!—were ancient when I was a teen. And they're still on air. Our demographic might skew older, but Channel 13's doesn't even fit a demographic.

But they are a hardworking news station, I think, glancing over at Polly Sue preening. They earned their stripes.

When the whistle blows, Polly Sue picks up a snowball and hits Rocky hard and square in the side of the head.

"Hey!" I say. "He didn't even have time to react."

"Fair and square," she says. "Whistle blew. And which side are you on anyway, Amberrose?"

I pick up my snowball and dearly want to throw it at her, but I stop myself.

She smirks at me, picks up another snowball and fires it at Rocky.

It's not even a contest. We win in under ten minutes, poor

Rocky saying how badly his ear aches, and move on to play Channel 2, our archrivals.

"This is our year!" Lisa cheers.

"No deadweight," Polly Sue says, staring at me.

Channel 2's snowball team resembles an issue of *Sports Illustrated* meets Chippendales poster. In fact, two of them are shirtless in the cold and snow. Women cheer and catcall from the stands. They flex and strut. One of them calls, "You're dating the wrong reporter, Polly Sue!" Another bellows, "Scared any young children lately, Sonny?"

Polly Sue laughs.

In the near distance, Channel 2's team huddles up. "We pick Sonny first!" one yells. The others laugh. "Yeah! Let's go! Take her down! Make her pay! It ain't sunny today!"

"You're up," Lisa says.

I position myself in front of the low snow wall and eye the enemy.

Why do the bad guys always win so much in the world? How do we stop them? Why does this cycle of meanness continue?

I've been professional. I've been unprofessional. I've taken the high road. I've taken the low road. And yet the road never ends. It just follows the same, ugly path.

The mean guys come out on top. The good guys go down.

I think of Cliff, Icicle and myself. I think of Joncee, my dad and Andi. I think of Ramey, Ronan, Polly Sue, the Channel 2 goofballs.

"We're doomed," Polly Sue groans.

I consider my nemesis. What battles has she waged in her life? What has she fought for? Who has she lost? What has made her this way?

I may never know, but I know there is a lesson for her—and me—in all of this.

I think of my mom, who is likely with someone right now whose life is nearing the end. For years, she has been the bridge, the one to help others transition from this world to the next. My mom has long believed in what she calls the "Two Ps": penicillin and prayer. When there is little more that doctors and hospitals can do to prescribe treatment, my mom embodies palliative care, keeping the sick as pain free and as hope-filled as possible.

What secrets has she heard? What secrets does she know?

No wonder my mother has little patience for Ronan's antics or Polly Sue's theatrics. She knows the value of life. The importance of each moment.

How short our journey here truly is.

And then suddenly I remember Joncee. I can see her right here in the snow as clearly as I can see Polly Sue standing a few feet away from me.

Mean girls, Joncee had said to me so long ago.

She had not been her boisterous self, doing her homework in a rush so she could go play in the snow even in the dark, sliding around the house in her socks, annoying me to get up early on a Saturday to build a snow fort.

And then one day when I opened her notebook sitting on the kitchen counter to steal a piece of paper, I saw it: a folded-up wad of notes—folded together to create a thick triangle. I carefully undid them. One note read:

"TOMBOY!"

Another read:

"Are you a girl?

Or a boy?

Pick one."

Another stated:

"JOHN, SEE, I knew you were weird. Why do you play with the boys at recess?"

What are you doing? she screamed, catching me in the act.

I was just borrowing a piece of paper, I had said. *Swear. Didn't mean to snoop. But I did.* I looked at her. *Tell me what's going on?*

Mean girls, she said.

Joncee began to cry, which she rarely did, telling me about the clique of girls—led by Tiffany Laney—who had been tormenting her in grade school because she didn't want to spend recess jumping rope or trying on Lip Smackers the girls had stolen from their older sisters' purses.

Should I just give up and be their friend? she sniffed.

They don't want you to be their friend, I said. *They just want you to give up who you are.*

Why?

People are threatened by anyone who is different, I said. *We want everyone to be the same. But don't you ever stop being who you are. That's what makes you* you. *And, one day, everyone will appreciate that. But not if you give in to people, hear me?*

She nodded. *But what do I do until then?*

I have an idea.

That Saturday, Joncee and I begged mom to give us a ride to the little shopping center downtown, telling her we were meeting friends. It was a lie. When she left to pick up a few groceries, we hid behind a big delivery truck and waited for Tiffany and her friends to come out of Claire's, the boutique for girls, where Joncee said they went every weekend. When they came out—bags in hand, hair perfect—we began to throw snowballs at them. Tiffany screamed and ran, leaving her friends there alone.

See? I said. *She didn't even try to defend herself or her friends. What's that say about her? What would you have done?*

Stood up for myself, Joncee said. *Protected my friends.*

Exactly. Don't you ever change.

Joncee beamed. *I won't*, she said. *Where did you learn to do this?*

We've been studying Greek mythology in school, I said. *It's really cool. Our history teacher taught us about the Trojan Horse. It's when Greek warriors hid inside this huge wooden horse to get inside the city of Troy. Once in, they jumped out in a surprise attack to defeat the Trojans. Sometimes, it's all about the art of surprise.*

A snowball whacks me squarely in the face, literally knocking me from this memory.

"Ooooffff!" I say.

Snow scatters in front of my eyes, and I can feel my cheeks shake. My head moves in slow motion, and I stumble, seeing stars. I was so lost in my own thoughts, I never heard the whistle blow.

"I told you we were doomed!" Polly Sue yells. "She's too old to move much less be on air."

I stretch out my arms and stand as still as a statue, eyes shut, never moving even as snowballs pelt me from every direction.

"What are you doing!" Polly Sue screams. "You idiot!"

I walk back to my team. Even Lisa is looking at me like I'm crazy.

"Let me show you how it's done," Polly Sue says, brushing by me in a huff.

No, let me show you how it's done.

Channel 2's buff sports anchor cocks his arm and fires a fastball. Polly Sue leaps sideways into the air. The snowball whizzes under her body as she lands with a thud.

"See?" she says, yelling at me. Polly Sue turns toward Channel 2 and screams, "Bring it on!"

The health reporter throws a knuckleball. It arcs in the air. Polly Sue waits and then spins in a circle, the snowball missing her by inches.

"C'mon!" she taunts.

The weekend anchor, who resembles Liam Hemsworth, was a former football quarterback. He doesn't so much smile at Polly Sue as leer. His snowball is big. He moves around for a few seconds, as if he's dancing in the pocket, trying to avoid the rush, and then launches a tight spiral that moves at the speed of light. Polly Sue makes a circle with her arms, an actual moving target, and the snowball flies through the center of them.

She laughs like a madwoman. "No one can take me down!" she yells.

When the consumer affairs reporter moves to the front, I turn toward the closest end zone. I begin to spread my arms and fly like an eagle.

Lisa looks at me. "Are you okay? Do you have a concussion?"

I don't even look at her.

I don't tell her that Icicle was intent on choosing this cockamamie signal because he saw it in an old movie and became convinced this should be our secret code. I laughed but agreed because somehow—in all of its stupidity—it seemed totally appropriate for this moment.

It is finally time to soar.

Just as the consumer affairs reporter pulls his arm back to throw, phones ping, sing and beep all at once, like a cellular orchestra.

Everyone stops, as if God Himself has hit pause on the remote, and reaches for their phones. I can read their faces: reporters at every news station receiving a message all at once. There must be breaking news of epic proportion. I grab my phone, too.

On my cell—on everyone's cell—grainy footage of Polly Sue begins to play, showing her sneaking into an office, the flashlight from her cell illuminating the scene. She looks around guiltily. She opens a laptop and begins searching it.

"Got it!" she says.

She picks up her cell phone and calls someone. "I just accessed all the location footage of Sonny Dunes," Polly Sue says, clear as day. "I can edit it to make her look crazy and mean. This is perfect. There's footage of her where she's actually concerned about the well-being of a girl who looks like she's falling off a dune. But the family doesn't know that. I'll make her look worse than Miranda Priestly. Everyone will hate her as much as I do. I gotta go before someone catches me."

Polly Sue hangs up.

More footage of her doing the same pops up.

I turn from my cell to look at Polly Sue. Her mouth is open as she stares at her phone. Her face is whiter than the falling snow. I smile. She sees me, and her face contorts with rage.

"You!" she screams. "You…"

Polly Sue can't finish her sentence because her mouth is full of snow.

The Channel 2 reporter has hit Polly Sue smack dab in the piehole.

In fact, every member of every team on the field is racing toward her, snowballs in hand. It is war, and Polly Sue is a team of one. They fire, and Polly Sue covers her face, then her body, before hightailing it off the field, snowballs continuing to whiz in her direction, the stadium echoing in boos.

Before I can react, members from the TV stations' teams surround me, apologizing. Other teams gather and cheer my name.

When it finally quiets, Lisa approaches.

"Why didn't you tell me?"

I look at her and cock my head like the RCA dog.

"Okay, I understand," she says. "We'll talk Monday."

Mason runs up. "Well, you certainly made this an unforgettable year."

"I'm honored," I say.

"Your team is also disqualified," he says.

"Another year we didn't win." Lisa shrugs.

"Oh, we won," I say. "Women won."

Mason and Lisa look at me.

"I'm really sort of enjoying being fifty," I say. "In control. Not taking any BS. Doing my thang."

I stick out my hip and dance.

"Okay, stop talking like that," Mason says.

"And dancing like that," Lisa says.

Icicle appears to great applause, and before I know it, we are both swept into the arms of the Channel 2 team and lifted into the air.

"How'd you do it?" someone asks Ice.

"I have all your numbers," he says innocently. "All I did was just hit send."

Sneak attack, Joncee, I think. *It worked yet again.*

chapter 15

"I'm down to a weather team of one."

Lisa is talking to her lamp. She can't even look at me.

"And that *one* is the talk of the town."

"In a good way," I interrupt.

"No, no," Lisa says, turning to wave a hand at me. "It's not your turn yet."

I nod.

"And I also had to let a nightly news reporter go because he was in cahoots with a turncoat spy. And management wants to know what I plan to do with a station that has suddenly become the news equivalent of Jerry Springer. And I have five newscasts to air every day along with a morning show and a staff that doesn't trust anyone or know whether they will be next on the chopping block or victim of a surprise snowball attack."

Lisa pulls her cardigan around her as if she's warding off such an attack. She reaches into her desk drawer and pulls out an Oreo. Then another. She shoves them in her mouth as I stare.

"They're Oreo *Thins*, okay!" she says, spitting cookie. "They're like mini candy bars on Halloween. It takes a dozen to equal one."

She takes a seat in her chair with a big sigh. She finally swivels to look at me.

"Why are you sitting there looking like the cat that ate the canary?" she says.

"Because, one, it's good she's gone. We can all move on now in a positive way. And because, two, I have a plan."

"Oh, really!" she exclaims, her voiced etched with sarcasm. "Is the plan as good as the one you just pulled that's about to cost both of us our jobs? Is your plan as good as the one I had to bring you here?" Lisa stops and takes a deep breath. "Unless your plan involves erasing what has been a total nightmare of a winter and putting us both into a wayback machine, then I'd suggest shelving said plan."

"I want to address what happened, on the air," I say, unfazed. "I want to do a full top-of-the-news segment about the polar vortex before anyone else in the local area beats us to the punch. CNN and The Weather Channel have reported on it, but not in a big way yet. We still have the chance to be first here. I want to restart my 'Sonny in the Winter' segments, especially now that we have a chance to lead with the polar vortex. And I have a replacement for Polly Sue."

I say all of this in a rush, like when I was in high school and trying to convince my parents to let me stay over at a girlfriend's house "to study" even though they knew that meant "party with boys."

Lisa reaches for another cookie.

"Icicle," I conclude.

She spews cookie again.

"What? I might as well go ahead and put in my application at the Dress Barn because my career here will be over."

"Lisa," I say, remaining calm, "the kid is smart. He is driven. He is trustworthy. He does every single job here—from camera to research to writing—exceedingly well and always on time. He never complains. He loves his job and this station. I've been around a long time, and I can recognize talent. When you combine that with someone who desperately wants to prove himself, you have someone who has the potential to be great." I stop. "And he's an actual meteorologist. Polly Sue just played one on TV."

"Sonny," Lisa says, sighing, "I know you two have bonded. It's been very sweet to watch, but he doesn't really have an on-air persona. I mean, Icicle looks like the kid who dresses up as the Statue of Liberty alongside the highway and spins signs for Liberty Tax. He doesn't have the look of a trusted weather person." She stops. "He has the look of someone who could fix your computer."

"Give him a chance," I say. "You gave me one."

My voice trembles. I didn't want to get emotional.

"What have we got to lose?" I press.

"Um, everything," Lisa says. "By the way, you've said all of this before, and the winter ice just keeps getting thinner for both of us as we get closer to spring ratings."

"Please," I say.

"No."

"Please."

"Let me think about it."

"Please." I draw the word out like a kid begging for a toy.

"Sonny."

"Lisa."

"This could go on all day, couldn't it?" she asks.

I nod.

"I believe in him. Or I wouldn't be doing this."

Lisa sighs and shakes her head.

"Okay."

"Yes!" I cry. "Thank you!"

"But I need to see an audition tape before I fully approve," she says. "You need to polish him up more than a Petoskey stone, got it?"

"Got it."

I stand. "You won't be sorry."

"You've said that before, too."

"You'll see," I say, opening her office door.

"And you've said that, as well."

I shut the door. I can still hear Lisa talking to herself.

"What?"

"I thought you'd be ecstatic."

Icicle looks as though he wants to run as far away from me as he can, but he's paralyzed. The only movement I see is the nervous twitching of his cheeks. Whereas Lisa couldn't stop talking, Icicle can't seem to open his mouth.

"Icicle?" I finally ask. "Are you okay?"

"I have to go," he says.

"What?" I ask, now sounding like he just did. "Where?"

"I don't know," he mumbles. "Just go."

He starts to leave the weather office, but I grab him. Icicle may be wiry, but he's strong, and he drags me toward the door.

"Okay, enough!" I say, digging my heels into the floor.

Icicle stops.

"I can't do this, Sonny," he says, his voice scared, his head down.

"Yes, you can."

"No, I can't."

Icicle finally looks at me. His eyes are wet.

"Oh, Icicle," I say. "I thought…"

"I could do this? Well, sorry to disappoint you, but you were wrong."

"Sit," I say. When he doesn't, I repeat it more emphatically. "Sit!"

"Talk," I say, walking back to take a seat in my chair.

"Were you a dog trainer in a previous life?" he asks.

I laugh, and he cracks a small smile.

"Look, you know me. I've never been in the spotlight," Icicle says. "I'm not comfortable with it." He looks up at me with sheepdog eyes. "My parents have always been the center of attention. You and all the anchors enjoy being on air. Some people thrive under pressure. I don't."

"Really? Because you have thrived under pressure since the day I met you," I say.

His eyes widen.

"You've managed to navigate a swamp without being eaten alive. You've performed your job with incredible skill, professionalism and decorum. You've worn so many hats so well, you could be a fashionable Hydra. You never complain. You're an accomplished writer, editor and researcher, and you have a knack for location, history and detail that make stories memorable."

"But I'm not an on-camera guy," he protests. "People just don't see me that way."

I look at him and shake my head. "No, *you* don't see yourself that way." I stop. "But that's going to change right now."

I walk to the tiny space that serves as storage room and coat closet. "Voilà!" I say.

Inside are a variety of clothes.

"What are those?"

"Clothes," I say. "For you."

"What's going on?"

"We have to make an audition tape for Lisa," I say. "Management wants to see you on air before they sign off on everything."

Icicle stands abruptly. "I told you! No one believes in me. No one has ever believed in me."

"I believe in you."

He stops at the door.

"I'm risking my career for you," I say. "So is Lisa. This is your moment, Icicle. Take it, because they don't come around very often."

He sighs. "What do I have to do?"

"Nothing," I say. "I'm handling everything. In fact, we have to go right now. You have a haircut appointment at Front Street Salon, followed by a facial. Then I'm going to dress you in some clothes I picked out for you..."

"How did you know my size?" he asks.

"I have reporting skills. I snooped. And then I called your mom. This is what we call a makeover. It's like *Pretty Woman*, and you're Julia Roberts." My voice continues to rise in excitement. "My whole life has led up to this moment. You are my creation." I laugh like Dr. Frankenstein.

"Help me," Icicle calls out as I drag him through the newsroom.

Four hours later, we return to the newsroom, and staff members literally do double takes to see who I am with.

Icicle's shaggy hair has been cut short and groomed into what I can only term as professionally hipster: longer on the top, gelled back in a swoop, and the sides have been razored very short and high. His face is shaved smooth, and it is glowing after a facial. He is wearing a touch of bronzer to make him look a bit tanner, and we purchased a pair of vintage half-frame glasses that make him look older and more refined, as well as making his cheekbones look like buttah.

Icicle is dressed in a navy suit with a bright white shirt that make his eyes pop. And, although he fought me, I got him to wear a navy bow tie with little snowflakes on it.

"Bow ties can be your signature," I say. "For every season."

In short, Icicle doesn't look like the same man.

"Everyone is staring at me," he mutters. His shoulders sag, his spine bends, and he tries to make his tall frame invisible. He slouches toward the weather office.

But he's still acting like the same man.

"Look at yourself," I say, steering him toward a mirror on the far side of the office. "Go ahead. Look at yourself."

He stands before the mirror.

"Who do you see?"

"Icicle," he says.

"Who do you see?" I ask again.

He looks again, as if for the first time, but doesn't say a word.

"Everyone is staring at you because you look great. They see you differently already. But it's really not about the way you look. It's all about the confidence you project."

Icicle again is silent.

"All right, let's go."

I lead him to the newsroom. It is early afternoon, and it is quiet. Everyone is at their desks working on stories for the evening newscast. I position him at the anchor desk. I have everything set up: a camera is stationed in a tripod, and the green screen is readied with the latest maps and forecast. I hand him the clicker.

"You know what to do," I say. "Refer to the monitor just off-screen when you need to so you know you're motioning in the right place, but keep looking into the camera to connect with the audience."

"Which is Lisa and management," he says.

"Yes, but think of them as your audience. At home in their pajamas."

Icicle smiles. I continue. "But more than anything, be yourself."

"Is that such a good idea?"

"Yes. There is no one else like you. That's what makes you *you*, Icicle." I walk over to him. "Take it from me: hiding who you truly are and everything you feel is just as bad as running away. You're still distancing yourself from the world. I've denied myself the life I wanted *and* deserved. I've wasted the opportunity to be truly, deeply happy. Most importantly, I've been unable to make others happy because I wasn't. I don't want you to be like me and waste all those precious years." I walk back and turn on the studio lights and the camera. "That's living in the shadows. The strong live in the light. It's time for you to shine."

Icicle takes a deep breath.

"Ready?"

He nods tentatively.

I count down from the three, hit record and point at him.

"Hi, everyone. I'm Icicle, and I'm here..."

He stops.

"Can I start over?"

I count down again, hit record and point.

"I'm Icicle, and I... I... I..."

He stops again.

"Sorry. Again?"

I nod.

I might have been wrong about all this.

Icicle dips his head.

Is he saying a prayer? Looking within himself?

Finally, he looks up and points at me. I hit record.

"Hi, I'm Ron Lanier, TRVC's newest meteorologist."

I look at him, my eyes wide with surprise. His voice is confident. His face is beaming.

He continues. "I grew up in Michigan, and I love Michigan. I love our four seasons, I love the stunning, natural beauty of our state, but mostly, I love all of you. You represent what is best about our state—good people trying their best to lead good lives."

My heart pitter-patters. The kid has got it. He's a natural. I knew it.

"I'm honored to work alongside Sonny Dunes, one of our nation's most respected meteorologists. And I promise to honor you by doing the very best I can. Every day." He turns toward the green screen. "It may be cold, but it's downright balmy compared to the frigid temperatures headed our way. A historic polar vortex looks to make its way into our vicinity within the week, and Sonny Dunes—who was the first to report on this—is here with a special report. We'll be covering this story live and in depth in the coming days, bringing you not only updated weather reports but also ways to keep your homes, families, farms and orchards safe. So stay tuned to TRVC for the latest weather news. For now, we'll have temperatures in the twenties with light snow tapering off by late afternoon, which is good news for the evening commute."

When he finishes, I stop recording and look at him.

He is no longer a kid. He is no longer a joke. He is no longer Icicle. He is the man he dreamed of being.

"Sonny?" he asks. "Was that okay?"

I don't say a word.

"Sonny?"

"That was..." I hesitate, trying to pick the best word to convey what I'm feeling. Finally it comes to me. "Perfect." I stop again because it still doesn't feel like enough. And then it comes to me. I smile.

"Sorry. I meant to say, that was perfect, *Ron*."

The crew is antsy, much like when a celebrity or dignitary is scheduled for a live interview on set.

How will she act? Will she be like I dreamed? Or will she act like a diva?

This is the way I imagine every single person working at TRVC tonight feels right now.

Lisa is letting me have three minutes at the top of the newscast to address what happened with Polly Sue and my on-air meltdowns since I arrived as chief meteorologist. In essence, Lisa has agreed to let someone with a history of erratic behavior kick off the nightly news with her job on the line. It's the equivalent of handing the keys of a bus to a toddler who just walked off the playground and saying, "Have a nice ride, everyone!"

I have not even given her the text of my remarks as I begged her to trust me. I have not given the text of my remarks to anyone. I want it all to be a surprise. Even to me.

Ironically, the majority of a meteorologist's career is unscripted. That's the one thing viewers often don't comprehend about our jobs. We ad-lib from start to finish, our "scripts" are the graphics we create. Anchors read the news from monitors. Reporters—unless they're live or covering breaking news—have taped, edited stories. Meteorologists are like Cirque du Soleil performers: we practice and know what we have to do—after a while—by instinct alone. And yet we are still flying solo. Anything could happen.

I have slipped and fallen on air. I have accidentally cursed. You try saying "Fork's Sake, North Dakota" when you're utterly exhausted. I once broke down in hysterics when I tossed a Sonny sun that swerved last minute like a boomerang and managed to adhere to Cliff's head instead of the green screen. When he yanked it off, the sun left a clean circle that revealed how much makeup he wore on air.

When our entertainment reporter left for a job at an LA station two days before the Palm Springs International Film Festival, Eva and I were tapped to interview Oscar-winning actors and actresses on the red carpet at the Palm Springs International Film Festival, including an iconic actor who was so haughty and condescending to me that I turned away from him and began to interview a local citizen who had slept in a lawn chair all night just to get a front row seat.

"I don't think it was worth it now, do you?" I asked.

That unscripted moment not only led every entertainment news report the next day, but it also garnered me a dozen roses as an apology from the actor and a penthouse suite in a fancy hotel for the lawn chair interviewee.

The ironic thing is that—even with all our missteps—this is what viewers enjoy the most. They love it when we mess up. They love it when we fumble. It's because we're human, and they like to be reminded of that. Even though we appear composed on air almost every night, coming to them in their homes at every hour of the day and talking to them as if we're family members, people like to know that their local TV personalities and favorite celebrities are just like them—human.

And though they may want us to screw up on occasion, they also want us to overcome our mistakes. They root for us. Because we become part of their lives. We become trusted friends. We become family.

I check my makeup and take a deep breath. The anchors are watching me. Even Lisa is pacing around in the studio like a nervous cat.

"How do I look, Ron?"

"Call me Icicle," he says. "When we're not on air. We're friends. Friends still have nicknames for each other, right?"

I nod.

"You look great. Are you ready?"

I shrug.

"You're always ready, aren't you? You live for moments like this, don't you?"

He winks, and my nervousness deflates.

"Take your position, Sonny," I hear Lisa call.

I position myself in front of the green screen.

"And we're live in three, two, one..."

The anchors introduce me with all the gravitas of a state senator who wants to address a personal scandal. The world spins. I am live.

"Thank you," I say.

I turn toward the camera and click. A black-and-white image of a snowstorm appears behind me.

"I was seven years old when the Blizzard of 1978 hit Michigan."

I click again. An old photograph of a girl sledding off the top of her roof and down a giant bank of snow pops up.

"That's me. The snow was so intense and the wind so strong that I could climb out of my second-story bedroom window and sled right off the roof like I was on the mountain of a ski resort."

Another photo pops up.

"This is Front Street during that blizzard. As you can see, snow engulfed downtown, making the storefronts disappear. And right here—" I point "—you can see on the marquee the movie that was playing at the State Theatre that day. *Oh, God!* Remember? With George Burns and John Denver?"

The anchors chuckle and nod.

"I had just gone to see that movie before the blizzard hit, and it became a long-running joke in our house because my dad would look out the window every half hour. The snow just wouldn't stop. It was coming down in heaps. He would groan and say, 'Oh, God.'"

Crew members laugh.

"The Blizzard of 1978 raged for two straight days, the result of two massive storm systems colliding over Michigan, with lake-effect snow contributing to the natural disaster. When it was over, some areas saw as much as three feet of snow. Here in Traverse City, our snowfall was around two feet. Winds gusted as high as seventy miles an hour. Windchills fell to thirty below. Drifts were as high as fifty feet. Three people died, including an eleven-year-old girl. It took days for residents to shovel their homes clear. Many still consider it to be the worst winter storm in living memory." I turn to look at the photo before continuing.

"That was the first time I remember noticing—even as a little girl—the incredible power of weather. I was fascinated by it. I watched this very station around the clock to see what was happening. It was my window to the world. The blizzard was so daunting that firefighters worked alongside plow drivers—including the man who still plows my mother's home—driving in front of them to open up the roadway. I remember watching a firefighter jump into a snowbank so deep that he just disappeared. The other men had to pull him free before they could run in to do their jobs. I remember people creating makeshift dogsleds—with their own dogs—to get to the grocery so they could bring stranded neighbors and elderly friends food. Roughly one hundred thousand cars were stranded on Michigan's highways. Snowmobile patrols helped those who were stranded. Volunteers shoveled highways and overpasses clear."

I stop again.

"What I remember—in the most difficult of times, in tragedy and hardship—was our resourcefulness and kindness to those who needed it the most. We met that challenge with hard work and great humor, and we continue to do that to this day."

Another photo appears behind me. It is of me and Joncee making snow angels in the backyard.

"This is my sister, Joncee. She loved snow and winter more than anything in this world. She was my angel on earth." I can feel tears rise, and I take a deep breath. "She died when I was sixteen. She was still a little girl. It was a tragic accident, in the middle of winter, and it stays with me to this day. She is the reason I became a meteorologist. The fact that perhaps I could save a life—maybe even yours—with a forecast or a warning fills me with purpose. I have made a number of mistakes in my life and my career. But choosing to be a meteorologist and choosing to return home are not among them. And I've never apologized for being human. I've never apologized for fighting for myself, my family and what is right. I've learned that you can take the girl out of Michigan, but you can't take the Michigan out of the girl."

The cameraman actually whoops.

"We have some tough weather and days ahead, including

a massive polar vortex on its way that we're forecasting here first, which I'll be back to bring you the latest on in just a few minutes. But I know that we can and will get through this together because the only thing greater than a Great Lake is us. Thank you from the bottom of my heart for standing with me through what has been a tough winter for Sonny Dunes. And thank you for welcoming me home again and making me a part of your family."

I throw it back to the anchors. "We'll be back in a moment."

We cut to commercial and the set explodes into applause. Icicle rushes over and lifts me into the air, swinging me in a circle.

"Well done," Lisa says. "You just might have pulled our frostbitten rears from the fire."

When I return to do my weather segment, I glance at the monitor. It now reads, SONNY DUNES, TRVC CHIEF METEOROLOGIST.

I glance quickly off-screen at Lisa. She smiles ever so briefly and then rolls her hands to remind me to keep going.

"As I mentioned earlier, a brutal polar vortex—which could be historic in terms of cold and length—is headed our way..."

When I head home in the bitter cold night, I turn on the defroster but not the heat. I am already warm enough inside.

"How do you feel?" I shout over the wind.

"Like an icicle."

"Icicle feels like an icicle," I yell. "Very funny."

We have spent the day shooting segments on the polar vortex, rushing in and out of the news van, heat cranked, to stay, well, not just thawed but alive. The current temperature is minus eleven. That's the high for the day. The windchill is sixty-eight below. We are taking turns shooting segments about the polar vortex, and we have one remaining, which will require the most time.

"I can't feel my fingers," Icicle says as we jump back into the van. He removes his gloves and shakes his hands. He sticks them in front of the vents.

He looks over at me, clearly irritated.

"What?" I ask.

"Okay, what's going on? I've lived here my whole life. You've lived in the desert the last few decades. You should be freezing, complaining, screaming right now. And yet you seem warm as a thermal blanket."

I shrug. "Inner strength?"

Icicle looks at me. And then he leans over and grabs my arm, squeezing it under my coat. He reaches for my back.

"I am so reporting you to management," I joke.

"What do you have on?" he asks. "Give it up!"

I look at him. "I learned from my mentor at WGN that you have to stay warm and dry when you cover winter storms and are outside for long periods of time," I say. "So I go to the pharmacy and stock up on the patches and heat wraps that athletes wear when they have muscle aches. I stick them all over my body and then put on a wet suit. That keeps me warm and dry all day. It's like I have a fireplace burning inside my clothes."

"Why didn't you tell me that?"

"Rookies need to learn some things the hard way."

"Who's the one who caught Polly Sue?"

"Who's the one who got you this job?"

He eyes me warily before holding out his hand. "Truce?"

"Truce."

I start to shake his hand, but Icicle pivots and grabs my bag off the seat. He yanks a box of heating therapy patches from my purse.

"Hey!" I yell.

"Is for horses," he says. "Get out for a minute. I need to strip and stick these on my body."

"I've dressed you," I tease. "You're like my little brother."

He looks at me. "Get out. You're just saying that because you don't want to get cold again. Payback stinks."

I open the door and the wind smacks me in the face again. I hop around for what seems like an eternity until he honks a minute or two later.

"Icicle is warm." He sighs contentedly.

I laugh.

"Before we freeze again, let's review some of our footage. I just want to make sure we don't have to do this all over again."

He grabs the camera and hits play.

For the last few hours, we have shot multiple segments of varying subjects about the polar vortex. Some pieces are only fifteen or thirty seconds and will run as PSA's during prime time. We covered topics ranging from how to protect your pipes, pets, livestock, car and home during this epic cold spell, to how-to's: how to make your own emergency-survival kit for your vehicle, how to avoid frostbite, which can occur in mere minutes in such extreme temperatures, and how to locate the nearest warming center should you lose power.

We spent a couple of hours in and out of the studio so that Icicle could tape his special segment for kids, "Ice, Ice Baby." The title—and accompanying Vanilla Ice song that introduces it—was totally his idea, a wink-wink at his winter history as well as the polar vortex. He taped a segment in which he demonstrated how cold it was by tossing a cup of boiling water into the air that crystallized into ice and snow before hitting the ground. He also taped a science experiment for kids to try at home with school canceled demonstrating how a soap bubble freezes.

Icicle was exceedingly nervous at first, though I convinced him this idea was brilliant, not only in educating kids about science and the weather but also in drawing in younger viewers, which the station desperately needs. His first segment will run during Saturday morning cartoons, and I already know in my gut the initial response will be very strong.

But I had as much to teach him about the art of weather forecasting as he had to teach the kids about the science of weather.

"A meteorologist's job is to break down complicated scientific facts into something the general public can easily understand. I approach the weather like I did as a journalism student at Northwestern: I ask, 'Who? What? When? Where? Why?' And I treat each segment as both news and entertainment," I explained to him. "We are journalists, teachers *and* entertainers. But never forget that we meteorologists are usually the only real scientists a viewer encounters every single day."

When he was still having difficulty, I said, "I always pretend like I'm talking to my mom. If she gets it, I know everyone else will, too."

His segments soared after that.

"Water is so cool," he said in one of his segments after our talk. "We're surrounded by water in Traverse City." He went on to explain how water can exist as a liquid, a gas and a solid at the same time, and then he demonstrated to kids how boiling water droplets—when tossed into the air at such extreme temperatures—fall as ice crystals.

"Yes," I had cheered, so enraptured and enthused by what he was saying.

After that, I continued my series on how the polar vortex is impacting life in our local resort towns. This morning, we went to Leland, famous for its Fishtown filled with historic weathered fishing shanties, smokehouses and fish tugs along the Leland River. One can imagine what it would have been like in the early 1900s to live and work in this small fishing village nestled by the shore of Lake Michigan, which still operates as one of the only working commercial fishing villages in the State. I interviewed the head of the Fishtown Preservation Society about the dramatic and necessary measures they're taking to protect the historic area from the incredible ice forming on the Great Lakes, which—in the wind—could cause significant damage to the historic shanties when it moves inland. The Great Lakes are so vast that it is extremely rare for the entire lake to freeze over, but my prediction is that nearly 90 percent of Lake Michigan will be frozen over before winter ends.

And that is where we are headed next, for our final segment: to the beach on one of the coldest days in the last hundred years.

We pull into the snow-drifted parking lot of a public beach in Leelanau County. We bundle back up, gather our equipment and head across the cold, crunchy sand and hike along the ice-strewn beach. My eyes are watering so much in the icy wind that when I first see what we came to film, I think it is an icy mirage. I wipe my eyes, and then stop cold—pardon the pun—in my tracks.

The ice caves of Leelanau.

"They're so beautiful," Icicle says.

A local photographer reached out to me about this rare winter phenomenon in which massive caves of ice form, hollowed out and worn by the waves. Different kinds of ice formations occur because of a variety of reasons, including meteorological conditions, the location and the wave action, so ice caves can vary greatly along the shoreline. But it's rare that anchor ice builds up to such great heights—two stories!—that one can explore the caves as if they were spelunking.

"I feel like I am in another world," I say.

"We *are* in another world."

To say that the ice caves are spectacularly beautiful would be akin to saying that Sophia Loren was *cute*. They are breathtaking. Unique. Surreal, as if Dr. Seuss had drawn them.

The caves rise from the water and the shoreline. Many are as thick as castle fortresses, while some are as fragile and as translucent as a piece of paper. Many of the caves have ten-foot icy stalactites dangling from their tops. Many are big enough to drive our news van through, while others are barely big enough for me to squeeze my body into them.

There is a bit of danger, so we are careful. But the ice is thick, and the photographer has shot here many times already and told us it is safe to explore.

"Sonny!" Icicle yells. "Over here!"

He is as giddy as a kid, rushing from spot to spot. His camera is out, and he is shooting, his enthusiasm as palpable as the first time I saw the Eiffel Tower and took pictures of it from every angle.

But I feel the same: we are witnessing a rare natural event that might not occur again in our lifetime.

Suddenly, the world brightens. The clouds clear. The ice comes alive. The world shimmers, glimmers and shines. The ice takes on a life of its own. It reflects the blue of the sky; the lake water becomes glitter under glass. I stand in the middle of an ice cave and stare out at the lake, frozen for miles.

It is one of the most beautiful things I have ever seen. I take a picture in my mind and then shut my eyes to store it forever. I have seen countless sunsets in my life. I have seen the sky turn so pink over the mountains in Palm Springs that I have felt my knees quake. I have watched the sun melt into Lake Michigan like a Dreamsicle while holding my sister's hand. I have sipped wine in Amalfi as the sun slunk sexily into the sea under *Vesuvio*'s eye.

But this, this is so unreal, so spectacular that I begin to cry.

We shoot until sunset, and as we finish, I can't help but sing the song that keeps coming into my mind.

"'The cold never bothered me anyway!'"

Icicle laughs. "Really?" he says. "Suddenly you're Elsa from *Frozen*?"

I look at him. "You know *Frozen*? Impressive."

"My mom loves that movie. She told me there were zombies in it, and I believed her."

I laugh. "I've always been Elsa. Just took winter to thaw me."

I realize the camera is pointed directly at me.

"Got that all on tape," he says. "I think that's a perfect ending to the segment and our day."

We begin to head home as darkness overtakes the frozen shore.

I turn one last time to see the ice caves glistening in the day's last light, a frozen soul coming to life for all to see.

It took only a few miracles and a once-in-a-lifetime occurrence to make it happen.

The weather has warmed. It is fifteen degrees. The polar vortex is still in effect, but it's had a couple of stiff drinks and is finally ready to slink off to bed.

I am on Front Street doing a live "Sonny in the Winter" segment. It is the Cherry Capital Winter Wonderfest, and the event's main attraction is the Michigan Ice Festival, which attracts some of the state's and nation's most accomplished ice sculptors. The downtown is lined with icy works of art, many of which have taken days to create, some sculpted by hand from fifty thousand pounds of natural ice.

I am speaking with last year's winner, a third-generation ice sculptor who re-created the winning entry, a ballerina twirling atop rippling water, as if the lake itself had birthed the dancer. It is ten-feet-tall and dwarfs its sculptor, who crafted it from an eight-thousand-pound ice block.

When I finish, I hear a voice.

"Fancy meeting you here."

"You invited me. This is your gig."

"Oh, yeah. I forgot."

Mason laughs and leans toward me. "Is it okay to kiss you in public? I wouldn't want anything to go viral. Seems like you've finally gotten your life under control."

"Now that's funny," I say. I lean in and kiss him on the lips.

"Don't melt the ice sculptures."

I look up. "You have great timing, Mom."

"Mason," she says, hugging him.

"It's good to see you again, Patty Rose," he says, hugging her tightly. "Isn't this beautiful?"

"It is," I say.

"Been years since I've come down for this," my mom says. "It is simply magical."

And it is.

I feel like I'm in a Hallmark movie where the town is alive with the wonder of winter. People mill about in the cold, bright night sipping coffee and cider, taking photos of the ice sculptures and shopping. Traverse bustles with activity, nearly as much as it does in the summer.

"Over one hundred entrants this year," Mason says, gesturing around. "Front Street is filled."

"I'm glad I forecast a polar vortex for this," I say. "Perfect weather."

We walk up and down the street. I see Icicle shooting footage of the sculptures so we can include that in the lead-up to my next segment: the announcement of the winning entry.

"I bet I know as much about ice sculpting as you do now," I brag to Mason.

"Oh, really?" he says. He stops in front of a sculpture of a salmon swimming upstream. The sculpture is breathtaking: half of the fish is shown breaking the surface, and its head is sculpted in great detail. Its body is underwater, struggling hard against the current.

Mason's eyes are breathtaking, too. Juxtaposed against the blue ice at night, he looks like a sculpture come to life. It only takes my kiss to breathe warmth into him.

I kiss him.

"Get a room," I hear someone call.

I turn. It's my mother, again.

"Get a coffee!" I yell.

"I'd be up all night," she says. "Maybe some cider." She winks. "With a little somethin' somethin' in it."

Mason laughs. "Cherry doesn't fall far from the tree."

"That's an apt analogy for these parts," I say.

"I've missed you."

"Me, too."

"I'm glad everything has taken a turn for the better."

"Me, too."

"Now tell me all you know, ice guru."

"The time spent preparing, drawing, designing, engineering and producing sculptures like this can take months," I begin, as we move from creation to creation. "Sculptures can be incredibly delicate and weigh just a pound, or be massive in size, and weigh up to fifty thousand pounds or more. The average weight of a two-block ice sculpture is roughly three hundred to five hundred pounds."

Mason looks at me, nodding and smiling. "Go on."

I continue. "There are three types of ice that can be used in sculpting: basic canned ice with a white feather in the core, crystal clear ice block, which cost the sculptor two to three times more than the canned ice. And naturally made ice. Quality conscious sculptors primarily use the crystal clear ice that is made in a controlled environment. This skill is often passed down through generations in a family. Today, many sculptors often learn their techniques in culinary school or at specialty classes dedicated to ice carving. They learn how to use tools, including chainsaws, chisels, torches and angle grinders. It takes a great deal of practice, experience and time to reach a level like these sculptors demonstrate."

Mason stops on the sidewalk. "I'm impressed. You've done your homework for this segment. I don't even know that much about it, and I organized this whole thing."

"Oh, I'm not done," I say. "I was saving the most important thing for last."

"Which is?" he asks.

"They eventually melt," I say. "You can't keep something in a controlled environment forever. It's not natural."

Mason stops walking again. This time, he reaches out and puts his hands on my shoulders. He smiles.

"Winter has a way of making us see the world from a different perspective," Mason says. "In winter's bare bones fragility, we either see the beauty or we see the harshness. We feel the warmth or the cold. We witness a season of stunning change or experience a season of exhausting repetition." He gestures to the sculpture behind us, which gleams. "We see a season of light or we see a season of unending darkness."

His words again move me. "That's beautiful."

"So are you." He kisses me on the cold night, and I know that I am fully thawed, completely unfrozen. I am winter warm.

When he releases me, I finally notice the massive sculpture covered with a giant drop cloth. The sculpture is huge—probably ten-feet tall—and the draping gives it a mysterious, nearly mythical feel.

"Is that the winner?" I ask.

"That's the winner," Mason says. "The one you're going to announce live. We covered it to build suspense. Works, doesn't it?"

"You already know the winner, don't you?" I ask. "Give it up. I can have the scoop first!"

"I do know, but I can't tell you, or I'd lose my job," he says. "And you already have the scoop. You're the only station I invited tonight, and you get to reveal the winner live on air. Remember?"

"It's never enough for TV news," I say with a wink. "But thank you. This is so fun. And viewers love the suspense."

My mother appears with a cup of cider. "Want a sip?"

I take it and lift it to my lips but hesitate. "This smells like something Foster Brooks would drink," I say, handing it back. "I've made a vow to stay sober on air."

"Wow, that's quite a promise to your viewers," my mom says with a laugh.

"Gotta start somewhere." I shrug.

"It's nearly 9:00 p.m.," Mason says. "Time to announce the winner. You should go get set up."

I see Icicle waving at me from in front of the covered sculpture. I scoot across the street, check my hair and makeup, and take my position. I can hear Lisa's voice in my earpiece.

"We'll do five minutes of news and then go to you live, okay?" she says. "You can talk about the Winter Wonderfest and Michigan Ice Festival, then intro the winning piece and talk to the sculptor about it. Sound good?"

"Got it," I say.

"Back in a few," Lisa says.

Mason's voice booms across downtown. He is standing on a podium.

He is so handsome standing there above the crowd. Friendly, smart, sweet, funny.

I look around. He's right. This whole area in winter feels like Mayberry during the holidays, and Mason is my Andy Griffith.

I need to stop watching old TV shows with my mom, I think, or every reference I make will only be understood by people over fifty.

"Welcome, everyone, to the tenth annual Cherry Capital Winter Wonderfest and Michigan Ice Festival. We're honored to have with us some of our state and nation's best ice sculptors whose talents are on display on a perfect night to showcase them."

The crowd applauds.

"This was a juried festival. Only the top talent was invited to participate, and tonight's winner was selected by their peers.

So, without further adieu..." Mason stops, and a woman in a bright red coat hands him an envelope. He smiles and pauses.

He's good at drama.

"Read it!" someone yells.

"Yeah!" the crowd calls.

"The winner of the tenth annual Michigan Ice Festival is..." He opens the envelope. "Winter Sisters by Stefan Koster."

A team of people pull the giant cloth from the sculpture. The gust from its removal sweeps across me at the same time as the crowd gasps.

I look up and do the same.

It can't be?

The sculpture is of me and Joncee as kids.

I am building a snowman, half snow, half human, which resembles my little sister. I look more closely. I am not just building a snowman, I am re-creating Joncee from the winterscape, bringing her back to life from snow and memories and love.

The expression on Joncee's face—pure joy in the winter—captures the spirit of my little sister perfectly. And my expression—pure joy that she is with me again—brings me to tears.

Staring at our icy likenesses is like finding an old photo buried under ice.

"My sculptures have always depicted family," the winning sculptor is saying into Mason's mic. "My work is meant to connect people to their histories and memories. They are meant to remind us all of what matters most in this world. More than anything, I hope that my work fills those who see it with love and hope, which we need more than ever these days. Thank you for this honor."

Mason escorts the sculptor down to talk to me as the crowd applauds and gathers around the winning entry.

"How did you—" I look at Stefan and then at Mason "—*know*? How did you pull this off?"

"I was inspired by the story you shared on air when I was

doing research of the area," Stefan says. "It made me change my entire design. I contacted Mr. Carrier who put me in touch with your mom. I hope it was okay. Your history moved me greatly."

I can only stare at him, and then the sculpture.

It is then I notice the crowd is doing double takes, looking curiously at me, then the sculpture and then me again.

"And we're live," I hear Lisa say in my ear. "Sonny?" Her voice is slightly alarmed now. "We're live!"

I take a deep breath.

"I'm here with the winner tonight," I finally manage to say. I stop and look directly at the camera. "And it's me. It's always been me."

Suddenly, a few people in the crowd break into applause. It's slow and scattered at first, but it grows into a thunderous ovation.

I begin to cry.

"Keep shooting, keep shooting," I hear Lisa saying in my ear.

My mother races up and hugs me. "Isn't she beautiful?" she asks.

I don't know if she's talking about me, Joncee or the sculpture, but I see that she is crying, too.

"She is," I reply.

I look at the sculptor.

"Do you know what I learned tonight from you?" I ask.

"Tell me," he says with a smile.

"I learned that you cannot prevent an ice sculpture from melting in an average room temperature of seventy-degrees. Only if the ice sculpture is displayed in a climate-controlled environment below thirty-degrees Fahrenheit or outdoors in conditions below freezing may an ice carving be preserved for a period of time."

Stefan cocks his head at me.

I keep going. "It's like our memories. We try to freeze them in time." I stop. "I've lived my life in a climate-controlled environment for a long time now. I've stayed frozen even in the warmest of climates. But it's okay to melt just a little bit. The memories still remain. I just feel them now."

Stefan opens his arms and hugs me tightly. Mason and my mother join in.

I open my eyes and look up.

Joncee is with us, too, laughing in the winter night.

chapter 16

MARCH 2022

"Well, if it isn't Jennifer Garner!"

"Hi, Jo," I say to my agent. "Why am I Jennifer Garner?"

"You've suddenly become one of America's most beloved personalities," she says in her New York accent and inimitable style. "You're as liked nearly as much in the Great Lakes as Dolly Parton is around the world right now."

"How do you know that?" I ask.

"Your Q Score, sweetheart, is off the charts."

Ah, I think. The famed Q-Rating everyone in show business fawns over, the measurement of a celebrity's appeal. The higher the Q-Rating, the more beloved you are.

"My Q-Rating used to be a Z-Rating," I say.

"Not anymore!" Jo crows. "You're the comeback kid. Told you everybody loves a comeback story."

I hear her take a sip.

"What are you drinking?" I tease.

"We're celebrating!"

"We are?" I ask. "What exactly?"

"Are you sitting down?"

I take a seat in my chair at TRVC. When Jo asks you to sit, you sit.

"I am now."

"Good, because I have news!"

I hold my breath. She never calls unless the news is really good or really bad. And I can never tell which it is until she decides to tell me. Moreover, she hates it when I ask which one it is before she has a chance to tell me.

"It's good news!"

I exhale into the cell.

"You're so dramatic," she says.

"Me?"

She laughs, then coughs, then takes another drink.

"So?" I ask.

"*Good Morning America* called." She pauses.

"And?"

"And…they want you to interview."

"What! For…?"

"For a weekend anchor and fill-in for Ginger Zee," Jo says. "They love how you scooped almost everyone on the polar vortex, and they really loved the reporting you did on it. More than anything, they just love how real you are. They love how viewers respond to you. They just love you, period."

I am silent. I am stunned. The room spins.

"Hello?" she asks.

"I don't know what to say."

"Well, you can start by thanking me for resurrecting your career. You can thank me for that *People* magazine interview a few weeks ago. You can…"

"Thank you, Jo."

"You're welcome."

Jo takes a sip.

"You know, we've been together since day one. Ever since Vic Victor recommended you to me when he was on WGN. 'This girl's got spunk,' he told me. 'I hate spunk,' I replied."

"*Mary Tyler Moore* reference, right?" I ask.

"You got it," she says. "But you did. You had spunk. And more. You were vulnerable. It only took a few decades for you to show that side to the world."

"A lot has changed," I say.

"A lot is *going* to change," she says. "I saved the best part for last."

She pauses again.

"For Pete's sake, Jo, spill the beans."

"Love making you beg," she laughs. "Okay, okay. The gig would be on the West Coast. LA. You could even move back to Palm Springs and commute in for the weekends. And with the salary I'm going to demand—and the amount you'll earn from endorsements, hosting and speaking gigs—you'll only need to work a few days a month. Everybody wants Sonny, honey. And they're going to pay to get you."

"They have no idea what they're up against, do they?"

"Jo's going to row, row, row Sonny's boat gently up to the bank vault."

I laugh.

"I'm so, so proud of you," she says, suddenly serious, her voice actually soft and tender for once. "You are one strong woman."

"Thank you," I say. "That's a compliment coming from one of the strongest women I know."

"So, what works for you? They want to talk to you ASAP. I'm thinking Saturday. You don't work weekends there, right? You could say you just want a few days away. Or that a friend in the city needs to see you. What do you think?"

I can feel my heart pound in my ears.

"Okay," I agree. "What do I need to do?"

"Buy the most flattering outfit you can. Get your hair done. Get some rest. I'll take care of the rest. They're going to put you up somewhere great. What do you like? The Ritz with a room overlooking Central Park? The Four Seasons? St. Regis? The Peninsula?"

"You pick," I say.

"Dinner will be on me after your interview. It's going to be an epic celebration."

"It always is with you."

"Damn right." She laughs. "Got another call. Talk soon. Congratulations."

Before I can say goodbye, Jo is gone.

I hang up. My head is spinning so much that I have to check to make sure I am not rotating in circles in my office chair.

"Got a sec?"

I yelp.

"Overreact much?"

Lisa is standing at my door. She sees my face, and a look of concern comes over hers.

"I'm so sorry. I didn't mean to startle you. I knocked." She walks toward my desk. "Is everything okay?"

I nod idiotically like one of those old-school drinking birds with the red head and blue hat I had sitting on my desk when I was a kid. I'd play with it when I was bored doing my homework.

"Totally," I say, still nodding. "Just tired. Long week." I try to stop myself, but the lie is already coming out of my mouth. "I was actually going to ask if you would mind if I took Friday off. A friend of mine invited me to New York for a last-minute girls' weekend. I haven't been anywhere in a while."

"Except Palm Springs, remember?"

I feel my cheeks flush at the memory.

"I'm just joking," Lisa says. "Jeez. You look all wigged out right now. Are you sure everything's okay?"

I nod again.

"Of course, it's fine. You deserve it. You've worked nonstop the last few months. I'll ask Icicle to cover. He's ready for a shot during the week. He's just been outstanding, Sonny. You were right about him. I can never thank you enough." A smile crosses her face. "And it's actually good timing for your weekend because after what I'm about to tell you, you're going to be in the mood to celebrate."

How much good news can I take today?

"Well, I'm glad you're sitting," she starts. I think of Jo. "I just got the first quarter ratings. We're number one."

"What? Really?"

"And it's largely because of you. We've never seen numbers like this. I mean, we are solidly number one. From worst to first."

I get up and open my arms to hug Lisa.

"I can never thank you enough, either," I say. "For believing in me. For giving me this opportunity." I look at her for the longest time. "This second chance changed my life. Personally and professionally."

I am so emotional that I can't stop my voice from trembling.

"Thank you, Sonny," she says. "That means the world." She holds me at arm's length. "You really do need a few days off. I think you're exhausted. Now get ready to celebrate all this good news with your friend. I actually might need a weekend in the city soon, too."

She turns to leave as Icicle enters.

"Good timing," Lisa says, telling him the ratings news.

Icicle pumps his fist in the air and yells, "Yes!"

He looks at me, a huge smile plastered across his face.

"To the best weather team in Michigan!" he says. "No one will ever be able to bring us down! We're going to be number one forever!"

His words cause my heart to break. My stomach drops. I bite my cheek to hide my emotions.

"Right, Sonny?" Icicle asks.

If I say a word, I will cry. So I nod and nod and nod just like that stupid bird.

If I were wearing a hat, I would take it off and toss it into the sky just like Mary Tyler Moore.

"'If I can make it there, I'll make it anywhere…'"

I look around Times Square.

New York, New York!

I feel as bright and tall as the billboards flashing up and down the street. Typically when I come to New York, I rarely venture to Times Square. It's too crowded, too noisy, too jammed with tourists taking selfies, buying sneakers and shopping at the Hershey's Chocolate World or the Disney Store.

But today, walking out of *Good Morning America*'s studios, I feel as big as the advertisements for McDonald's and *Mamma Mia!*

My interview didn't just go well, it went toss-my-hat-into-the-sky-like-Mary-Tyler-Moore-and-Frank-Sinatra-singing-"New York, New York"-well!

I turn around in a circle and take it all in.

Jo told me to take a moment when I was done—no matter the outcome—and just stop and relish it.

"Too many people rush through the big moments in their lives and careers without stopping to take a mental picture," she had told me.

I think of doing the same thing with the ice caves, slowing down and taking a mental photo.

I stop in the middle of Times Square, a big no-no in New York City. New Yorkers expect you to just keep moving. Stopping in the middle of a sidewalk is akin to stopping your car in the middle of the highway at rush hour. For once, I don't care.

I look back at Times Square Studios, the home of *GMA*. I see the faces of Robin Roberts, George Stephanopoulos and Michael Strahan streaming across the state-of-the-art video screen. News tickers scroll just below them. The building, I learned in my interview, was meant to symbolize a "looking glass" and represent the idea of "media as architecture."

I picture my face on the video screen, like Ginger Zee's is right now.

I discovered in my interview that we had so much in common. She was raised in Michigan, graduated from high school in Michigan and worked as a meteorologist in Grand Rapids.

I could barely breathe sitting next to my idol. She told me to breathe and to remember it was just a couple of Michigan gals talking about the weather. I had laughed. She then told me she chose to be a meteorologist because she saw a waterspout on Lake Michigan when she was eight and that it was the coolest thing she had ever seen.

She also told me that my story about why I became a meteorologist—because of Joncee—had moved her greatly and that women needed role models on TV who were "real, over fifty and fighters."

My interviews with the anchors and producers had gone just as smoothly.

I feel my phone vibrate against my body. I can't hear it in all the hustle and bustle, but I feel it shake. I grab it as quickly as I can. I see who's calling. I take a deep breath.

"You got it!" Jo screams. "Get ready to party! Pick you up for drinks at five!"

I barely have a chance to say "Really?" before she's gone.

I am too jazzed to sit, too hyped to have any more coffee, and—even though it's New York City—it's still a bit too early for me to have a celebratory drink.

So I do what I love to do when I'm alone in New York City: I just walk. As if I'm floating on a cloud.

I did it!

I am as alive as the streets of New York, and nothing is more alive than that. It is a video game come to life, action surrounding you at every corner, the world at your fingertips.

Visiting the city's different neighborhoods is akin to going on a tour of the world every few blocks. I missed many things when I moved from Chicago: I missed the diversity of the city. I missed the hustle. I missed the restaurants. I missed the endless culture. I missed the shopping. I could have all of that again in LA. I would come to meetings here in New York. I would be back home in Palm Springs. It would be the perfect balance.

An ambulance siren blares. Taxis honk. Construction pounds every few storefronts.

I didn't miss any of that, though. The crowds. The noise. The constant intensity.

As I aged, I loved the quiet beauty of Palm Springs. I loved that I could have the fun of the city and then retreat into the shadow of the mountain. I loved seeing the hummingbirds at my feeders every morning, the mountain goats standing on the ridge of the mountains, the roadrunners that zipped across my yard just like in the old cartoons.

I love that about Michigan, too. Mother Nature is a friend you can visit any moment. She is in control, not people.

It is a brisk March day—cold, blustery but sunny—and the skyscrapers pop against their bright blue canvas. I am dressed to the nines, but people don't notice much of anything in New York. They just want you to keep moving. So I do.

I walk and window-shop, popping into a few stores.

I get jostled and feel the need for a bit of space.

And then it hits me. A quintessential New York winter moment.

I head to Forty-Ninth Street, passing the famed Magnolia Bakery, where I stop and buy a red velvet cupcake—and then another—eating them as I walk. I don't stop again until I reach my destination: The Rink at Rockefeller Center.

When I used to visit New York City in the winter as part of network meetings, I would always come here on my own to skate. It wasn't as much a way for me to spend time alone in all the hustle and bustle, it was more a way for me to reconnect with Joncee and my Michigan roots without anyone ever realizing it.

Rockefeller Center is iconic. From the lighting of the Christmas tree to Radio City Music Hall, The Rock—as it is known—covers nearly twenty-two acres of Midtown Manhattan.

I enter. Although it is the weekend, it is still early, and the rink is fairly quiet. It will be packed soon.

I get my skates, lace them up and head onto the ice.

It is surreal to skate in the middle of New York City. I feel so at home here and yet so out of place.

I skate across The Rink, the cold breeze that whips across my face no different from the one that does in Michigan. No matter where we live, we all have that in common: the wind, the sun, the rain, the snow, the weather.

I glance up as I skate and laugh. I had forgotten that NBC's *Today* show is filmed here.

My would-be rival. How ironic.

I race around The Rink. A massive bronze statue of Atlas, located on Fifth Avenue, rises over the skating rink like the mythological god it is. Atlas glows in the light. If I remember my college mythology correctly, Atlas sided with the Titans in their war against the Olympians and when the Titans were defeated, Zeus condemned him to stand at the western edge of the Earth and hold up the celestial heavens on his shoulders for eternity.

I spin around the rink, faster and faster, but I cannot avoid the gaze of Atlas. I slow and, without warning, am overwhelmed with emotion.

For the majority of my life, I have punished myself for the death of my sister. My guilt was akin to carrying the weight of the world on my own shoulders.

And yet I now have the world at my fingertips. By accepting this job, my life will have come full circle. I would be an Olympian, victorious. My lifelong sacrifices would finally have paid off.

But by saying yes, would I be saying goodbye to everything I have gained so far?

Can I say goodbye to my mother yet again, knowing I will likely spend the winter of her life far away?

Can I say goodbye to Mason, who patiently thawed my heart?

Can I say goodbye to Icicle, who has become the younger sibling I need in my life?

Can I hurt Lisa again?

Can they survive another setback, another loss, another goodbye?

Can I?

When I finish and return my skates, I stop and look around.

Atlas—and the city—is aglow.

This is what I've worked for my whole life.

As I begin to exit The Rink, a quote from John D. Rockefeller Sr. catches my attention.

"I do not think that there is any other quality so essential to success of any kind as the quality of perseverance. It overcomes almost everything, even nature."

The sun wakes me in my bedroom at home.

As I do most mornings, I grab my cell from the nightstand and check the forecast. I smile when Icicle pops up on the video.

"'This shocking March warmth will last for a few more hours…"

Of course, while I was gone, Michigan experienced a heat wave, relatively speaking. The temperatures warmed into the upper fifties, as the cold front pushed onto the East Coast.

More irony, I think. *Of course, I would leave when it got warmer.*

I pull on my robe and slippers and head downstairs.

"Morning."

My mother's voice makes me jump.

"You're up early," she notes.

"You, too," I say.

I head to the cabinet, pull out a mug and pour a cup of coffee.

"That's become a favorite mug," my mom says with a smile.

I look. I grabbed the mug featuring Michigan as a winter mitten on the side of it.

More irony.

"Sit," my mom says.

I take a seat on a barstool at the counter beside her and take a drink of coffee.

"How's was your girls' weekend?"

I look over at my mom. If a question could have a sarcastic wink attached to it, my mother's would.

"Talk," she orders.

"Okay. It wasn't a girls' weekend."

"I'm stunned," my mother says, clutching her chest. "Don't know a lot of girls' weekends where everyone stays at The St. Regis. And you don't really have any close girlfriends, either."

"Ouch, Mother," I say.

"You're a meteorologist, dear. Not Keith Morrison unraveling a murder on *Dateline*. It wasn't hard to figure out." She looks at me and takes a sip of her coffee. "You're more like the killers he covers who can't hide their tracks. You left clues everywhere."

"Busted," I say.

"Tell me everything."

When I finish, I stare at my mom. It is impossible to read her. She is like the world's best poker player. I can't tell if she has a full house or a pair of threes.

"What do you think I should do?" I ask.

"Oh, no," my mom says. "No, no, no."

"You're not going to tell me?" I ask.

"You already know," my mom says. She reaches over and shakes my leg. "For all of history, children have come to their parents seeking advice. They ask and listen, and they go off and do what they want. That's not a bad thing, but I know I can't—and shouldn't—change your mind or influence your decision in any way. I asked my parents if I should get married, when I already knew. I asked you if I should go back to work after your father died, but I already knew. You already know, sweetheart. And I can't make that decision for you. It wouldn't be fair to either of us."

My mom continues. "I help my patients transition. I give them medication, I nurse, I pray, I ease their pain, but—much of that time—the final decision is still theirs. Often, I don't know how their bodies can last an hour longer, and yet sometimes a mother will go on for days until her daughter finally arrives to say goodbye. Or a father will hold out until his son rushes in the door to grip his hand. Even at the end of our lives, we are often still making our own decisions. We are still fighting. We are still holding on to hope and love." She stops. "Because we're still alive, and we know what we want."

I start bawling and cannot stop. My mother opens her arms and hugs me, and she sways me back and forth atop my stool.

"I have so many regrets, Mom. I regret not picking up Joncee that day. I regret turning my back on so many people who loved me and tried to help me. I regret not being a mother like you. I regret wasting so many years fearing I might get hurt again when I was hurting myself every single day. I regret missing years of conversations like this. I regret not being me. Amber-rose Murphy. Daughter, sister, Michigan native."

"Nearly every patient I help transition is filled with regrets. The only solution is to start living your life with an open heart and an open mind. Today."

"I'm glad I'm home, Mom."

"Me, too. So?" she finally asks. "What are you going to do?"

"I'm going to call some of my friends and seek their advice, too," I say, "and then I'm going to go for a walk in the woods."

"Smart. What was the old Robert Frost poem?" my mom asks.

"'The Road Not Taken'?"

"Exactly," she says. "You can only choose one path at a time."

My mom lets me go.

"Where are you off to?" I sniff.

"I have to help a client prepare for a walk, too."

"Oh, Mom. I'm sorry."

"Thank you," she says. "It's okay. She's a mother of six. Grandmother of nine. Great-grandmother of three. Husband died young. She became a postmistress. But now she says she misses her husband. Says she has for decades. She told me last month that she missed dancing with him." My mom stops. "She told me last week he was reaching for her hand, and that she could feel it and she could hear the music. She's made her decision."

My mom kisses me on the forehead.

"I know you'll choose your path wisely."

My mother pulls on her coat, grabs her purse and heads to the garage.

I listen to her leave. It is silent in the house.

I pick up my cell.

"Hi, Eva. It's Sonny. Got a minute?"

And then I call Tammy Lynn, Becky Jo and Jenny.

I head upstairs and get dressed for my walk. Not as many layers today are needed. Spring is coming, then summer.

And there is nothing like summer in northern Michigan.

Clouds are beginning to build over the bay. I walk the opposite way and into the woods. The ground is spongy, and my boots leave suction marks as I walk. Snow still lines the shaded areas on the wooded hillsides. Memories come flooding back as I walk. I see a stand of bent, gnarled sassafras twisted like witches fingers.

Aliens were here, Joncee used to say of these weird trees spotted with knots and growing in odd directions.

I used to laugh at her description, but it seems accurate, and I scoot past them quickly.

As I walk, the sun angles through the woods, giving them a magical feel. The darkness is sliced with light, and I follow it as if it were the Yellow Brick Road leading me to an answer.

Home.

I am warm as I walk, the first time I've felt this warm outside in ages.

Since Palm Springs?

Since I danced with Mason in the snow?

I look around. I no longer know where I am.

Which direction?

Clouds begin to choke out the sun, and I am suddenly standing in darkness. The wind shifts to the north and begins to gust. I can feel the temperature drop, quickly and precipitously. Instinct tells me to turn around, but I search for a different path home.

I head toward a stand of barren birch, white and light in the darkness. When I reach them, I stop and smile.

A hillside of daffodils is blooming, yellow, bright and happy.

The recent spate of warmer than average weather has forced them to bloom much earlier than usual.

I take a seat on the stump of a tree that has fallen and broken off over the winter.

Was I meant to find you for some reason? I think. *Am I meant to see you right now?*

I sit for a moment and shut my eyes. The cold wind cuts through me. Joncee loved daffodils. But she hated that people often thought she was named after jonquils, a type of daffodil with a strong fragrance.

Why did our parents give us such stupid names? she'd complain.

I would always shrug. I didn't much care for Amberrose, either.

A way for us to carry on their history, I'd say.

That would always appease her. Makes sense I guess.

I sigh.

What should I do, Joncee? I ask the daffodils. *Tell me. Please.*

The wind whistles through the branches.

No regrets, my mother always says. *Do not end your life with regret, Amberrose.*

What will I miss when my time here is over? Will I regret not taking this job, or will I regret leaving home once again? Will I regret not being a huge success, or am I one already?

Will I regret not being on national TV every weekend, or will I miss making snow angels with my mom?

Will I miss being recognized on the street everywhere I go, or will I miss dancing in the snow with Mason?

Will I kick myself for not making more money than I ever dreamed, or will I be sick to my stomach when I have to send my regrets to Icicle's wedding because I have to work?

"What should I do, Joncee? Tell me. Please."

I say this out loud, and the sound of my own voice in the quiet of the woods surprises me. My voice is lost, sad, trembling.

I take a mental picture of the daffodils and shut my eyes.

I can see myself as a girl picking a bouquet of them and rushing home to put them in water. *How many times did Joncee turn the sprayer on me and laugh while I was filling the vase at the kitchen sink?*

I can hear her infectious giggles in the sound of the wind.

Suddenly, I feel water.

My imagination is out of control, I think.

I sigh.

And then I feel it again.

I open my eyes, and snow is falling. Not just falling but coming down in wet, heavy sheets.

I look up, through the trees, toward heaven.

Lake effect, I think. *Lake-effect snow.*

A cold air mass is passing over the lake's warmer waters.

I start to giggle. And then laugh. Finally, I am doubled over.

Joncee and the weather have answered the question I already had answered in my heart. I just needed my brain to play along.

I walk home through the snowy woods, taking a path I'd never taken before, feeling exhilarated at being both lost and found.

When I get home, I pick up the phone and I call Jo.

"Are you sitting down?" I ask.

"Don't play my game on me," she says.

I tell her my decision.

She doesn't say a word to me for seemingly forever, a first in her life.

"I'm not a magician," Jo finally says, her voice hoarse.

"Yes, you are," I say. "You could sell underwear to a nudist."

She laughs. "Are you flattering me?"

"Yes." I stop. "I know it's a hard sell, but I know I'm making the right decision. I'm proud of who I've become: strong, independent, happy."

"Oh, good Lord," Jo says. "You've become a Kelly Clarkson song." She takes a sip of something. "Okay, let me see what I can do. I can't promise you anything." She hesitates. "Are you sure?"

"I've never been more sure of anything in my life," I say. "I'm ready to take this leap."

"Then I'll be your parachute," Jo says.

"Now you're the one who sounds like a Kelly Clarkson song."

Jo hangs up.

I sit in the kitchen, make a cup of hot chocolate and watch it snow. The snow falls, heavier and heavier. I crack the patio door. The world is silent.

When the snow covers the patio, I head outside to play in the lake effect.

chapter 17

APRIL 2022

"I'll miss you!"

"I'll miss you, too!"

Lisa and I look at one another.

"For two weeks!" we say at the same time.

Lisa opens her arms, and I hug her.

"Thank you for the recommendation," Lisa says. "I still don't know what to say."

"You don't need to say anything, my friend," I say.

"Do you really mean that?" she asks.

I look at her, confused.

"That I'm your friend?" she clarifies.

"Of course you are," I say. "With what we've been through, I can't imagine being closer to anyone."

Lisa beams.

"And I still need friends in high places, too."

Lisa laughs.

"I'm just a segment producer, remember." She stops and looks at me.

"For *Good Morning America*!" we scream again at the same time.

I think of the snow and the daffodils. I think of my life then and now. I think of who I was, who I am and who I want to be.

"Blame the lake effect," I say.

Lisa doesn't shoot me a concerned look; rather, she nods, seeming to understand exactly what I mean.

That winter can change a person. It can show you the delicate structure of the world when everything is stripped clean. It can illuminate your soul when the world is cloaked in darkness. It can warm your heart when everything else is frozen. It can let you hear your own thoughts for the first time when the earth finally falls silent.

But mostly winter can let you see the silhouette of your body's branches—like a tree in February—when all the leaves are off, the green is gone, the adornment stripped away and, for the first time, you can appreciate all the knots, bends, broken limbs and lightning strikes.

You can see the beauty that has been created in harsh times.

But to see all of this you first must be willing to stand alone in the cold.

I see the stand of sassafras in my mind, and I smile.

I made it happen, I think, before amending that thought. *No, Jo made it happen, too. She took my dream and made it reality.*

When I called Jo, I told her that *Good Morning America* was my dream job. But it had to be on my own terms. I didn't want to leave Michigan. I didn't want to leave my job at TRVC. But I did want to do the job they offered. So, what if I were to stay in Michigan but commute to LA twice a month to shoot live? In the meantime, I could shoot my segments here—and bring the beauty and four seasons of Michigan to the world—without upending the world I had created.

"Without leaving my mom, my friends, and Mason," I had told Jo.

"Mason?" she had asked in her inimitable way. "Be still my heart."

"You still have one?" I had joked, before adding a bonus: And what if I brought along the most talented news director with whom I've ever worked, a woman who took our TV station from worst to first—as my segment producer? If they were to hire me, they also had to hire the woman I trusted to be the LA glue that held my segments—to be titled Sonny Skies Ahead, a show that would be equal parts weather and feel-good human interest stories—together?

Jo did it, of course. Like *GMA* ever stood a chance.

Lisa will now be responsible for scheduling interviews with guests, reviewing scripts, editing footage, pulling together my stories and lifestyle vignettes, and creating a seamless viewing experience for my Sonny segments.

She will be working in LA. I will be working here and there. We will be working together.

Why can't women have it all?

"Oh, that reminds me," I say, reaching out to touch Lisa, who is now being mobbed by guests at her going-away party. "I have a gift for you."

"A parting gift?" she asks.

I pull a little box from my bag and hand it to her.

"It's so pretty," she says, unwrapping the velvet bow on top. Lisa opens the box and looks at me. Her eyebrows raise in confusion. "What is it?"

"It's a key," I say.

"To your heart?"

"No, to my house in Palm Springs," I say. "I thought if you needed a weekend getaway you could use it."

"Really?" she says.

"It's the perfect getaway from LA. Believe me, you'll need it. It's a stressful job in a big city with a lot of pressure. Palm Springs is the perfect paradise to unwind."

"Again, I don't know how to thank you."

I smile. "Well, actually, this time you can. I have a list of things that need done when I'm there. It would save me a lot of time, worry and money if you could." I grab my cell and hit send. "I just sent you the checklist for the house."

"I knew there was a catch."

I lift my phone and show her a picture of the glimmering pool in the sunshine, magenta bougainvillea in bloom, the mountains looming in the near distance.

"And consider your checklist complete," she says with a laugh, taking the key, putting it back into the box and shoving it into the pocket of her long sweater.

Music begins to blare, and suddenly the lights in TRVC's conference room go dark. A song comes on with a familiar beat. One I knew from my younger days.

"Ice, Ice Baby" by Vanilla Ice.

I look at Lisa. She looks at me and shrugs.

A spotlight appears at the door.

Icicle appears in it. He lip syncs for a moment before grooving to the beat. Finally, he moonwalks across the floor.

The lights come on, and the entire news team bursts into applause.

"What's going on?" I ask.

Lisa shrugs again, but then moves forward to join Icicle.

"We," Lisa starts, putting her arm around Icicle, "couldn't think of a better way to announce the following news—I'd like to introduce everyone to our new news director, Ron Lanier."

The room explodes.

"Ron?" she prompts.

"Thank you, Lisa," he says. "I'm beyond honored to serve as the new TRVC news director. And I must thank Lisa for recommending me. Once you say you work for *Good Morning America*, you can pretty much get anything you want."

The room titters.

"That said, I know I'm young. I know I'm still unproven. But I have done every job at the station, from sweeping the floors to writing news, from being cameraman to being on air. And with my 'Ice, Ice Baby' performance, I am officially retiring my nickname. It's who I was, not who I am. I hope you will respect me—and that decision—by calling me Ron, which is what I use on air. It doesn't change a thing, and yet it changes everything." He stops and looks my way. "Right, Sonny?"

I nod.

"I want this to be a newsroom filled with trust, respect and hard work. Lisa has built the number one news team in northern Michigan, and I plan to keep it that way. I am so, so proud to help lead us into the future. Thank you! And now let's have some fun!"

I am not only bursting with pride but my legs are shaking from emotion.

I make a beeline for Lisa and Ron. "Why didn't you tell me?" I ask them. "How could you keep this a secret?"

"Really, I'm-just-going-on-a-girls'-weekend-but-actually-interviewing-with-*Good Morning America*?" Lisa says. "Are we playing that game?"

I turn to Ron. "I'm so overwhelmingly proud of and happy for you!"

"But," he says. "There's a but in there."

"But what about us still working together?"

"Don't worry. I'm continuing as weekend meteorologist. What choice do I have? You'll be gone twice a month."

"That's a lot of work," I say.

"I know. I can't wait."

I hug him.

"You're the little brother I never had," I whisper to him.

He looks at me, his chin quivering.

"You can't make the news director cry," he says. "It won't look good."

"Our secret," I whisper.

I turn to Lisa and hug her, too. "You're the sister I still need," I whisper.

Someone hands us three glasses of champagne and slices of cake, and we toast one another before cramming icing into our mouths.

Suddenly, the lights go dim again, and another familiar song begins to play.

A circle gathers around me and Lisa.

"What's going on?" she asks.

"You don't know?" I ask her.

She shakes her head.

"California Girls" by Katy Perry plays.

"Now I get it." I grin. "This is for us."

We hand off our plates, hold on to our champagne and begin to dance as the crowd shouts and applauds. We sing. On the last verse, however, Lisa and I look at one another as if we're reading each other's minds. We smile, nod and sing at the top of our lungs:

Michigan girls
We're unforgettable

"Happy New Year!"

I kiss Mason.

"What a year, huh?" he asks.

The ball drops in Times Square in New York City.

"You can say that again," I say.

"Any regrets?"

I think of my mom, who is at a friend's house right now. She had asked me the exact same question earlier today.

"None," I say.

And I mean it.

I glance again at the TV. People are kissing and tooting horns while confetti swirls in the streets.

I glance outside Mason's windows. Snow, winter's confetti, is swirling over the lake.

The two worlds couldn't be any more different.

And I would choose mine any day.

"Auld Lang Syne" plays, and Mason grabs me, and we sway

in the firelight. When the song finishes, Mason pours two more glasses of champagne.

"To a new year!" he says. "Filled with new beginnings."

I lift my glass and begin to drink. Mason grabs my wrist.

"You're supposed to sip Veuve," he admonishes. "And notice how the beautiful bubbles form."

I give him a funny look. "I'm not that classy," I say.

"No, look at the bubbles!" he says.

I gave him a strange look. It is then I finally notice the champagne flute.

Or, rather, what's in it.

At the bottom, amid all the golden bubbles, is a gold ring.

I sip—okay, I slam—the rest of my drink and then reach for the ring.

"Is this…?"

Mason goes down on one knee.

"It is," he says. "I love you more than anything in this world. Would you do me the honor of becoming my wife?"

I shake my head.

"Yes?" he asks.

"Yes!" I say.

He stands, kisses me and places the ring on my finger.

"I didn't want to wait any longer, Sonny. I know I love you. I don't want any more regrets in my life, either. I don't want to live in fear, or play 'what if' one more day. I want you to be by my side forever." He stops. His voice is quavering. "You are the sun in my winter sky."

Mason looks me in the eyes. His eyes are the color of ice against a clear winter sky. My knees feel weak. He is the most handsome man I've ever seen. He is one of the kindest men I've ever known. He is a good man who loves me.

I kiss him as the music continues to play in Times Square.

"I have one more surprise for you," he says.

"Was there something else in my champagne glass that I mistakenly ingested?"

He laughs.

"No. But put on your coat, scarf and boots."

"Where are we going?"

"Outside."

"It's snowing," I say. "It's freezing."

"I know," Mason says with a big smile. "The weather is perfect."

I pull on my winter garb and follow him outside. Although the snow is falling at a steady clip, it is a light snow with little moisture. The breeze kicks it around with little effort.

"Where are we going?" I ask.

Mason takes my mittened hand and guides me to into his yard. We stop at the top of his bluff, which overlooks Omena Bay. The snow is two-thirds the way up my boots.

"I talked to your mom today," Mason says. "I got her blessing. She also told me about your New Year's tradition."

I look at him.

"You mean snow angels?"

He nods.

I think of arriving home last year with my tail between my legs. I had tried so hard to forget about my past, our traditions, winter. And when my mom led me into the backyard and reminded me it was not only okay to remember my past but also to remember my pain, my year—in spite of all the turmoil—began to change for the better.

"Oh, honey," she had said. "You need to remember. You *have* to remember."

"We're going to jump into a clearing, okay?" Mason says, like my mom always does.

He tightens his grip on my hand.

"Together." Mason looks at me. "One, two, three... Go!"

Mason pulls me through the air.

"Now we're going to fall straight back in the snow," Mason says.

"I know the drill," I say. "Are you nervous?"

"No," he says, although his voice is filled with excitement.

"Don't worry," I say. "The snow is fresh and powdery, so it'll be like a pillow. Trust me. I'm a weather professional."

He laughs.

"Try to land in a T, with your arms out. Makes for a better angel. I'm going to let go of your hand now, okay?" Mason looks over at me. "Your mom told me to say all of that."

"I'm sure she did," I say. "Are you ready? One, two, three..."

We fall backward together, and I can't help but scream from the adrenaline. We land with a big *Poof!* and snow billows up and around our bodies. My heart is racing, and I giggle.

"Just move your arms and legs like you're doing jumping jacks..." Mason starts.

"My mom taught you well, didn't she?" I ask. "But I got the rest. Now, gently press your head into the snow to make an indentation."

We push our arms and legs through the powder, and I can feel chunks of powdery snow sneak into the back of my coat and underneath my shirt. The chill takes my breath away but makes me feel incredibly alive.

I look over at Mason. In the moonlight, his cheeks red, his breath coming out in big puffs, his hair wet and mussed, he looks like a kid.

I stare into the sky. Snow falls on my face. It tickles my nose, and it covers my lashes.

My life comes to me in flashes: child, teenager, young adult, working professional, middle-aged.

Happiness, loss, guilt, denial, hiding, discovery, honesty, happiness.

I blink, and snow falls from my lashes.

Our lives, as my mother once told me, are as brief as one blink of God's eye. It is up to us to decide how to best use His gifts and make our short journey here important and memorable. It is important we never forget, as we too often do, what matters most in that blink: family, friends, each other.

I think of Joncee. Her blink was much too short, and yet the importance of her brief life impacted and changed so many lives.

Her life, I realize, was not a blink. It was eye-opening.

It is hyperbole to say that our lives are like the weather, or the four seasons, but some truth lies in that or such statements wouldn't become part of our vernacular. I am likely nearing the winter of my life. And I am proud of that. Because it is a beautiful season in which to live.

I stick out my tongue and catch the snowflakes.

Stick out your tongue, I can hear Joncee say as clearly as if she were next to me. *Eat some snow, it'll make you grow.*

It'll make you look like a snowman, I remember saying.

Perfect!

"What's next?" Mason asks. "I forgot what your mother told me."

"You have to pick a star, and then we have to recite the poem."

"How do I pick?" Mason asks.

"Pick one that calls to you," I say. "It may be the brightest star, or one that is barely even noticed in the sky by people. As long as it calls to you. Got one?"

"I do," he says.

He is looking at me.

"No, a star in the sky," I say. "Not Sonny."

"The Sun is a star," he says. "You should know that. There are lots of stars, but the Sun is the closest one to Earth. It is the center of our solar system." Mason stops. "You, Sonny, are my star. You are the center of my solar system."

I can feel my face flush even in the cold.

"'When you wish upon a star, makes no difference who you are…'" I say to Mason.

"My dream has already come true," he finishes.

"Me, too."

I think of my sister as I did one year ago when I was lost and with my mom. Joncee believed there was nothing purer than newly fallen snow, and that if you made an angel on New Year's Eve then God would most certainly see it and all your wishes for the new year would come true.

You were right, I whisper to her.

"Now, we have to stand up as carefully as we can, so our angels—and our wishes—remain intact," I say.

I sit up and position my legs underneath me, so I can stand without messing up my creation.

"Here," Mason says. "Take my hand."

He reaches out, his arm sliding across the snow. I take it, and we stand. Together.

We leap from our snowy silhouettes and turn around. There is a muddled line attaching the two angels, thanks to his assistance in helping me stand.

My mom and I did the same thing one year ago tonight.

"I think we ruined them," I say.

"No, Sonny," he says, as if my mom told him exactly what to say. "We made them better. They're connected."

"What did you wish for?" he asks.

"You know I can't say. Then it won't come true."

"Mine already has," Mason says.

I look at my snow angel. I've wished for so many things in my life, I didn't know if God could ever make heads or tails of it. I wished for a life I used to have, I wished for a new start, I wished never to know winter again.

I look up at the sky and find the star I selected.

I used to stare at the sky—here and in the desert—and try to realign the stars so that my sister would be with me again.

And then, out of nowhere, I see it from the corner of my eye: a falling star blazing across the winter sky.

Joncee!

You've always been with me, haven't you?

I just want to spread my wings and fly, I can hear her say like she did when she was a little girl. *Just like an angel.*

"You are an angel," I whisper out loud. "Fly, angel. Fly!" I stare into the sky. "I love you!"

"Did you say something?" Mason asks.

"I love you," I say.

"Me, too."

He takes my hand, and we head back home through the snow.

★★★★★

A PERSONAL LETTER TO READERS

When I was growing up, my family personified the holidays. My father was a real-life Clark Griswold, digging up Christmas trees that were too tall for the living room and overdecorating them in a single color (only ONE color, which varied year to year: green, red, blue, silver). My mother was Mrs. Claus. She put out manger scenes and bought enough tinsel to drape the Rockefeller Center tree. My grandma (Viola Shipman, my pen name) loved Christmas most of all. Her home was absolutely drenched in lights, and her yard and roof were filled with inflatables dancing to holiday music. She had the most beautiful heirloom Christmas ornaments and bought so many gifts for our family that she had to create a walkway in her living room to get through them all. And don't get me started on the holiday cookies—shaped like Santa, holiday wreaths and bells, reindeer—topped with icing as thick as snow.

I loved Christmas, too. And I loved winter as well, from making snow angels to sledding down the biggest hill in our little town. One of my favorite memories is of standing up to my waist in snow as a kid after a historic snowfall. My older brother, Todd, had carried me out and—plop!—dropped me into the middle of the snow as if I were as weightless as another flake. Then we built a snowman that was the envy of the entire neighborhood. Our Frosty was mammoth. My dad brought out a stepladder so we could build it to the sky, and my brother let me adorn it in any way I wanted. So I designed my snowman—as I describe in *The Secret of Snow*—to resemble the two of us. Our Frosty sported the mittens my grandma made for me, and its top hat was my brother's favorite ball cap.

And then tragedy struck our family. Todd died when he was only seventeen. I was thirteen. As you can imagine, his loss shattered our family. It not only redefined our lives but it also changed the way we celebrated the holidays. For many years, my family sleepwalked through the holidays, hoping they would pass as quickly as possible. Christmas became a shadow of its former self, devoid of decoration, celebration and emotion. In time, we tried to kick-start the holidays again, but it wasn't the same because my brother was missing. Todd wasn't there to sneak into the living room to unwrap and rewrap his Christmas gifts. He wasn't there on the Fourth of July to show me how to shoot bottle rockets into the caves that surrounded our cabin or toss cherry bombs into the water to watch them smoke. He wasn't there at Thanksgiving to steal a piece of pumpkin pie and blame it on me.

He wasn't there.

There was an empty chair at the Christmas table. There were no more snowmen. There was a void under the tree where his gifts should have been. There was a hole in all of our hearts.

Two people returned Christmas to me: my grandma and Gary.

I remember sitting on the couch watching TV one Christmas with my grandma. It was just the two of us, and *A Char-*

lie Brown Christmas came on. I got up and changed the channel immediately.

"I thought this was your favorite holiday special of all time?" she asked.

"It was," I said. "When I used to watch it with Todd."

"No, it is," she said, "and it always will be."

My grandma told me that running from my memories would never change what happened—it would only erase what Todd had meant to us and always would mean to us. She told me we needed to celebrate who he was again as well as the holidays, or we would never be whole.

"He helped make you who you are, didn't he?" she asked. "And that's not only worth remembering at the holidays, it's worth celebrating every day."

I wept that year when Charlie Brown saved that little tree, and I wept when Linus reminded us of the true meaning of Christmas. It was healing and cathartic. I felt whole again, not halved. I felt my brother with me for the first time in decades.

Decades later, after my grandmother had passed, I met Gary, who returned the spirit of Christmas to my parents. Gary embodied Christmas. He decorated more than Martha Stewart, he sang holiday songs twenty-four seven and he believed in embracing holiday tradition.

And so we commenced decorating seven trees—and still do to this day (we've even added a few more!)—in different-themed ornaments (family heirloom, Radko, midcentury, cabin, beach…). We baked cookies, we volunteered, we shopped and lit candles and went to church and drank eggnog and made holiday cookies with my grandma's holiday cookie cutters. We moved to Michigan, and I reembraced winter. I went sledding and snowshoeing and all the things Sonny does in *The Secret of Snow*.

And in the last years of my parents' lives, they celebrated Christmas with all of the spirit they had done decades before. My mom and dad were able to embrace their son's memory again, all because of the power of hope and the holidays.

The Secret of Snow is based on these deeply personal memories. I think it might be my favorite novel to date because it is so meaningful to me. I hope it speaks to your heart.

A few years ago, my friend author Nancy Thayer said, "Wade, if anyone should write a Christmas book, it's you."

I knew exactly where to start. I love the holidays—from Christmas books to *Peanuts* specials to the carols to Hallmark Channel movies—and I'd always wanted to write a holiday novel. *The Secret of Snow* is very funny and very sad, but most of all, like all of my novels, it's filled with oodles of hope, family memories and heirlooms. It's filled with characters from my own life: Sonny's mother is very similar to my own mom (who was very wise and funny and also a hospice nurse), and Joncee is a replica of my own brother. And, well, Sonny is a lot like me.

I truly hope you love reading *The Secret of Snow* as much as I loved writing it.

There is a passage in the novel that sums up the power of winter as well as the struggles and pain we all endure in life.

> Winter can change a person. It can show you the delicate structure of the world when everything is stripped clean. It can illuminate your soul when the world is cloaked in darkness. It can warm your heart when everything else is frozen. It can let you hear your own thoughts for the first time when the earth finally falls silent.
>
> But mostly winter can let you see the silhouette of your body's branches—like a tree in February—when all the leaves are off, the green is gone, the adornment stripped away and, for the first time, you can appreciate all the knots, bends, broken limbs and lightning strikes.
>
> You can see the beauty that has been created in harsh times.

Wishing you the merriest of Christmases and happiest of holidays! And I will see you this spring with another brand-new novel.

XOXO,
Viola

ACKNOWLEDGMENTS

Considering this is the holiday season, there are many Christmas elves I must thank whose gifts not only made this book possible but also make my life immeasurably better.

To my agent, Wendy Sherman: thank you for being my advocate, guide, fighter and friend since 2005. We've been in the trenches together, and we've sipped champagne. There is not a book I've written that would have made it into the world without you. I can never thank you enough.

To Callie Deitrick, Wendy's incredible assistant, who keeps my multiple book contracts on track and is also a wonderfully keen reader.

To Jenny Meyer, my foreign-rights agent, who has overseen my books being translated into twenty-one languages now. (Twenty-one! My twenty-first is a Hebrew translation in Israel!) You have brought my books to the attention of readers around the world, and there is no greater gift.

To Susan Swinwood, my editor, who champions my work and makes each and every book infinitely better with her deeply insightful edits—from a micro and macro level. Her deep affection for the characters and even deeper respect and appreciation for what I wish to accomplish and relay to readers with every novel cannot be thanked enough.

To the entire Graydon House team: Heather Connor, for the difficult and too-often thankless job of publicizing my work; Randy Chan is a marketing genius (when you see my books at your favorite bookseller, say thanks to Randy); Pam Osti, you are tireless and creative; and Lindsey Reeder is a prime reason my social media is growing by leaps and bounds. I've said it before and I'll say it again: working with this team is the best publishing experience of my career.

To all of the indie bookstores across America, THANK YOU for your support and love! You are the hearts, souls and minds of our communities, and you're going to rock this next year with our collective support. (A special thank-you to all the bookstores in Michigan who are not only my biggest cheerleaders but also my dearest friends: Saturn, McLean & Eakin, Forever, Schuler, Brilliant, Horizon, Bay Books, Readers World, and on and on and on…)

And heartfelt thanks to all the libraries across America who buy my books in droves for their readers every single time. Libraries changed my life. And though they've undergone a huge sea change the last few years (and need our support more than ever), the foundation remains the same: books change lives. And they always will.

Personal thanks to the following people, whose love and support literally kept me sane and kept my head above water this past year. You have been my buoys in the publishing ocean. Ron Block from the Cuyahoga County Public Library; all the Friends & Fiction authors (Kristy Woodson Harvey, Kristin Harmel, Mary Kay Andrews, Patti Callahan Henry and Mary

Alice Monroe); Brenda Novak; Nancy Thayer; Susan Mallery; Danielle Noe; Meg Walker and Gretchen Koss; the amazing bookstagrammers; and SO many more.

To my readers: this past year has been extraordinarily difficult and extraordinarily beautiful. You were my silver lining in a dark time. I feel as if I've gotten to know you on a more personal and meaningful level than ever before. I write the types of books I do because of you. "You keep writing, and we'll keep reading!" you email me EVERY SINGLE DAY. I didn't know if the types of books I wanted to write would resonate—books that are inspired by my grandma's heirlooms, life, love and lessons; books meant as a tribute to family and our elders; books that inspire hope; books that are meant to remind readers of what's most important in life; books dedicated to "the simple things"; and books whose characters are inspired by good, kind, hardworking women like my mom and grandmothers, women too often overlooked in literature and life. I'm constantly happy and humbled they have touched you so deeply. You give me as much hope as I pray I give you. THANK YOU! I cannot wait to get back out on tour to hug each and every one of you. Get ready! I ain't lettin' go, either!

Finally, to Gary, the King of Christmas, the one who restored my and my family's faith not only in the holidays but also in life itself. The one who taught us there could be light again after all the darkness. If you watch *Wine & Words with Wade* every Thursday at 6:30 p.m. ET on the Viola Shipman Facebook page, you know his talent, from the set decorations to dressing up as Santa, a leprechaun or the Easter bunny. You can also see that he is one of the world's brightest lights, and he shines through me and illuminates the best in my soul and the best in others.

Here's wishing you a beautiful, blessed holiday season with family and friends! I know this year is going to be extra special now that we can all be together again. As my grandma Shipman always said, "Life is as short as one blink of God's eye, but we too often forget in that blink what matters most: each other." We have been reminded of that again, and I know this will be a magical Christmas and winter for us all.

QUESTIONS FOR DISCUSSION

1. Many of the memories and traditions shared in *The Secret of Snow* are inspired by the author's own life. What are your favorite holiday traditions and why? What memories do they conjure?

2. People either love or hate snow in the winter. What are your feelings about it? Are you a summer or a winter person? Do you have any favorite winter activities?

3. Loss plays a major role in *The Secret of Snow* and can often amplify our feelings of loneliness and sadness. Has the loss of someone in your life affected the way you celebrate the holidays?

4. How have you coped (or not coped) with the loss of a loved one?

5. Sonny and her mother have a wonderfully complicated relationship. They love one another deeply, but the pain they've experienced has made Sonny build a wall around her heart. What is or was your relationship with your mother like? What made it that way?

6. Sonny and Lisa are what we might refer to as frenemies. Have you ever had a frenemy? How did they hurt you? Or how did you hurt them? Did you ever repair your friendship?

7. Some of the author's dear friends are meteorologists, and he always thought if he wasn't an author, he might have been be a meteorologist like Sonny! What career or lifestyle might you have chosen if you weren't doing what you're doing now?

8. Do you believe women are treated differently than men in the workplace, especially women "of a certain age" like Sonny? Do you have any personal experiences to draw from?

9. Society often treats women in the media (celebrities, TV personalities) differently than it treats men. Do you agree that we judge women more harshly based solely on their appearance? Discuss.

10. In the novel, Mason lost his wife to depression. Have you known anyone with depression? How did you try to help? How did their illness impact you?

11. Have you or a friend ever experienced a later-in-life romance like Sonny and Mason?

12. Have you ever been to Michigan or Palm Springs? What are your impressions of these two beautiful locations that are so special to Sonny (and to the author!)?